Duty, Honour, Truth, Valour

The tenets of the Knights of Champagne will be
sorely tested in this exciting Medieval mini-series by

Carol Townend

The pounding of hooves, the cold snap of air, a
knight's colours flying high across the roaring crowd—
nothing rivals a tourney. The chance to
prove his worth is at the beating heart of any knight.

And tournaments bring other dangers too.
Scoundrels, thieves, murderers and worse are
all drawn towards a town bursting with deep pockets,
flowing wine and wanton women.

Only these powerful knights stand in their way.
But what of the women who stand beside them?

Find out in
Carol Townend's

Knights of Champagne

Powerful swordsmen for passionate ladies

Author Note

Arthurian myths and legends have been popular for hundreds of years. Dashing knights worship beautiful ladies, fight for honour—and sometimes lose honour! Some of the earliest versions of these stories were written in the twelfth century by an influential poet called Chrétien de Troyes. Troyes was the walled city in the county of Champagne where Chrétien lived and worked. His patron, Countess Marie of Champagne, was a princess—daughter of King Louis of France and the legendary Eleanor of Aquitaine. Countess Marie's splendid artistic court in Troyes rivalled Queen Eleanor's in Poitiers.

The books in my Knights of Champagne mini-series are not an attempt to rework the Arthurian myths and legends. They are original romances set around the Troyes court and the town of Provins, which is also in Champagne. I wanted to tell the stories of some of the lords and ladies who might have inspired Chrétien—and I was keen to give the ladies a more active role, since Chrétien's ladies tend to be too passive for today's reader.

Apart from brief glimpses of Count Henry and Countess Marie, my characters are all fictional. I have used the layout of the medieval cities to create the Troyes and Provins in these books, but the stories are first and foremost fictional.

LADY ROWENA'S RUIN

Carol Townend

MILLS &
BOON

Published in Great Britain 2015
by Mills & Boon, an imprint of Harlequin (UK) Limited,
Eton House, 18-24 Paradise Road, Richmond, Surrey, TW9 1SR

© 2015 Carol Townend

ISBN: 978-0-263-24823-4

Harlequin (UK) Limited's policy is to use papers that are natural,
renewable and recyclable products and made from wood grown in
sustainable forests. The logging and manufacturing processes conform
to the legal environmental regulations of the country of origin.

Printed and bound in Spain
by CPI, Barcelona

Carol Townend was born in England and went to a convent school in the wilds of Yorkshire. Captivated by the medieval period, Carol read History at London University. She loves to travel, drawing inspiration for her novels from places as diverse as Winchester in England, Istanbul in Turkey and Troyes in France. A writer of both fiction and non-fiction, Carol lives in London with her husband and daughter. Visit her website at caroltownend.co.uk.

Visit the Author Profile page at millsandboon.co.uk.

To Susie with love and sincere thanks
for many years of help and encouragement.

Chapter One

May 1175—Jutigny Castle, near Provins in the County of Champagne.

It was some time since Sir Eric de Monfort had visited Jutigny Castle and it was strange to be back. As a boy, the place had once been his home. Leaving his horse in the capable hands of one of the grooms, Eric crossed the bailey with his squire, Alard, and headed for the steps leading to the great hall.

Jutigny hadn't changed much, the keep towered over everyone just as it always had done, and the pale gleam of new wood on the walkway up on the curtain wall proved that Lord Faramus de Sainte-Colombe was keeping his defences in order. There was the familiar string of outbuildings, the chapel, the cookhouse…

Sir Macaire, the castle steward and an old friend, was standing in the hall doorway, talking to a castle sergeant. His face lightened. 'Eric, thank God you're here! Lord Faramus is getting impatient, you can go straight in.'

'I need a mug of ale first,' Eric said, going to a side table and picking up the ale jug. 'I've been at the fair in Provins all morning and I'm parched. Lord Faramus didn't mention that the matter was urgent. What does he want?'

Sir Macaire grimaced. 'I'm not at liberty to say, lad, but your ale will have to wait. Lord Faramus and Lady Barbara have been waiting for you up in the solar for nigh on an hour and as you know, the count is not known for his tolerance.' Sir Macaire threw a dark glance in the direction of a knight sprawled on the bench nearest the stairwell. 'Besides, if you don't go up straight away, I've orders to send in Sir Breon. And that would be a travesty.' He shook his head. 'A travesty.'

'A travesty?' Eric searched the steward's face. That was surely a curious choice of words. Pouring ale into a mug, Eric took a quick draught. Eric knew Sir Breon from his time at Jutigny and he'd never much liked him. Not that Eric could level anything specific against the man. Sir Breon had a bullying manner and he was crude, but then so were many knights. What was odd was that Eric couldn't recall Sir Macaire being troubled by Sir Breon before this. 'Macaire, what in hell is going on?'

'It's not for me to say.' Sir Macaire jerked his head at the stairwell. 'For the love of God, Eric, hurry straight up.'

'They're in the solar, you say? Doesn't Lady Barbara usually reserve the solar for herself and her ladies?' Eric was becoming more intrigued by the moment. Sweat was breaking out on Macaire's brow and his manner—Macaire looked decidedly panicked—was mysterious, if not downright worrying. 'What's the problem?'

'The solar, lad. Get to the solar and you'll have your answers.'

In the solar, Lord Faramus was pacing in front of a low fire, pulling at his beard. His eyebrows were drawn into a deep frown. His wife, Lady Barbara, was sitting beneath the window, long white fingers gripping a scroll of parchment.

Eric had fond memories of Lady Barbara, who had always treated him with kindness. Her usually clear brow was crossed with lines and her face was pinched with worry. She looked deeply distressed. A pang of sympathy shot through him. Had she and Lord Faramus quarrelled again?

'Good morning, my lady, my lord,' Eric said, bowing.

Irritably, Count Faramus waved the niceties aside. 'Where the devil have you been? I've been waiting for you all morning.'

'I've been at the fair in Provins, my lord.'

'The fair?' The count's expression lightened. 'Oh, yes, I remember. You are looking for a stallion, as I recall. Did you find one?'

'Not yet, *mon seigneur*.' Eric wanted a brood mare as well as a stallion, thus far he hadn't found either. At the Provins fair he had learned that he might find both at Bar-sur-Aube. Given that horses with good breeding lines were almost impossible to track down, Eric had wanted to go there directly from the fair. And then he'd remembered the count's summons. Eric felt a certain loyalty to his former liege lord and he'd felt bound to come to Jutigny first. As soon as this meeting was over he would set out for Bar-sur-Aube.

'My apologies if I kept you waiting, my lord. You have something to ask me, I believe?'

Eric found his gaze returning to Lady Barbara. She was not usually present when her husband discussed his affairs with his household knights. Come to think of it, in his time at Jutigny Castle, Eric's orders had invariably been issued in the great hall or the armoury. What was going on?

Lord Faramus sucked in a breath and Eric

caught an exchange of glances between man and wife. 'Eric, *Sir* Eric, before we get to the meat of the matter, I should like your word that what is said between these walls will remain confidential. At least for the moment.'

'As you wish, my lord.'

'Eric, this concerns my daughter, Lady Rowena. You remember Rowena?'

Alarm tensed every muscle in Eric's body. *This was about Lady Rowena?*

Of course Eric remembered Lady Rowena— as Lord Faramus and Lady Barbara's only child, how could he forget her? Lady Rowena was a shy, fair girl, a handful of years younger than he. Until Lady Rowena had professed a desire to become a nun, she had been heiress to the Sainte-Colombe acres and every eligible knight in Champagne had been suing for her hand. At times it had seemed as though Jutigny Castle was under siege. Count Faramus had eventually come to terms with Count Gawain de Meaux, but there had been some scandal and the marriage had never gone ahead. Eric didn't know the details. 'I heard that Lady Rowena entered the convent outside Provins?'

'St Mary's Abbey.' Lord Faramus's mouth was grim. 'Aye, so she did.'

Count Faramus had made no secret of his displeasure at his daughter's decision to take the veil. But Lady Rowena was the king's god-daughter and once the king—himself a religious man—had endorsed her wish to become a nun, there'd been little the count could do about it.

The skin prickled at the back of Eric's neck, he was beginning to feel very uneasy.

'Sir Eric, I am well aware that I am no longer your liege lord and I cannot command you, but I do have a favour to ask.' His fingers curled into a fist. 'A very large favour. It's a task I believe you will find distasteful.'

'Mon seigneur?'

'Sir—Eric—I want you to get my daughter out of that convent. Take her to your manor at Monfort. Hold her there until she agrees to marry you.'

Appalled, Eric drew his head back. He must have misheard. 'I don't think I understand you, my lord.'

Lord Faramus made an exasperated sound. 'I want you to ruin Rowena. Get her out of that convent and seduce her. Make love to her. Make it so that she has no choice but to marry you—'

'My lord, I can't do that!' No wonder Lady Barbara was so ill at ease!

'Why the devil not?'

Eric stepped closer. 'It would be wrong, my lord. Your daughter has a religious calling, I cannot come between her and her vocation.'

'Rowena *thinks* she has a religious vocation,' Lord Faramus said curtly. 'It is not the same thing, not the same thing at all.'

Firmly, Eric shook his head. 'I will not do it.'

The count's jaw worked. 'For pity's sake, you have to, it's the Visitation of Our Lady next week.'

Eric gave the count a bemused look. 'My lord, I do not see the connection.'

Lady Barbara leaned forward. The parchment rustled. 'Eric, Rowena is to make her preliminary vows that day.'

Lord Faramus cleared his throat. 'De Monfort, Rowena's about to become a novice. You have to get her out of the abbey before that happens.'

Eric stepped back and bowed. A tight knot formed in the pit of his stomach. 'My lord, I am conscious that I owe you and Lady Barbara a great deal, but in all honour I am afraid I must refuse you.'

The count's expression darkened. 'De Monfort, I feel sure you are forgetting how lucky you were to end up at our gate.' He gestured at this wife. 'Who else but my Barbara would have taken in a half-starved child? Who else but Sir Macaire would have taken you—a complete unknown—under his wing and trained you the way he did? Lord, I myself knighted you. And you have the gall to refuse me?'

Eric held firm. 'I shall never forget the kindness I have found in your household, my lord, but all that you taught me did not include seducing virgins! It would be wrong to abduct Lady Rowena. She has a calling.'

'Like hell she does.' Lord Faramus narrowed his eyes on Eric. 'Don't you want more lands? Marry Rowena and you will be count yourself one day.'

Eric huffed out a breath, he couldn't believe what he was hearing—Lord Faramus was asking him to ruin his daughter. To force her into marriage. To say the least, it was a desperate plan. And to make matters worse, the count seemed to be ignoring the fact that if Lady Rowena were to marry him, the king ought to agree to the match first.

Had Lord Faramus lost his senses? Of course it was beyond flattering to think that the count would welcome him as a son-in-law, not to mention that it was temptation beyond his wildest dreams—him, to become a count one day!—but he couldn't do it.

He glanced towards the lady sitting by the window. He couldn't read her expression, she had set aside the parchment and was bent over some needlework. Surely Lady Barbara didn't condone this foolhardy idea?

'The king himself has approved Lady

Rowena's desire to enter the convent,' Eric said, mildly.

'Well, I am her father and I do not. Stop quibbling, de Monfort. Get her out of St Mary's and get her to marry you. I don't care how you do it, just do it. It might inspire you if you tell yourself that when I die, you will be Count of Sainte-Colombe.'

'I am truly sorry to disappoint you, my lord, but I will not do it. It simply would not be the act of an honourable knight.'

'Eric, we chose you because we recalled that as a child you were kind to my daughter.'

We? So Lady Barbara was in on this ridiculous plan, was she? Eric felt a muscle flicker in his jaw. 'As I recall, my lord, you warned me about being over-familiar. In fact, you forbade me to speak to her.'

Lady Barbara's needle stilled. 'Sir, you are referring to the time when you and Rowena were found in the plum tree. You must forgive my husband for that. He tends to be over-protective and hasty in his judgements. And you must not forget that you were, at the time, young and untried. You were unproven.'

'And now I have won a manor and a few acres you consider me proven?'

Lord Faramus looked him straight in the eye.

'De Monfort, I trained you myself, I know you are an honourable man.'

'What you ask me to do is dishonourable!'

Lady Barbara made a sharp movement. 'Please, sir, you have to help us.'

'My lady, I am sorry, I will not do it.'

The count's shoulders sagged. 'Very well, de Monfort, you may leave.' He waved a curt dismissal. 'On your way out, send Sir Breon up.'

Lady Barbara's eyes filled with anxiety. The knot twisted in Eric's stomach. What would happen next? Telling himself it was none of his business, Eric was halfway to the door when he remembered Macaire muttering about how it would be a travesty if Sir Breon went up to the solar. Obviously, Macaire must be aware that the count was determined to get his daughter out of the abbey and he didn't like the idea of her being handed over to Sir Breon.

Lady Rowena's face as Eric had last seen it, beautiful in its innocence, flashed into his mind. The idea of that sweet child being forced in to Sir Breon's company—for life—was utterly repugnant. Eric had always had the impression that she was afraid of the man. Lord, his stomach turned at the thought. That child with that lout…it simply would not do.

Sir Breon might refuse to agree. He might.

Briefly, Eric closed his eyes. He was deluding

himself, there was no way that Sir Breon would turn down the chance to wed the heiress to the Sainte-Colombe acres.

Lady Rowena, that lovely girl, forced into marriage with Sir Breon?

Rather me than him.

Eric stopped in his tracks, turned and looked intently at his former lord. 'You would foist Sir Breon on Lady Rowena?'

'Since you are clearly not the man I took you for, yes. Sir Breon knows where his loyalties lie. I feel confident that he will be less of a disappointment.'

'My lord, you cannot be serious.'

Lord Faramus glowered. 'Someone has to marry her. I'll be damned before I see my lands fall into Armand's hands.'

'Armand?'

'Sir Armand de Velay, a distant cousin.'

Eric was beginning to understand. With the count's only child taking the veil, the County of Sainte-Colombe would fall into this cousin's hands. Unless Rowena married.

'My lord.' Eric forced himself to speak calmly. 'It is natural for a man to want his lands to go to his child, but I cannot think that force is the way to achieve it.'

Lord Faramus's mouth thinned. 'Do you think we haven't tried persuasion? Rowena is the most

stubborn wench in Christendom. She will not
see reason.'

Eric had never seen Lady Rowena's stubborn
side. It came to him that even if she were stubborn she was only taking after her sire. Wisely,
he held his tongue on that score, saying merely,
'My lord, in my view Lady Rowena mislikes
Sir Breon.'

Lord Faramus lifted an eyebrow. 'So? Sir
Breon will get her agreement.'

Eric shook his head, frowning. 'Aye, he probably will, Sir Breon is not a gentle man. My lord,
have you thought about the methods he might
use to persuade her?'

'Sir Breon will do my will. Send him in.'

'*Mon seigneur*, Lady Rowena wants to become a nun.'

'*Tant pis*. She will marry one way or the
other.' With a sigh, Lord Faramus clapped Eric
on the shoulder. 'No hard feelings, de Monfort,
I won't hold this against you.'

'Wait.' Eric put up his hand. He wasn't sure
why, but the thought of Sir Breon forcing himself on Lady Rowena was unbearable. Naturally,
the thought of one day being count of Sainte-
Colombe was tempting, but it was the thought
of Lady Rowena in Breon's hands that pushed
him to accept. 'I'll do it.'

Lady Barbara gave him the tiniest of smiles. If

Eric had blinked he'd have missed it. Oddly, her smile gave him heart. It made him realise that he was her choice, Lady Barbara wanted him for her daughter. Lord knew Eric had never looked to force any woman into marriage, let alone Lady Rowena, but if he didn't agree then Sir Breon surely would. Eric must spare her that.

The count's eyes glittered. 'You agree?'

'Aye.' Eric thought fast. Agreement would buy time. Clearly, Lord Faramus hadn't had time to accept Lady Rowena's decision to enter the convent. That much was understandable, the realisation that his cousin would inherit his lands rather than his daughter must be hard to swallow. Given more time, Lord Faramus would surely come to his senses.

Eric had to admit it was flattering to think that Lord Faramus and Lady Barbara had chosen to put their extraordinary proposal to him first. It showed a measure of trust. Of approval. Lord Faramus was a hard man, hard and determined, but he must love his daughter.

And there sat Lady Barbara, smiling that small smile. Eric looked directly at her. 'I will keep your daughter safe,' he said. He wouldn't marry her though, he couldn't. It would be sacrilege to come between Lady Rowena and her calling.

'I know,' Lady Barbara murmured.

'I am not sure she will remember me.'

'She will.' Lady Barbara bent over her sewing.

Yes, if Eric kidnapped Lady Rowena, he could keep her safe. And then, when Lord Faramus came to his senses, he would return her to the abbey. Count Faramus must see reason in the end. Even a great lord like him couldn't force the king's goddaughter into marriage.

'I'll do it, on these terms,' Eric said. 'I'll not hurt her. And I want your word that you will not meddle.'

Lord Faramus stroked his beard. There was a pause. 'Yes, yes, I shall leave everything in your hands.'

With a bow, Eric left the solar.

As the door swung shut behind him, Lady Barbara set her sewing aside. 'I told you he'd agree.'

'He had me worried for a while. Rowena is a stubborn wench, but God knows I wouldn't wish Breon on her.'

'I wouldn't wish Sir Breon on any woman,' Lady Barbara said drily. 'I knew Sir Eric would agree if faced with that. He has a kind heart.'

'It's nothing to do with his heart, orphans always make the best recruits.'

'Faramus!'

'Don't delude yourself, Barbara, for de Monfort this is the chance of a lifetime. He was a foundling, for pity's sake. He's done well to win his manor, but he wants more power, more land.'

'He wants Rowena.'

Lord Faramus sent his wife a pitying look and shook his head. 'Barbara, you've been listening to too many ballads. That boy wants land, this is all about land.'

Lady Barbara looked at her husband and didn't reply.

At St Mary's Convent the next morning, Lady Rowena de Sainte-Colombe dressed as quickly as she could. 'Hurry, Berthe,' Rowena said.

Outside the sun was shining. Rowena couldn't bear to be inside a moment longer. She lived for her morning rides or, more precisely, she lived for those few brief moments of each day when she could delude herself that she was in charge of her life. She eyed the door to their cell, as ever she was half-afraid that one of the nuns would appear and ban her from taking her exercise in the open air.

'Very good, my lady.'

Berthe set about binding her hair into the simplest of plaits and Rowena tried not to fidget. Berthe seemed to take for ever covering her head with the grey veil deemed suitable for a girl who was shortly to take her preliminary vows. She adjusted it and pushed a golden tress out of sight.

'*Ma dame*, please keep still, I almost stabbed you with a hairpin.'

'Sorry, Berthe, I'm longing to be outside.'

Berthe gave the veil a final twitch and stood back to admire her handiwork. 'There. You look lovely, my lady. Fit to face the world.' Her face fell. 'Not that it matters, they'll be confining you inside these walls soon enough. And cutting off all that beautiful hair. It's a crime, if you ask me, my lady.'

Rowena gave her a straight look. 'You don't like it here, do you?'

Berthe glanced around the chamber. On account of her mistress's status it was larger than most of the nuns' cells, large enough to contain a bed for Lady Rowena and her maid. The walls were roughly plastered and lime-washed. The only ornament was a wooden crucifix on the wall opposite Rowena's bed.

Berthe shrugged. 'Doesn't matter much what I think, does it, my lady? You're the one who'll be staying here, not me.'

Rowena's throat tightened. 'That is true.'

Rowena picked up her riding crop. She wanted to ask Berthe to stay with her at the convent. The difficulty was that Berthe showed no signs of liking convent life, rather the reverse. It was a pity, as Rowena liked Berthe and ladies were allowed maids in this convent, even if they were not called maids as such. But Berthe had shown no sign of a calling. Indeed, Berthe seemed to dislike the place as much as she did…

Rowena drew a sharp breath. No! What was she thinking? She didn't dislike it here. It was quiet. Peaceful. It was far more restful living in a convent than in a castle. In convents the person in authority was a woman, and here in St Mary's Convent Mother Pauline was most definitely in charge. The few men allowed through the gate—a couple of gardeners, the grooms—wouldn't dream of crossing her. Within these walls, women were most definitely in charge.

Rowena was pulled two ways. She had told the world she wanted to be a nun; she'd told everyone that she had a calling. Her father was a practical man rather than a religious one and she'd had to cross swords with him to get here. She stared blindly at her riding crop. Soon she would be taking her preliminary vows. The bishop was coming to the abbey to say mass on the morning of the Feast of the Visitation and she would be clothed as a novice afterwards.

Briefly, she closed her eyes. She did have a calling, of course she did. However, she wouldn't be human if she didn't sometimes have doubts. She had made such a fuss to be accepted as a nun, how in the world could she confess that she didn't fit in as well as she had imagined? The

trouble was that her father wanted her to marry.
And she could never marry, the wound left by
Mathieu's death was too raw. Poor Mathieu. He'd
had such a sweet, loving nature, she'd never
forget how they would sit for hours among the
daisies in the meadow by the river, talking and
making daisy chains for each other.

'My lady, is something amiss?'

Rowena clenched her riding crop and prayed
for a stronger sense of calling. She must make
this work. When she had first arrived at the
abbey, she had been resigned to the idea of taking the veil. She'd been too busy grieving to face
marriage to Lord Gawain and the convent had
been her only escape. It had been a rebellion
against a world where she had been viewed as
a chattel to be married off at her father's whim.
At the beginning, life here had felt satisfying.
But now…

Despite her determination to take the veil,
there were doubts. Lord, the days turned so
slowly. The quiet, once so pleasantly peaceful,
sometimes seemed like the quiet of the grave.

'My lady?' Berthe caught her by the arm and
looked deep into her eyes. 'Thank the Lord,
you've realised you weren't meant to take the
veil.'

'No. *No.*'

'Yes, you have, I can see it in your face.

You've changed your mind about becoming a nun.'

Vehemently, Rowena shook her head and reached for the door latch. 'You're imagining things.'

'I don't think so. Look at you, desperate to get beyond the convent walls.' Berthe gave her a kind smile. 'It's no shame, my lady. In truth, it's better to decide you're not suited to the convent before you take your vows. That's why the nuns insist that you spend time with them before becoming a novice. It's a test of sorts. You want to go home, you want to become Lady Rowena again. Your father won't be angry, he hates the idea of you mouldering away in here.'

'My father hates the idea of Sir Armand getting hold of his land.' *And he will force me into a marriage I do not want. I will become a nun.*

Rowena opened the door and stepped over the threshold. She understood very well that the months spent at St Mary's had been some form of a test. But Berthe was wrong if she thought she was eager to return to her former life. Lady Rowena de Sainte-Colombe would be made to marry at the behest of her father and Rowena refused to marry. She missed Mathieu. 'You're wrong, Berthe. Wrong. I can see that you hate it here, but you mustn't assume that I do too. Life here is better than life in a castle. It might not be as exciting, but it is peaceful. And that is all I ask for. Peace. I want to rest my head in a place where women are in charge.'

As Rowena hurried down the corridor, Berthe's voice followed her. 'They won't let you ride out at whim once you've taken your vows, my lady. They'll cut off your hair.'

One of the convent grooms had Rowena's grey mare, Lily, saddled and waiting when she arrived at the stable. 'Thank, you, Aylmer,' Rowena said, leading Lily to the mounting block.

Aylmer swung on to another horse. 'Where to today, my lady? Do we ride into town?'

'Not today. Today I've a mind to ride north.'

'As you wish, my lady.'

Rowena and Aylmer trotted out through the gates and took the path leading up through the convent orchard. Rowena was discomfited to realise that her spirits weren't rising as they usually did. Finding herself staring down at Lily's head, she frowned.

Novices, like nuns, weren't allowed any possessions other than their habits, their crosses and their psalters. When Rowena took her vows, Lily would no longer be hers, she would belong to the convent as a whole. Rowena swallowed down a lump in her throat. Lily had been given to Rowena when she was a foal and she was glad they weren't actually going to be parted. She would miss the rides though. Novices weren't permitted to roam through the abbey estate as she'd been doing these last weeks.

Leaning forward, Rowena patted the mare's neck. 'Lily, you form part of my dowry to the convent. Soon you will belong to all the nuns in common. I may not be allowed to ride you, but I'll still be able to see you every day.'

Lily's ears pricked, for all the world as though she was listening.

With the convent and the town at their backs, the track wound steadily up through the apple trees. They were about a mile from the main road. A couple of horsemen had drawn rein at the top of the rise. They were looking towards the convent.

A knight and his squire? Rowena's fingers tightened on the reins. She only had instinct to tell her that she was looking at a knight and his squire, but she was certain she was right, even though the horsemen bore no insignia that she could see. They were too far away for her to make out their features. She marked the flash of a gilt spur—yes, that larger man was definitely a knight—and felt a flicker of unease. He had dark hair. She would feel happier if she could make out his features.

The knight was mounted on another grey, a

stallion. Rowena found herself staring at it. She knew her horses and the stallion on the rise put her strongly in mind of a grey she had seen years ago in her father's stables. No more than mildly alarmed—she was yet on convent lands and if this knight was one of her father's, surely she had nothing to fear—she spurred up the hill.

As she and Aylmer approached, the knight jammed on his helmet, and again Rowena felt that flicker of disquiet. The man wasn't wearing chain mail, just a brown leather gambeson, and the way he had shoved his helmet on—it was almost as though he didn't want to be recognised. Held in by a strong hand, the stallion sidled.

Rowena glanced at the squire, a lad of about fifteen. He had honest brown eyes and a scatter of freckles across his nose. He looked like a choirboy playing at being a soldier. This time something about him was definitely familiar. When she drew level with the squire, Rowena came to a halt. 'Do I know you?'

The boy blushed to his ears and made a choking sound. His hand was curled firmly round the hilt of his sword. Familiar or no, the way he stared at her had Rowena going cold.

The knight's horse shifted. A large hand caught her wrist and held it in an iron grip. Choking and spluttering in outrage, Rowena dropped the reins and wrestled to free herself. 'How dare you? Release me this instant!'

Aylmer cried out, 'My lady!'

The knight tightened his grip. Rowena flailed about with her free arm and Lily snorted and sidestepped.

Rowena was conscious of the knight's squire closing in on Aylmer, but she was too busy fighting to free herself to pay him much attention. She heard a thud and then Aylmer's voice again, faint and full of distress. 'My lady!'

Poor Aylmer was on the ground, his sword lay some feet away. The choirboy squire had him at sword point.

The knight captured Rowena's free hand and immediately set about tying her wrists together. Icy fear shot through her veins. Fury had her choking in anger. She twisted and wriggled, but it was impossible to see the face behind the gleaming visor of his helmet, just the faint glitter of green eyes. The knight shifted his hand over her mouth even as she began to scream.

'Let me go!' she cried. 'Let me go!'

Her heart thumped as she fought to escape that iron grip. Then, just as she was certain matters could hardly get any worse, she was hoisted from her saddle and thumped face down—like a sack of wheat—in front of the knight. The wretch had shoved her across his saddle-bow.

The harness clinked and his horse began to move. The knight was abducting her! The blood rushed to her head, she could see the grey's threshing forelegs, the ground rushing past— the grass, a daisy, a buttercup…

'Who are you?' she gasped, jolted by the movement of the horse. Dismayed as she was, she was certain this man was in some way connected with Jutigny. Who was he?

A large hand settled in the small of her back. She felt his fingers curling around her belt, holding her firm. 'Never fear, I won't hurt you. You're safe.'

She knew herself to be outmatched, and a sob escaped her.

'My lady, you are quite safe. You have my word.' Amazingly, his voice sounded soothing.

'Let me down!'

'I'll let you down when we are out of sight of the abbey. Be still, my lady.'

Chapter Two

Eric kept a firm hand on the wriggling bundle of fury that was Lady Rowena. He had hardly recognised her as she had ridden towards him through the orchard. How long had it been since he had seen her? Two years? Three? She must be eighteen by now.

Rowena de Sainte-Colombe had been a pretty child and Eric had heard she'd grown into a beautiful woman. However, nothing had prepared him for the sight of her, slender and elegant even in a drab gown and veil that could only have come from a convent. The grey that should have muted her looks did nothing of the kind. It framed a beauty that was simply breathtaking. Her eyes seemed brighter, bluer than they had done when she was a child. Her skin was flawless, perfect, and as for her lips, Lord, Eric had never seen such rosy, kissable lips.

They were the lips of a woman who wanted

to become a nun, he reminded himself as he gripped her belt. Lips that wanted to do nothing more than chant litanies and sing psalms. Heavens, this woman had chosen life in a convent over life as the Countess of Meaux and, one day, Sainte-Colombe. She'd certainly looked prim as she had ridden towards him. Prim and aloof. There'd been no sign of the carefree child he'd once known.

As they moved off, Lady Rowena's grey veil streamed out like a pennon. Eric stifled a grin. She didn't look quite so prim now. Fearful her veil would become tangled in Captain's hoofs, Eric leaned forward to gather it out of the way. He found himself holding more than he had bargained for, Lady Rowena's blonde hair, bound in a neat braid, came too. He juggled with veil and braid, struggling not to pull on her hair. In the tussle, the ribbon fell from the tail of the braid and the long, golden tresses began to unwind.

Holding her firmly, Eric pulled up and glanced over his shoulder to see that Alard had dismounted. Arm looped through his reins, his squire had Lady Rowena's groom at bay. The two other horses, Lady Rowena's and the groom's, were placidly cropping grass under one of the apple trees.

Eric nodded at Alard, it was a signal they had arranged earlier.

'On your way,' Alard said, dismissing the poor groom.

The groom hesitated, rubbing his skull. His expression was pained. 'What about Lady Rowena?'

Alard's sword caught the light as he leaned towards the groom. 'On your way. Come back for your sword later.'

The groom stumbled over to the horses under the tree.

'You may take your horse. Don't touch Lady Rowena's,' Eric said. The groom would, Eric was certain, report what had happened the moment he was back at the convent. Eric was relying on him to do so. Word would be sent straight to Jutigny and Count Faramus would know that Eric had his daughter. Sir Breon would not be called into play.

All was proceeding exactly as Eric had planned.

It had been almost too easy, particularly once Eric had discovered Lady Rowena had not lost her habit of riding out every morning. He'd known that then would be the best time to strike. And with it being broad day, he thought and hoped she would be less fearful. Of course she would be alarmed at what had happened to her and as soon as they were out of sight of the convent, he would reassure her that she was safe.

Eric watched the groom hobble towards the convent gate with his horse and grimaced. It was a pity he'd had to suffer that crack on the head, but he didn't look to be much the worse for it. Doubtless the convent would soon be in uproar.

Uneasy, he looked at the woman slung across his saddle bow. Even though Lady Rowena was unmistakably a woman, she was still tiny. Petite. She would mistrust him for a time, but it had to be better than her becoming Sir Breon's captive. Realising that his gaze was resting rather too appreciatively on the gentle curve of her buttock, Eric heeled Captain into a walk and headed for the stand of chestnuts over the brow of the hill. He would set her down in cover of the trees and do his best to explain.

Eric wasn't looking forward to the moment he took off his helmet. She'd be bound to recognise him, after all he'd been one of her father's household knights for years. Why, when Lady Barbara had heard Lord Faramus turn down his request to learn to read and write, she'd run the gauntlet of her husband's displeasure by allowing Eric to sit in on her daughter's lessons. Eric and Lady Rowena had known each other quite well in those days.

He would ensure Lady Rowena understood

that she must stay away from the convent for a time, then he would take her back to his manor at Monfort and there they would wait until Lord Faramus came to his senses. Though the idea of marrying Lady Rowena and one day becoming Count of Sainte-Colombe was tempting in many ways, he couldn't in all conscience force her into marriage.

Rowena felt the wretch who had abducted her take her veil and hair firmly in hand. The knight's spurs flashed and his horse lurched into a trot. It was a struggle to find air—with every step the horse took the breath was pushed from her lungs. Rowena supposed she should be grateful the knight was riding an ordinary saddle rather than one designed for battle. Otherwise she'd be wrapped round a horrible pommel and then it really would be impossible to breathe.

He planned this. What is he going to do with me? Can he really be one of my father's household knights? Father will kill him!

The lack of a large pommel was small comfort as they made their way up the rise. Fear felt like a lump of lead in her chest, constricting her breathing every bit as much as the saddle digging into her ribs. The irony of her position flashed through her mind—to think that a short while ago, she'd been wishing for more excitement! Twisting her head the better to see, gasping with the effort, Rowena saw they had reached the small copse. Shadows dappled the grass as they rode in between the chestnut trees.

'Keep still, my lady. Not much further,' the knight said.

True to his word, a couple of heartbeats later the grey stallion came to a standstill and the knight dismounted.

'With your permission, my lady,' he said.

Warm hands took her by the hips and Rowena was half-lifted, half-dragged from the grey and set on her feet next to a tree. Her veil floated to the ground. Her hair was in her eyes. The knight was yet wearing his helmet and his visor remained down so she couldn't see his features. Save for the helmet and the knight's spurs, he was dressed as a huntsman, with a brown leather gambeson over a blue tunic and hose. He towered over her. Determined not to be daunted by his height, Rowena took in a shaky breath and glared up at him.

'My father will kill you,' she said. 'I know you are one of his household knights. You might have the decency to show your face.'

'Very well.' Calmly, he unbuckled the strap and removed the helmet.

He shook his head and ran his fingers through dark, tousled hair. He wore it slightly long for a knight. He had warm, unforgettable eyes.

Rowena remembered them well, they were green with bright flecks that appeared gold in some lights and amber in others. Here in the copse, they were gold.

She felt her jaw drop. 'Eric? Sir Eric?' Her mind raced. Sir Eric de Monfort hadn't been her father's man for a few years, but he had indeed been a Jutigny knight. A favourite of Sir Macaire's, Eric had earned his spurs early. Then he had won his manor in a tourney. Shortly after that he had left her father's service—a landed knight had no need to be at another man's beck and call.

Rowena had been delighted by Eric's success. There was a world of difference between the life of a knight who had won lands and that of a landless knight. A knight with land had some measure of security, he had revenues he could call upon and a place to call home. For someone like Eric—a foundling—that must mean much. If Eric had remained landless, his life would have been very different. He would have been reliant on short-term contracts with men like her father, in short, Eric might have ended up being little better than a paid mercenary. Landless knights too old or too weary to fight often ended up in the gutter. She wouldn't have wanted that for Eric.

She scowled up at him, she had been fond of

Eric. Unusually so. When he'd been a youth she had had a crush on him. Before he had won his manor and gone away, sight of him had filled her with secret longings. Surely he couldn't have changed that much? 'I demand you untie me.'

'You won't scream or try and run back to the convent?'

'No.' Her chin lifted. 'Not immediately, at any rate.'

His eyes danced and Rowena remembered something else about Sir Eric. He could be charming when he chose, the castle maids had adored him. With a slight huff, she turned to face the tree so he could reach her bonds. Leaning her cheek against the bark, she felt his fingers on her wrists.

'Hold still, my lady, I don't want to cut you.'

The rope gave. Turning, Rowena rubbed her wrists and glared at him.

'Why are you doing this, sir?' She searched her mind for possible explanation. This was Eric, for heaven's sake—he had played with her as a child, they had learned to read together. It was hard to believe ill of him. 'Is this a wager of some kind?'

His jaw tightened. Gesturing her towards a patch of sunlight, he spread his cloak on the ground. 'Please sit, my lady.'

Rowena stood firm. Her foot tapped. 'Sir?'

'No wager.' His eyes held hers. Above them, leaves rustled in the breeze. Dappled light played over his hair.

She looked back down the hill. 'What happened to Aylmer?'

'He's your groom?'

She nodded. 'Did you hurt him?'

'Aylmer will be safely back at the convent by now.'

She felt her brow crease in puzzlement. 'You do know that Aylmer will send word to my father?'

'I am rather hoping that he will.'

'Are you mad? My father will kill you.'

A small smile lifted one side of his mouth as slowly, Eric shook his head. 'I doubt that, my lady. You see, I am doing this at the behest of your father.'

She felt the blood drain from her face. 'Father asked you to carry me off?'

'Please, my lady.' Again Eric gestured at the cloak. 'Sit down and I will do my best to explain.'

Stunned into silence, Rowena sank on to his cloak. Her father had asked Eric to do this? Her father?

Eric sat on the ground beside her and rested his arms on his knees. Rowena noted the sprinkling of dark hair on his forearms and found herself studying him. She couldn't remember when she had seen him last, and there were differences as well as similarities. He looked older, although traces of the boy she had known remained. His features were more clearly defined—the line of his jaw, his nose, his lips. A fluttery feeling made itself felt and she jerked her gaze away from his mouth. His hair was as thick as ever, dark brown with rich auburn glints that caught the light when he moved. His shoulders were wide, he looked strong and much more masculine. A man, a real man. Rowena didn't like many men and she hadn't been in the company of men as powerful as Eric since she'd entered the convent. It felt strange. Oddly, it didn't feel as alarming as she had imagined it would, she had known him for many years after all. With a start, she realised the fear she had felt when he flung her across his saddle had gone the moment she'd seen his face. Her heart was still thudding—with excitement rather than fear. She felt more alive than she had in weeks.

Except—there was only one reason she could think of for Eric abducting her. She swallowed. 'My father doesn't want me to take my vows.'

'No.'

'He's asked you to take me back to Jutigny?' Despite herself, her voice cracked. 'He's found someone he wants me to marry?'

Eric shifted, he looked decidedly uncomfortable. Reaching for a blade of grass, he picked it and twirled it between his fingers. Fingers that for no reason that Rowena could think of held her gaze. Eric had capable hands, with blunt fingers. His hands were the hands of a successful knight, and as long as she had known him they had never been put to any dishonourable task. She did not think he could have changed that much and yet snatching her from the convent was hardly the action of a man of honour.

'Eric?'

'Aye?'

'Take me home. Please?'

'I take it by home you mean the convent, not the castle?'

'Yes.'

Not meeting her gaze, he shook his head. 'I cannot. My lady, it pains me to admit it, but Count Faramus has indeed found another man for you to marry.'

Rowena shivered and wrapped her arms about herself. 'Do…do you know who it is?'

Green eyes lifted, held hers. 'It's me. Lord Faramus has asked me to marry you.'

'You?' Rowena blinked and her heart started to race. 'Eric, you do know I am set on being a nun.'

His mouth twisted and Rowena felt her cheeks

burn under the intensity of his gaze. He sighed and looked away. 'Aye, the whole of Champagne knows of your wish to take the veil.'

She leaned forward, running her gaze over his face, the face that was so familiar and yet so changed. Had Eric's character altered as much as his features? When she was young, he had been an entertaining playmate. She bit her lip. He had taught her chess and she had enjoyed the games, even if Eric had wearied of her company far too soon. Once he'd been made squire, it had been impossible to wring so much as a smile out of him.

'Father can't make me marry,' she said. 'I got the king's agreement to enter the convent. The king—he is my godfather, if you recall—approves of my wish to take my vows.'

'Sadly, your father does not.'

Rowena chewed her lip, conscious that even as they were speaking her excitement was rising. She couldn't understand it. God was surely testing her resolve again, tempting her by offering her a way out of the convent, tempting her almost beyond endurance by sending Eric to her. 'Sir, I cannot renege on my decision to become a nun.'

No sooner had the words left her mouth than Rowena found herself wondering what would happen if she did indeed change her mind. What would the king say? She would be pleasing her father, and whilst Rowena couldn't forget her father had tried to force her into marriage with Lord Gawain when she wasn't ready, she hadn't enjoyed fighting him. It had really upset her mother.

And, most shocking of all, she even found herself wondering if marrying Sir Eric wasn't such a terrible idea—provided she could reassure herself that Eric wasn't going to turn into a tyrant like her father. How much had he changed in the years since she'd known him?

'Dear Lord,' she said, alarmed at how easily her thoughts had run away from her. 'I was certain that if I won the king's agreement to take the veil, even Father wouldn't dare go against him.'

'I agree, it's surprising,' Eric said, quietly. 'However, I should warn you that Lord Faramus is showing no sign of backing down.'

Rowena touched his sleeve and snatched her hand back as soon as she realised what she had done. She was almost certain she liked this man as much as she had done when he had been a boy. But she would never agree to marry him. Marriage was such a large step. If she married this knight, she would have to obey him for the rest of her days. This was a test of her vocation and she must resist. 'Sir, let me in on your plans. I need to know your mind.'

What she couldn't say, not out loud, was that she really needed to know whether Eric had mirrored himself on her father. What did he intend to do with her? Would he think nothing of riding roughshod over the needs of others to achieve his ambitions?

He smiled. 'My lady, I must confess I am reluctant to stand between you and your vocation.'

'Then why kidnap me?' She stared at his profile. There was more here that Eric wasn't saying and he seemed determined not to tell her. As a young man he had always been determined. Sir Macaire had once told her that Eric had been set on being a knight from the moment he'd arrived at the castle. He'd been—what?—six years of age. No one knew for sure.

Rowena hadn't been born then, so she couldn't remember Eric's arrival, she had to rely on what she'd been told. Everyone at Jutigny knew about the small boy her mother had found shivering in the snow one Christmastide. There had been no sign of his parents, so Lady Barbara had taken him in. Eric had been a foundling and he had risen to become a knight thanks to her mother's charity and his own formidable talents.

Eric had taken to castle life as though born to it. He was there in Rowena's deepest memories—practising swordplay with a wooden sword; sneaking out to ride horses that a boy double his size would think twice about mounting; teaching her to climb the plum tree in the herb garden because she had an insatiable fondness for ripe plums...

Eric was proud, he wouldn't like to be reminded that he'd been a foundling. To Rowena's knowledge, he never mentioned it. On the heels of that thought came the realisation that it had been stupid of her to ask why he had fallen in with her father's wishes. Eric was bound to feel beholden to her family. Her father had allowed him to rise through the ranks and win his spurs. Without her father, Eric would not be the man he was today.

She sighed. If only her father was less intransigent. He wanted her to marry and he had remembered that she had liked Eric as a child. And he must know how Eric coveted lands. Land represented security—every knight she knew wanted a larger estate and Eric was bound to crave security more than most.

Had Eric's nature changed? Had the kind boy grown into a kind man?

Eric tossed the blade of grass aside and gave her another of those intense looks. 'My lady, this is most awkward, I do not wish to tell you the whole. Suffice it to say that Lord Faramus put me in a position when I had no choice but to agree to snatch you from the convent.'

'Sir, there is surely always a choice.'

'Not this time.'

'Father threatened you.'

'Not precisely.'

'But he wants you to marry me?'

'So it would seem.'

'I can't help wondering what Mama would say if she knew.'

Eric's skin darkened. 'My lady, your mother knows about this. Lady Barbara was present at my meeting with Lord Faramus.'

A cool finger lifted her chin and green eyes looked earnestly into hers.

'My lady, you need not fear me.' Briefly, his gaze lingered on her lips and his lips quirked into one of those charming smiles she'd seen him direct at the castle maids. 'Much as I would like to fall in with your father's suggestion, I believe he is being over-hasty. I am sure that when he is given time to reflect, he will change his mind.'

The stab of disappointment was unexpected. 'You're going to take me back to the convent?'

'Sadly, I can't do that.' Eric shoved his hand through his hair. 'My lady, I didn't want to tell you this, but if you refuse to come with me, your father is holding someone else in reserve. Someone who may not be as forbearing as I when faced with your refusal to marry him.'

Rowena could hardly breathe. 'Do I know him?'

'Yes, my lady, it is Sir Breon de Provins.' His eyes were watchful. 'I do not think Sir Breon will hesitate to use force. And imagine the chaos he will cause if he has your father's blessing to enter the convent.'

'Not Sir Breon, the sisters would be terrified.' Rowena put her hand to her throat. A lump had formed and she was very much afraid that she might burst into tears. As a knight Sir Breon was efficient enough. Personally, he came over as brusque and cold and Rowena had always kept out of his way, she could never warm to a man like that.

She felt utterly trapped, exactly as she had done when her father had faced her with marriage to Lord Gawain. 'I thought Father would leave me in peace once I had the king's blessing to enter the convent,' she whispered. 'I thought I had escaped. I thought I had won leave to order my own life, but it would seem I've just swapped one tyranny for another.'

She stared at a spot of sunlight playing on the trunk of a tree and gritted her teeth. She should have known it wouldn't be easy to escape her father's will.

Unless she married Eric.

If she married Eric she would be obeying her father and escaping him. A voice in her head was muttering: *Better Eric than the convent. Better Eric than Sir Breon.* She couldn't bring herself to say the words out loud.

Mathieu's face swam into her mind and a pang went through her. It was obvious she wasn't going to be allowed to mourn him in peace.

Could she marry Eric? She gave him a sideways glance. His strong arms had had no difficulty overpowering her. The boy she had dreamed about so long ago was a successful knight, a landed knight. Doubtless the habit of command had become his second nature. Would he seek to dominate her as her father sought to dominate her mother?

'Sir Breon is as much a victim as anyone else,' she murmured.

Eric's eyebrow shot upwards. 'You like Sir Breon, my lady?'

Rowena shuddered and gave a swift headshake. She didn't like Sir Breon, but she thought she understood him. Over the years she'd watched Sir Breon's ambition warp his nature. He'd begun in a small way. There'd been an archery contest one winter—the men of Jutigny had been pitted against the Provins guard and Sir Breon had been put in charge. The Jutigny team had won, much to her father's delight. After that the rumours had begun, rumours which went something like this—Sir Breon had contacts in Provins and he'd bribed one or two of their archers to miss their mark. Provins had lost, not badly, just enough to ensure that the Jutigny team won.

'My father is a cunning man,' she said. It was clever of her father to offer Eric her hand in marriage. By holding out the promise of a county he was offering Eric everything he'd always wanted. If Eric married her, he would no longer feel like an outsider. 'He is also a cruel man.'

'Cruel?'

She shrugged. 'He is offering what you most want—land—and he is using your best quality—your loyalty—to bend you to do his will.'

'My lady, I will not marry you if you do not wish it.'

The gold cross at Rowena's breast flashed as she took in a deep breath. Eric's heart clenched. His aloof would-be nun was looking rather the worse for wear. Her hair streamed down her back like silk, she didn't seem to have noticed how it had unravelled. Her eyes, the colour of forget-me-nots, were shiny with unshed tears.

'Father is such a trial,' she murmured. 'Sometimes I think that he hates me.'

Eric shook his head. She looked so small and

defenceless. So hurt. He was taken with the urge to take her hand, he wanted to comfort her. *She wants to be a nun, don't touch her, it's obvious she dislikes men.* Eric could understand why. It took a strong man to hold on to a county and her father was just such a man. Sadly, Count Faramus could be extremely inflexible, certainly as far as his womenfolk were concerned. Yet it was more complicated than that. Her father had fought to keep his county and he wanted it to go to his daughter and in turn to her heirs.

'My lady, you are an heiress. The County of Sainte-Colombe could be yours one day.'

'I don't want to be an heiress.'

He smiled. 'Nevertheless, my lady, that is the role you were born to.'

Her chin lifted. 'What happens next?'

'Next, I take you back to my manor where we will wait. I swear you will not be forced to do anything against your will. I feel sure your father will reconsider. After that, you'll be safe to return to the convent.'

'And if Father doesn't relent?'

'My lady, I will take your part.'

Her pretty mouth set in a bitter line. 'Much good that will do me.'

'My lady?'

'Lord Gawain took my part when he released me from my betrothal. He went to Paris and convinced the king to let me enter a nunnery. If Father won't listen to the king, sir, I hardly think he will listen to you. He is determined to marry me off.'

Eric lifted an eyebrow. 'I too would petition the king on your behalf. Don't you trust me?'

'I trust you.' Blue eyes searched his. 'Up to a point.'

Eric stiffened. 'My lady, I take exception to that remark. You have my word that if all else fails, I will petition the king.'

'Thank you.' She pushed a strand of hair back over her shoulder and sighed. 'This is all because of my cousin, Sir Armand.'

'Yes, Count Faramus mentioned him.'

'Father hates him, he will do anything to prevent him inheriting the estate.' She looked pleadingly at him. 'So you plan to take me back to Monfort. And then?'

'We wait for your father to come to his senses.'

She shook her head and her hair rippled out over her shoulders. 'That day will never dawn. Father thinks to win you over by giving you a chance to step into his shoes. He's tempting you as he has tempted Sir Breon over the years.'

Eric stared at her. 'My lady?'

She shrugged. 'You must have noticed. Every time Father wants something unsavoury doing he goes straight to Sir Breon and offers him something he knows Sir Breon will not be able to resist. And however distasteful the task, Sir Breon always steps up to the mark. If silver is offered he accepts it. Every time.'

'I am not Sir Breon.' Eric's voice was gruff. It irritated him beyond measure that Lady Rowena should compare him to Sir Breon. Particularly since marriage with her would give him the security he had always longed for. Him? A count? Once it would have seemed impossible, yet now… 'You will have to trust me, my lady.'

She gave him a small smile that reminded him of her mother and shook her head. 'Sir, I can see I have little choice but to go with you.'

Eric breathed a quiet sigh of relief. Thank heaven, she was prepared to put a little trust in him, he didn't want to ride back to Monfort with her fighting him every step of the way.

As soon as Lord Faramus realised that he could not force her into marriage—after all, Lady Rowena was the king's goddaughter—Eric would do the right thing and send her back to the abbey.

Nearby, a horse whinnied. Alard had followed them into the copse and stood with the horses a little way off. Rising, Eric had extended his hand to help Lady Rowena up before he recalled that she would not like to touch him. To his surprise and pleasure her tiny hand took his and she came gracefully to her feet.

She straightened the cross at her breast, shook out her grey gown and started to tidy her hair. 'Goodness,' she said, flushing like a rose as she realised how much of it had worked loose. 'What a mess. You should have told me.'

Her hair looked beautiful to Eric—small golden tendrils framed her face, long shimmering waves cascaded down her back. A compliment hovered on the tip of his tongue. He folded his lips together and kept it in. A woman who was shortly to make her preliminary vows wouldn't appreciate compliments.

He cleared his throat. All in all, Lady Rowena was taking this better than he had dared hope. Nevertheless, the tremor in her hands as she plaited her hair told him that she was nervous. Was she afraid of him? Lord, he hoped not. It wouldn't be surprising if she were though. This—being abducted from the convent—had to be the most unnerving experience of her life.

Eric had considered her cossetted as a child. Now he realised how wrong he'd been. Not having parents himself had blinded him to the truth. Cosseted was definitely not the word to use for the count's treatment of his only child. Restricted would be a better word. When Lady Rowena had been young, Count Faramus had watched over her like a hawk and, as soon as she had left her childhood behind, she'd spent half her time in a convent.

The nuns must have been instructed to teach her the skills necessary to become some great lord's wife. Eric's mouth twisted. They didn't seem to have followed their instructions very well, all they seemed to have instilled in her was a desire to become one of them. And a dislike of her father and a wariness of men in general. Still, at least she had agreed to go with him to Monfort.

Eric looked at the small, shaking fingers deftly braiding all that golden glory into the tightest, most repressive braid he had seen. She must feel the world was falling apart around her. He should say something that would put her at her ease. 'Until I spoke with your father I had other plans for today.'

She gave him a brief glance. 'Oh?'

Eric picked up his cloak and shook it out. Crossing to Captain, he fastened the cloak to the back of his saddle and checked the girth. 'I intended riding to Bar-sur-Aube, to buy horses.'

She came to stand at his elbow and the rest of what Eric had been going to say flew out of his head. She really was a tiny thing and her father was a bully for trying to force her into marriage.

His chest ached. 'My lady, I swear I will do my utmost to help you.'

'Thank you, Sir Eric.'

He swallowed. 'You will ride before me?'

She glanced at her own horse. 'May I not ride Lily?'

'I am sorry, my lady, not at the moment.'

'You think I will gallop back to the convent?'

The grin was out before he could stop it. 'Something like that. Alard will look after Lily.'

Biting her lip, she nodded. Eric took the reins and mounted. Alard came forward to help her up and then she was sitting before him and they were riding towards Monfort. Eric kept one hand on the reins and the other on her waist. She sat before him, stiff-backed. Trying, no doubt, to keep space between them. Eric took a deep breath. It wasn't going to be the easiest of rides.

By the time they reached the main highway, Lady Rowena's body had slipped back against his. Eric's nostrils twitched. When he bent his head to hers, he could smell flowers, she smelt like a summer meadow. He kept his hand firm about that tiny waist. She shifted forward. Captain walked on and gradually she slipped back against him. No sooner had her body touched his than she shifted forward.

Eric ground his teeth together. 'My lady, it

will make for an easier ride for both of us if you
would relax. I am not going to hurt you.'

She muttered an apology—her voice was
strained—and allowed Eric to pull her more
firmly against him.

'Thank you, my lady. It will be safer this way.'

For the rest of the ride she remained quies-
cent, but Eric could feel the tension in her. She
had said that she trusted him. Why then was she
holding her back ramrod straight? She would
surely ache when they reached his manor. He
held his tongue, likely she would resent further
comment.

At least she had agreed to come with him. He
could keep her safe until he persuaded Count
Faramus to think better of his plans for her. Her
reaction when he had mentioned Sir Breon had
been telling—she loathed and feared the man.
That was some justification for the penance of
having to take her back to Monfort. A penance
that might go on for some time if her father
proved intransigent.

Eric wished Lady Rowena wasn't quite so
pretty; he wished her waist wasn't so tiny and
that she didn't smell of flowers; he wished that
she wouldn't keep squirming against him. It
made him think thoughts that would shock this
prim, would-be nun so much she'd never speak
to him again. It made him want to take up her

father on his suggestion and ask her to marry him, in truth. Not that she would accept him, of course. It just made him wish. She would be his wife and he would have the pleasure of teaching her that men weren't all monsters. He would enjoy discovering the delights of the marriage bed with Rowena de Sainte-Colombe as his partner. His blood heated at the thought.

Did Count Faramus realise what a temptation he had set before him?

Of course he did, the man was as wily as a fox, as his daughter had already pointed out. Except…the count was clearly of the opinion that the real prize was the lands that went with his daughter rather than his daughter herself.

A mule was headed for the market, laden with bales of cloth. As they trotted past it, a jay screeched somewhere in the woodland to their left. Eric focused his gaze on a large oak and tried not to think about what it would be like to really marry Lady Rowena.

He would think instead about what it would be like to be Count of Sainte-Colombe. It was an honour he had never looked for. Eric still felt stunned when he thought back on yesterday's interview in the solar of Jutigny Castle. Clearly, the count was desperate. Desperate and determined. Eric hadn't said as much to Lady Rowena, she was obviously worried enough already, she didn't need to be told that Eric suspected Lord Faramus might take some while to come to his senses. Lord, the count had suggested that he should seduce his daughter into marriage. He must really hate Sir Armand.

Lady Rowena didn't need to be told that Lord Faramus had asked him to ruin her. What kind of a father would do that? Eric shook his head. A ruthless one. Which brought his thoughts round to Sir Armand again. When they got to Monfort, Eric would make enquiries. What kind of a man was Sir Armand that he should drive Lord Faramus to have his daughter snatched from the nunnery she had chosen to make her home?

Dipping his head a fraction, Eric inhaled. Summer flowers. His hand shifted on her waist.

Mon Dieu, just thinking about marrying her made his blood heat.

Poor, innocent Lady Rowena. *She is going to take her vows. She is going to take her vows and I must not think of her in that way.*

Chapter Three

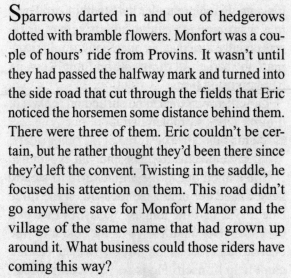

Sparrows darted in and out of hedgerows dotted with bramble flowers. Monfort was a couple of hours' ride from Provins. It wasn't until they had passed the halfway mark and turned into the side road that cut through the fields that Eric noticed the horsemen some distance behind them. There were three of them. Eric couldn't be certain, but he rather thought they'd been there since they'd left the convent. Twisting in the saddle, he focused his attention on them. This road didn't go anywhere save for Monfort Manor and the village of the same name that had grown up around it. What business could those riders have coming this way?

Cursing under his breath—Lord Faramus had promised that he would not interfere—Eric glanced at the squire riding at his side. 'Alard?'

'Sir?'

Eric jerked his head in the direction of the party behind them. 'Did you notice those horsemen?'

'Aye, sir.'

'How long have they been there?'

'They've been with us pretty much the whole way. I thought you'd seen them.'

Eric sighed, he should have noticed them as soon as they'd turned off the main highway—the scent of summer flowers must be fuddling his wits. He swore under his breath. Lord Faramus was going to meddle, he was sure of it. He was equally sure that his interfering would make matters worse. As things stood Lady Rowena barely trusted him.

Lady Rowena turned her head and looked at him. 'There's a problem, sir?'

'Behind us.' Eric gestured at the other riders. 'Your father seems to be keeping an eye on us.'

She leaned out, grasping his arm to steady herself, and her blue gaze focused on the three riders. She had the longest eyelashes Eric had ever seen. Her mouth—it was the colour of ripe cherries and just as tempting—firmed. 'Father can't help himself. He is so very controlling.' Her grip on his arm tightened. 'Eric, you won't let them take me?'

Eric's pulse jumped. When she'd called him Eric, it was as though the years fell away and they were children again. The lack of formality made him feel as though they'd been friends for ever. Tearing his gaze from her, he focused on the men behind them. If it came to a fight it was three against two. He was confident he could protect her, provided she wasn't sitting before him when they came to blows. 'They won't take you. My lady, you may be at ease, you are coming with me to Monfort.'

'I really don't want to see my father. Nor do I want to be given to Sir Breon.'

Eric was irritated Lord Faramus was checking up on him after promising otherwise, however, it wasn't her fault. And he supposed it showed some measure of care that the count wanted to know his daughter had come to no harm. He gave her as reassuring a smile as he could muster. 'You won't be. I am sure that your father has sent us an escort simply to make certain that I get you safely back to the manor.' His mouth twisted. It would be good to think Lady Rowena was happy to come with him because she had a sincere liking for him. He couldn't delude himself though—he and she had hardly spoken in years. She was only happy to accompany him because she disliked Sir Breon more than him. 'He wouldn't want you to be carried off by anyone but me.'

She gave him a straight look and surprised

him with a laugh that wasn't echoed in her eyes. 'Likely that's the truth. Father only asks knights he trusts to do his dirty work.'

It didn't sit well with Eric that Lady Rowena had decided he was doing her father's dirty work. 'My lady, I thought you understood, I am only appearing to fall in with your father's plans. He will change his mind, I am certain. You will be back at the convent before you know it.'

Those large blue eyes searched his before she gave a little shrug and released his arm. 'So you say.'

Her tone irked him. If she didn't believe him why was she agreeing to accompany him? Why had she called him Eric? As she turned to face forward once more, Eric put his hand carefully back on her waist. This time she made no move to ease her body from his. He wasn't sure what she thought of him—she had liked him when she'd been a child, but now? Had her view of him changed so much? If so, why? Was it simply that they were no longer children?

She dislikes men. Had she always done so? Her relationship with her father had always been fiery. In the past Eric had seen this as a sign of her spirit, two strong wills were bound to clash from time to time. Was there more to it than that? Had something happened in the years since he'd seen her? Something that had given her a mistrust of men?

Eric's thoughts regarding the woman sharing his saddle were rapidly becoming confused. It should be a simple matter to take her to Monfort and keep her safe until her father had cooled down. Sadly, Eric hadn't bargained for the effect she would have on him. Lady Rowena was a pretty child no longer, she had grown into a woman of rare beauty. There was no confusion there. The difficulty was that Eric found her convent aloofness something of a challenge. She was using it as a shield, too innocent to see that it made him ache to push it aside and see what lay behind. Was she as prim as she appeared? He was enjoying the neat way her body nestled against his far too much. He was enjoying the softness of her hair when it brushed against his face, not to mention the scent of summer. Her dainty, ladylike body was far too appealing for his peace of mind. This wasn't going to be as easy as he'd imagined.

She wanted to be a nun. He found himself staring at the back of her head, frowning as he wished he could see into her mind. It seemed so wrong. Did she really want to take the veil? Or was this just her way of thwarting her father?

As a young girl at Jutigny Castle, Lady Rowena had been a favourite with the retainers' children. She'd shown no airs and graces. Night after night the children had flocked round her, demanding stories before they settled down to sleep. She'd been happy to oblige, producing story after story. Naturally most of them had been Bible stories, but the occasional fairy story and chivalric tale had crept in among the parables. If it weren't for Lady Rowena's insistence on taking the veil, she would make a fine mother. *Mon Dieu*, it chilled his blood to think of her mouldering away in the cloisters until the end of her days.

Eric urged Captain on. As the fields slipped past, he glanced back from time to time. The horsemen didn't draw any nearer, nor did they fall behind, they kept their distance as though measuring it to the inch. When Eric's small party had passed through Monfort village and reached the manor, Eric hailed the guard at the gatehouse and glanced back up the road. Their unwanted escort had stopped about half a mile away on the edge of the village, near enough for Eric to see their horses' tails swishing to and fro.

Lady Rowena followed his glance. Her brow clouded. 'My father is the most stubborn man alive,' she muttered. 'I wonder which of his men he sent to follow us, it's odd I don't recognise the horses.'

Eric shrugged, hailed the guard at the gate-house and they clopped into the manor yard.

Lady Rowena looked about with interest and Eric wondered what she was seeing. She'd been to Paris; she was used to Provins with its upper and lower town, with its huge market and square. Compared to that, Monfort village was simple indeed—two straggling lines of cottages; a church; a smith; an alehouse. As for Eric's manor, it couldn't compare to Castle Jutigny or indeed to her father's other holdings in Sainte-Colombe. To her eyes—the daughter of a count—Monfort must seem a mean and shabby place.

Eric had had the stables repaired when he'd arrived; the main tower had been scoured top to bottom; a pair of extra privies had been built into the north wall, none the less he was achingly conscious that it lacked many of the comforts she had known at Jutigny or Sainte-Colombe. His household was relatively small. The cook-house was tiny and the food that came out of it was good, honest fare, if somewhat basic.

'Welcome to Monfort, my lady.' He found himself braced for her reaction.

'Thank you.'

He helped her down and she looked about with interest, giving him no sign that she saw anything amiss about her surroundings. She gave him a candid look. 'Eric, if you imagine my father will change his mind whilst I am lodged beneath your roof, you are very much mistaken. He means to make you marry me.'

He put his hand on his heart. 'My lady, I wouldn't dream of standing between you and your wish to be clothed as a novice. I swear you will be safe here.'

She gave him a faint smile. 'You intend to observe the proprieties.'

'But of course.'

'Where will I sleep?'

Eric gestured at the tower. 'There is a chamber off the minstrel's gallery, I have given orders for it to be made ready for you.'

'Thank you, sir. You've arranged for a maid?'

Eric felt his face fall. 'You want a maid?' *Bon sang*—good grief—naturally, she would want a maid. Likely Lady Rowena hadn't dressed herself in years. Swiftly he ran his gaze over her grey gown. The lacings were at the back. Tight lacings. She was probably too innocent to realise how those lacings showed off every curve. Beautiful.

She tipped her head to one side and the cross at her breast gleamed. Eric received the distinct impression that she had seen his gaze linger on her body. 'Sir, I am capable of dressing myself. However, if the proprieties are to be observed, you ought to arrange for a maid to sleep in my bedchamber. And most of my things are at the convent, I shall need more clothing.'

'It shall be arranged.' He offered her his arm. 'Do you care to see the bedchamber?'

The hall at Monfort was nowhere near as large as Rowena's father's hall at Jutigny, but it was well proportioned with heavy beams criss-crossing the roof. Rowena saw an oak table set before a stone fireplace. A young woman was kneeling on the hearth, shovelling dead ashes into a leather pail. The table was clean, though Rowena would swear it had never been polished—the mark of the adze showed clearly on the wood. She glimpsed side tables and a couple of stools by the fireplace. The walls were whitewashed, again they looked clean. However, there were no tapestries, indeed, no linens of any kind. There were no cushions to soften the benches. The lack of linens or wall-hangings told Rowena that Monfort was almost entirely a male domain.

As they approached the door at the far end of the hall, the woman laying the fire looked across at them. Eric gestured her over. 'Helvise?'

The woman brushed soot from her fingers and got to her feet. Rowena saw that she was about the same age as herself. She was far gone in pregnancy.

'Sir?'

'Helvise, this is Lady Rowena de Sainte-Colombe, she will be staying at Monfort for a time.'

'Yes, sir, I remember you told me last eve.'

'Is her chamber ready?'

'Yes, sir.'

Eric nodded. 'Thank you, Helvise.' His brow creased. 'I am going to show Lady Rowena up and I should like you to accompany us. For form's sake.'

The woman's gaze travelled slowly from Eric to Rowena and back to Eric again. For no reason that she could think of, Rowena felt her cheeks heat.

'For form's sake,' Helvise muttered. 'Of course, sir.'

They wound their way up a stairwell lit by slender lancets and stepped out on to a landing at one end of the gallery. Rowena could see right down into the hall. There were two doorways, Eric leaned past her and lifted the latch of the second door.

With Helvise hovering at their backs, Eric and Rowena squeezed into a shadowy bedchamber. It wasn't large, there was only room for the two of them. Rowena squeezed up against the wall next to a shuttered window whilst Eric flung back the shutters. Light poured in. The spring breeze ruffled Eric's hair.

The window looked out over a wooded area. Rowena could see the river gleaming through the foliage and a man leading a donkey along a narrow track. There was movement under the tree canopy, and one of the horsemen they'd seen earlier rode into a scrap of sunlight and said something to the man with the donkey.

Rowena sighed, her father's man was doubtless checking up on them. When the rider tipped back his head to examine the tower, instinct had her drawing back from the window.

'Well?' Eric was waiting for her reaction. 'Can you manage in here?'

In a corner of the bedchamber there was a tiny hearth; on the opposite wall a row of hooks. Other than the bed, there was nothing, it was as spare as her cell in the convent.

'This is fine. Thank you, sir.'

Eric shoved his hand through his hair. 'It is plain, I know, and the fireplace is small. You could have my bedchamber which is larger, but I didn't think you would be comfortable there.'

'No indeed, my father's request has inconvenienced you enough.' The bed here certainly swallowed up most of the space. The sheets appeared to be linen and a couple of blankets were heaped up at the foot. 'Truly, sir, this chamber will suit me well.'

Eric nodded and sent Helvise one of the smiles that Rowena remembered from his time at Jutigny. It was the smile of a man used to getting his way with women, full of charm and confidence. 'Helvise, do you know of anyone prepared to try her hand at being a maid? Someone who might be ready to take on some lighter tasks for a time.'

'You mean me, sir?'

'If you wish.'

'Thank you, sir, I would appreciate that,' Helvise said, in a cool tone that seemed to say otherwise.

'It will mean you bedding down here with Lady Rowena.'

'For as long as she's here, you mean, sir?'

'Aye.'

Rowena made a sharp movement. 'Eric, what about Helvise's husband? Surely he will object? He will want to be with her, particularly since Helvise is so near her time.'

The sudden silence told her she had blundered. Eric's face confirmed it, his expression seemed to freeze. He cleared his throat and opened his mouth, but Helvise got there first.

'Don't worry about that, my lady,' Helvise said. The girl lifted her chin so defensively that

Rowena understood without being told that Helvise wasn't married. 'I am more than content to act as your maid. I have had enough of shifting logs.'

Cheeks hot, embarrassed by her mistake, Rowena nodded. Helvise wasn't married and she was having a baby. It was very unorthodox, shocking even. Who was the baby's father? A horrible thought rushed in on her.

Could Eric be the father? It wasn't a line of thought Rowena wanted to pursue, but her father had forced her into a position where she might seriously have to consider marrying this man. She needed to know what sort of a husband he would make. Eric was known to be a terrible flirt, would he take his marriage vows seriously? The idea that he might stray didn't sit well with her. The question echoed through her mind. Was Helvise Eric's lover?

Eric was bowing her out of the chamber. 'If it pleases you, I will show you the rest of the manor.'

'Thank you.' Rowena followed him from the chamber and on to the minstrel's gallery, staring at his broad shoulders. He was so tall. She fixed her gaze on his dark head as he pointed out the doors at the other end of the gallery. He was saying something about building extra garderobes. Her thoughts rushed on. She really didn't like the idea that he might stray. She wasn't going to marry Eric, so why did she find the idea that he might take a lover so distasteful? It was most peculiar.

Last year, when Rowena had been betrothed to Lord Gawain she had discovered he had a long-standing mistress. Seeing that Lord Gawain loved the woman, Rowena recalled telling him that after their marriage she wouldn't mind him seeking his pleasure elsewhere. And it hadn't been because she had disliked the man, far from it. Grief-stricken though she had been, she had liked Lord Gawain, very much. He had seemed a fair-minded, reasonable man. Notwithstanding that, she wouldn't have minded him keeping a mistress. Why then was the thought of marrying Eric and having to watch him take his pleasure elsewhere so utterly repugnant?

She had idolised Eric as a child, that must have something to do with it. Each time she'd seen him teasing a Jutigny maid, her insides had twisted. She'd been jealous. Even today she could hear faint echoes of her childhood longings.

Her parents had tried to protect her innocence. In that they hadn't been entirely successful, Rowena knew full well that many married men kept mistresses. And when she'd given Lord Gawain leave to keep his lover after their marriage, she'd meant it, she truly wouldn't have minded.

Had she felt that way because she'd been reeling from the horror of Mathieu's untimely death? It seemed likely. Back then Rowena had been deep in mourning. It had been far too soon for her to think about marrying anyone else. Why, even the thought of kissing Lord Gawain had made her want to take to her heels.

Rowena heard Helvise take her leave and murmured her thanks. How odd that she could still hear echoes of her former childish longings. The idea of Eric being unfaithful really wasn't pleasant. In a way though, it was a relief. It must mean she was at last getting over the shock of losing Mathieu.

Eric was pointing at a doorway across the gallery, telling her that that was his chamber. Nodding, Rowena leaned on the gallery guardrail and looked down into the hall. A door slammed and shortly afterwards Helvise walked into view and crossed the hall.

'She's going to the cookhouse,' Eric murmured, following her gaze.

'Helvise runs your household?'

'Since I took over this manor, Helvise has been in charge of domestic matters, yes.' A frown brought his eyebrows together. 'She is very capable and very stubborn.'

'Sir?'

'Given that her baby will arrive soon, she does far too much.' His hand covered hers. 'She will not rest and I have been looking for a way to lighten her load.' He gave her one of his light-hearted grins and squeezed her fingers. Rowena's heart did a little skip. 'I never expected your father would ask me to kidnap you, but since he has, I am very pleased that you will accept Helvise as your maid. She needs to be made to do less.'

'I am happy to help,' Rowena murmured.

'I realise Helvise might not make an ideal maidservant, she will need training.'

Rowena searched Eric's face, looking for something that would reveal his feelings for Helvise. He was standing close enough for her to see that the flecks in his green eyes were amber up here in the dimness of the gallery. Were he and Helvise lovers? Was the child his? His expression gave nothing away. Rowena knew she must be patient, in time, she might learn the truth. 'Eric, who will run the household if Helvise acts as my maid?'

Eric looked blankly at her before his face cleared. 'There's a woman in the village, the smith's wife, Maude, I could ask her.'

Rowena found herself shaking her head. 'Sir, I

have been taught how to run a household, whilst I am here I would be glad to help.'

He stared. 'You, run this manor?'

'You think me incapable?' She stiffened, mildly affronted at his doubts. 'I assure you I have been trained to run households far larger than this one.' And if she did manage this manor, the insight she would gain about Eric would be invaluable. Servants revealed more about their masters than most men realised. She would learn far more about his nature if she put her hand to the wheel than if she sat idly by. With a start, she realised she was starting to take the idea of marrying Eric seriously. Could she marry this man? Could she?

'Rowena—my lady—you misunderstand, all I am trying to say is that I didn't bring you here to work. I brought you here to—'

'Save me from Sir Breon?' She lifted an eyebrow. 'Is that truly why you brought me here?'

'You know it is.'

'You think my father will change his mind? You think I will be able to return to the convent?'

He looked at her. 'If I had a daughter I couldn't possibly force her into marriage.'

'You might if you held my father's lands.' Rowena tipped back her head to hold his gaze. 'Eric, you have forgotten Sir Armand. My father loathes him, he will not change his mind.' She swallowed and the question she burned for him to answer slipped out. 'Do you wish to marry me?'

'My lady, have you forgotten the abbey? You are to take the veil.' He studied her face and lowered his voice. 'I was shocked when I heard about your decision to become a nun.'

'Shocked?'

'It seemed so much at odds with the girl I knew. You—a nun.' He shook his head. 'All I could think was that you made your decision to thwart your father.'

'In part.' Rowena saw no reason to tell Eric about Mathieu. Her relationship with Mathieu had been a secret. No one knew that she had fallen in love with him and that one day she had hoped to marry him. In any case, nothing had happened between her and Mathieu, a few stolen kisses didn't count.

However, there was something she did need to tell Eric. He had to be told that if he wished it, she might consider marrying him. Sir Breon was out of the question, but Eric had arranged for her to have a maid, exactly as she had asked. So far he was giving every sign that whilst she was under his roof he intended to observe the proprieties. She trusted him. Perhaps they might spend the next few days learning about each other. They might consider whether they might really make a match of it.

She took a deep breath. 'Eric, sir, there is something important I would ask you.'

'Aye?'

'If…if I was willing, would you marry me?'

Searching eyes looked into hers. 'You're serious?'

'Eric, you know I could never marry Sir Breon. Sadly, my father also knows it. That's why he put you in the position of having to rescue me. He was relying on your innate sense of chivalry.'

Eric's mouth twisted. 'My innate sense of chivalry?'

'He respects you too, of course. He would never have asked you to marry me otherwise.' Rowena gripped the gallery guardrail. This was beyond embarrassing, but since she had begun she would finish. Now she was away from St Mary's, she was beginning to see the world—and her place in it—with new eyes. She had believed she was made to be a nun and the thought of returning to the nunnery should please her. It didn't, it left her cold as stone. She didn't wanted to go back. Ever. How could this be? Her stomach felt jittery and her pulse was thudding. She drew in a breath. 'Eric, recently I have been ill at ease in the convent and I wasn't quite sure why.

I am beginning to see that I have been dreading taking my vows.'

'Go on.'

'I thought God was testing me.'

'It's possible you are not meant to be a nun.'

'Eric, I don't know. All I can say it that I have felt half-dead these past weeks. With your agreement, I should like to consider marrying you.'

He looked quizzically at her. 'You think marrying me would bring you to life?'

With difficulty she met his gaze. 'I don't know, but I would like to consider it. We were friends when we were young, we liked each other.'

'So we did.'

'Marriages have been founded on far less. I think we should use the next few days to see if we might suit each other.'

He drew his head back. 'You would be happy to become my wife?'

'I am happy to consider it, but only if you want it. I would not wish to marry you if you did not want me.'

Slowly, he looked her up and down. His eyes were dark and something in his expression brought warmth to her cheeks. 'Any man would surely be happy to call you his wife.' His face lightened. He took his hand in his and carried it to his heart. 'My lady, even if you hadn't a penny to call your own, you would be a desirable woman.' With a grin, he lifted her hand briefly to his lips. 'Lady Rowena, you are beyond compare.'

A pang went through her. Naturally, Eric would want her for her lands. As would any man. Rowena had always known her true worth as a daughter and heiress to the County of Sainte-Colombe. No man of any sense would ever put her person before her lands. Ignoring the pang—it couldn't be disappointment—she looked expectantly at him. She wanted to hear his agreement, she needed the words. 'So, you would be happy to consider my father's proposal?'

'If we came to an agreement, would it be a real marriage?' he asked, staring at her mouth.

Rowena shifted as an inexplicable wave of heat rushed through her. 'It…it should be in name only, I think, certainly at the beginning.'

He grimaced.

'Eric, it…it is a long time since we have seen each other. We have become as strangers.'

He cleared his throat and squeezed her fingers. 'If we decide to marry all shall be as you wish, my lady, though I give you fair warning the idea of a marriage being in name only holds no appeal. A marriage is not considered valid until it is consummated.'

She bit her lip. 'I do not feel ready for con-summation, sir.'

'I shall do my utmost to ensure you change your mind about that, and quickly. I want heirs.'

Cheeks burning, she nodded. 'Eventually, of course. I understand the duties of a wife.'

'We need to retreat,' he murmured. Backing her into the shadows away from the guardrail, he grasped her other hand.

Rowena's breath left her. She poised herself for flight as broad shoulders blocked her view of the hall. Eric's scent—a heady mix of leather and horse, woodsmoke and man—filled her nostrils.

'Relax, Rowena,' he said softly. 'If I may call you that?'

'Please do.' Managing to free one of her hands, Rowena had placed it against his gambeson with the vague intention of warding him off before she realised she wasn't afraid. Her throat worked. 'Wh…what are you doing?'

'I am going to seal our betrothal agreement, I am going to kiss you.'

Her gaze flew to his mouth. It was smiling. It was extraordinarily attractive. How strange, she wasn't afraid, she wasn't dreading his kiss. 'We are not actually betrothed, Eric,' she said as steadily as she could. 'We are merely considering becoming betrothed. We have to see if we think we will make a good match.'

His smile grew and his eyes danced. 'As you say.'

He lowered his head, still smiling, and Rowena's fingers curled into the leather of his gambeson.

Lightly, he kissed her forehead. Her stomach swooped. He kissed her temples equally lightly, and the muscles in her belly tightened. His musky male scent seemed familiar and something about it was sending messages to her brain, messages that spoke of safety. Of warmth. Of a haven in a world she had never understood.

And then his lips found hers and Rowena could no longer think. Here was warmth and gentleness. She heard flurried breathing, hers. There wasn't enough air. Her heart was racing and her fingers were itching to slide into his hair.

Taking her by the waist, he pulled her flush against him. When she heard a very male murmur of satisfaction, she realised that she had gone up on her toes the better to reach him. Something about this man—his kiss, the careful way he was holding her—made her feel as though she wanted to climb into him. Gripped by shyness, she hid her face against his leather gambeson. What was wrong with her? She had been lost in that kiss. Lost. Not once had she thought of taking her vows. Not once had she thought of Mathieu.

'Rowena.' The humour in his voice eased both shyness and shame, and she opened her eyes to see him shaking his head at her. 'Our marriage will be consummated quite soon, I believe.'

Frowning, she drew back. 'Sir, just because we have shared a kiss does not mean I will marry you. We have not yet decided, we might discover we loathe each other.'

A dark brow lifted. He tucked a wayward curl back under her veil and crooked his arm at her. 'As you say, my lady. Shall we go back into the hall and see what Helvise has found us in the way of refreshment?'

Chapter Four

That night, lying in bed in his bedchamber at the other end of the gallery, Eric couldn't stop thinking about Rowena. Lady Rowena de Sainte-Colombe was here at Monfort and he had her father's blessing—in a manner of speaking—to marry her.

Should he woo her? Since Rowena had confessed that she was prepared to consider him as her husband, he would be mad not to at least try and make her like him. If he courted her, if he gave her more reasons to want him as her husband, well, that could only count in his favour. He had hoped to marry some day. Why not Rowena?

Rowena wouldn't necessarily be a biddable wife. Her privileged upbringing guaranteed that, not to mention that she had her father's pride. Nor was Eric about to delude himself that she loved him, which made making her like him even more crucial. He must ensure that he made it impossible for her to refuse him. Such a chance would never come his way again.

Marriage to Rowena would give him the elusive sense of belonging he'd ached for ever since he'd stood shivering outside the Jutigny gate. He would have a family, a family he knew and understood. And maybe, just maybe, he'd have someone to stand at his shoulder when insults concerning his humble birth were hurled his way. He'd learned to stand up for himself, of course, and that had strengthened him, but it would be good to know he was no longer alone. Not to mention that he'd have the security of land in Champagne as well as in Sainte-Colombe. What a gift that would be.

Eric would be the first to admit that the events of the last couple of days had left him reeling. Lord Faramus's request had been so unexpected. Not only that, Eric had conflicting feelings about Rowena herself. He wanted her in the basest, most earthy of ways. With her delicate body, forget-me-not-coloured eyes and flowing golden hair, she was the personification of all that was feminine. In his mind, Eric conjured her image and smiled into the dark. She was such a fragile-looking creature.

However, he wasn't blind to her nature—that apparent fragility masked the most stubborn of wills. Rowena was strong enough to pit herself against her father. Witness her refusal to marry Lord Gawain; witness her using the convent as a refuge. She was also clever enough to know when she needed to back down. The woman had pride, but she was too sensible to allow it to trap her in the convent till the end of her days.

Dieu merci, thank God, it seemed she was prepared to change her mind about becoming a nun. He couldn't wait to see her lose some of that aloofness.

Dieu merci, she was prepared to consider him as her husband. He wanted to be the one to unravel that repressive golden braid, he wanted the right to run his fingers through those silken strands that smelt like a summer meadow.

Shifting on the bed, Eric put his hands behind his head.

Dieu merci, she'd grown so pretty. The trouble was that just looking at her had his thoughts in a tangle. He wanted Rowena and he wanted to belong, two desires that were twisted together so tightly there was no separating them. Marriage to Rowena would give him both of those things.

He let out an exasperated sigh. He didn't love her and she didn't love him. That didn't matter, what mattered was that he must make her like him. If he married her and their marriage wasn't to be blessed with love, so be it, few marriages were. He would, however, do his best to ensure that it would be harmonious. It would be a success.

He had passed the first hurdle, she had agreed to consider him as a husband. He was pretty certain that she liked him, he would build on that. It would be worth his while to set everything aside for the next few days and court her. Properly.

Remembering her skittishness concerning consummation, he frowned into the gloom and prayed her reluctance didn't go deep. Surely she had learned that from the nuns? He must show her she had nothing to fear. He would enjoy exploring the carnal aspects of marriage with Rowena de Sainte-Colombe. If that kiss had been anything to go by, she was more than ready to begin.

Mon Dieu, if he played this right, he might soon have a willing wife in this bed.

In the bedchamber on the other side of the minstrel's gallery, a single candle glowed on a wall sconce. Rowena was also finding sleep elusive, although for very different reasons. Helvise wasn't proving to be a very biddable maidservant. In truth, she was being so difficult that Rowena could only conclude that she had taken a strong dislike to her. Helvise was presently lying on a simple bedroll beside her bed, despite all Rowena's attempts to make her swap places. Leaning up on her elbow, Rowena frowned down at her. It wasn't that Helvise had actually disobeyed her, but…

'Helvise?'

Helvise's pallet rustled. Unlike Rowena's mattress which was filled with down, the bedroll they had found for Helvise was stuffed with straw and Rowena felt guilty. There was so little room in the chamber that in order to fit the bedroll in, half of it had been shoved under her bed. The result was that Helvise was squashed into a corner and the woman was great with child. She ought to be using the proper bed.

'Yes, my lady?'

'I cannot sleep.'

'I am sorry to hear that, my lady.'

'It is your fault I cannot sleep.'

'My lady?'

'You should not be sleeping on that lumpy pallet.'

'It's my mattress and I'm used to it.'

'Nevertheless, I insist you change places.'

'My lady, it wouldn't be right. Sir Eric would be most displeased.'

'For heaven's sake, Helvise, Sir Eric need not know. I won't tell him.' Rowena made an exasperated sound and flung back her bedcovers.

'You are with child and you need a good night's sleep. I insist we swap places.'

There was more rustling as Helvise sat up. 'Please, my lady, you must keep the bed.'

'I will not.' Pushing to her feet, Rowena caught Helvise by the hand and half-pulled and half-pushed, manoeuvring her on to the bed. 'Lie down and go to sleep. If you do not, I shall be forced to tell Sir Eric that you are unsatisfactory as a maid.'

Helvise bit her lip and Rowena suppressed a twinge of guilt. Her last comment had been a low blow. Helvise's manner had been distant all evening, it was plain she resented acting as Rowena's maidservant, but it was equally plain that whatever Helvise thought about her new role, she was anxious to please Eric. Rowena didn't like to think about the implications of that.

Helvise wrestled with the bedclothes, tugging off the top sheet which she offered to Rowena. 'Very well, my lady, but you must use this linen. Yesterday Sir Eric sent someone into Provins to buy it especially for you.'

Pleased that she had at last brought an end to the argument, Rowena accepted the sheet and thumped and pummelled the worst of the lumps into submission. 'Goodnight, Helvise.'

'Goodnight, my lady.'

Helvise's voice was so mournful, it struck Rowena that perhaps she was misjudging her. She had jumped to the conclusion that Helvise disliked her, she could be wrong. It was obvious that Helvise was deeply unhappy.

As Rowena closed her eyes she resolved that in the morning she would find out why. Rolling on to her side, her fingers curled into a fist. She willed them to relax. She might not like the answer, but she had to know. Who was the father of Helvise's child? If it wasn't Eric, who was it? What had happened to him? Why was Helvise on her own?

Rowena was in the habit of rising early and she and Helvise went down to the hall to break their fast shortly after dawn. A number of servants and soldiers were ahead of them. Rowena knew a few of them by name already.

'Good morning, Sergeant Yder.'

'Good morning, my lady.'

Exchanging smiles and greetings with Eric's household, Rowena took the place she had taken last night. Eric's seat was empty, neither he nor his squire were in the hall.

'Where's Sir Eric?' she asked.

A serving woman Rowena remembered as being called Pascale drifted over with a basket of loaves. 'Sir Eric's in the stables. Would you care for some bread, my lady?' With a smile, Pascale offered her the basket.

'Thank you, Pascale.'

Instead of turning away when Rowena had taken her bread, Pascale dipped into the basket herself and held out a posy of violets tied with green ribbon. 'For you, my lady, from Sir Eric.'

Conscious of Helvise's mournful gaze and Sergeant Yder's wry grin, Rowena felt herself flush as she took the violets. 'Thank you, they are lovely.' The flowers trembled as she set them down next to her bread. No one had given her flowers before. Even though she knew Eric had made the gesture to win her over, it was oddly touching.

'Sir Eric said that if you would care for a morning ride, my lady, he would be delighted to escort you,' Pascale added. 'When you have broken your fast, you will find him in the stables.'

Eric and Alard were talking in the yard when she emerged. Two horses—Rowena was pleased to see that Lily was one of them—had their reins looped round a ring in the wall.

'The violets are lovely,' Rowena said, lifting her skirts clear of some straw as she came across. 'Thank you.'

Eric swept her a bow. 'It is my pleasure. You would care to ride this morning?'

'I would love to.'

Eric ran his gaze over her, frowning. 'Alard, go and ask Helvise to fetch Lady Rowena's cloak, will you? There's quite a breeze.'

As Alard loped back towards the manor, Rowena went over to stroke Lily's nose. The mare whickered in greeting. 'I am glad you didn't leave Lily behind,' she said. 'I would miss her.'

'I know. You always did love your horses.'

Eric came to stand next to her, and once again Rowena was struck by his height, she found it slightly daunting. As a young man he'd been tall and lanky. He'd put on a lot of muscle since then, he looked so strong. Would he want to dominate her as her father dominated her mother? Then he gave her an easy smile and she glimpsed the friend that he had been and her fear dissolved.

'You should have let me ride Lily on the way here,' she said. 'It would have been more comfortable for you.'

Firmly, he shook his head. 'You might have galloped off.' His eyes danced as he took her hand and lifted it to his lips. 'I never thought to be asked to guard a gem as precious as you, I couldn't risk losing you.'

Slowly, green eyes watching her face, Eric turned her hand and pressed a kiss into her palm. Rowena's mouth went dry.

'Sir, please.' Embarrassed, Rowena tugged her

hand free. Saints, what was wrong with her? It seemed the man had but to touch her and she felt as though she was melting. Mathieu had never made her feel like that.

Eric's gaze lingered on her mouth. 'Besides, I liked having you ride with me. It was much more fun with you in my arms.' He stepped closer and leaned in to whisper, 'We could try it again today.'

Rowena caught one of the grooms grinning her way and stepped back smartly. 'I think not.'

'Pity.'

Rowena backed into Lily. Eric's shameless flirting was making it hard to breathe. 'Sir, you overwhelm me. We have not yet agreed we will actually marry. We should renew our acquaintance first.'

He drew back, expression sobering. 'My apologies.' He turned to his horse to check the girth and Rowena was once again able to breathe. 'I pray you will agree. Rowena, I swear that if you accept me, I shall do my utmost to make a good husband.'

Rowena gripped Lily's bridle. She couldn't help thinking about Helvise and it was on the tip of her tongue to ask him whether he considered being a faithful husband was a necessary part of marriage, but she said nothing. It was far too leading a question and their renewed acquaintance was of too short a duration for her to risk posing it. She wished she knew the answer though, because she really thought she could marry him. This was Eric, after all. Except, a sneaking fear lingered, she didn't want to become betrothed to a man who already had a lover. She had done it once before and, although her heart hadn't been engaged, it had caused no end of trouble.

Spirits sinking, she stared at Eric. She didn't think she could marry him if she had to share him. Her pulse speeded up. Apart from his tendency to flirt with every woman he met, the idea of marrying him was becoming more alluring by the moment.

Alard appeared at the head of the steps, her cloak over his arm. 'Here you are, my lady,' he said, hurrying over. 'I brought your gloves too.'

Eric intercepted him and took them from him. 'Thank you. Alard, please open the gates.'

'Aye, sir.'

Draping the cloak over Rowena's shoulders, Eric dropped a quick kiss on her nose before she had time to duck away. His lips twitched. 'Allow me to mount you, my lady.'

His tone was more than a little suggestive. Rowena's toes curled. Cheeks hot, she bit the inside of her mouth to hide her smile. Heavens, the man was incorrigible. While drawing on her gloves,

she made a show of tapping her foot. 'Stop it.
Eric, you must stop this at once, or I shall refuse
to ride with you.'

Green eyes gleamed. A dark brow lifted.
'Stop what?'

'You know exactly what I mean. The *double
entendre*. Flirting, I suppose. It might work on
the maids at Jutigny, it won't work with me.'

'*Dommage*,' he murmured. 'What a pity.'
Grasping her by the waist, he lifted her into the
saddle. His hands lingered.

'Sir Eric, please!'

Eric grinned. Alard heaved on the manor
gates and they groaned open. The horses surged
forward, trotting side by side away from the
manor. Eric had been right about the wind, it
was keen for May. Overhead, clouds billowed
in a blue sky. In the topmost branches of an ash
tree that was a swaying froth of green, rooks
were cawing.

'We will stop at the smith's first, I think,' Eric
said.

Rowena shot him a sharp look. 'If you are
thinking of asking his wife to act as your house-
keeper, I truly would like to help.'

'Rowena, you are my guest.'

Firmly, she shook her head. 'If we are to test
each other's mettle before coming to a decision,

we must do it properly. How else will you know whether I will make a good wife?'

Eric's mouth went up on one side. 'Rowena, you have nothing to prove here. I want you already.' A gloved hand reached out and briefly squeezed hers. When she frowned, he shook his head. 'There's no need to glower. I mean it.'

'You want my inheritance.'

Wide shoulders lifted. 'Only a fool would not want it.' He held her gaze, face softening. Releasing her hand, he ran his gloved finger briefly down her cheek and cleared his throat. 'Be assured that I want you. Rowena, you have become a very beautiful woman.'

Rowena's vision misted and she stared blindly at a passing cottage. 'Don't, Eric, please.'

That gentle hand was back on her again. 'What is it? Lord, Rowena, you're not crying, are you?'

'Of course I'm not crying.'

'What did I say? What did I do? *Bon sang*, I thought to court you this morning. I meant to make you laugh, not cry.' He leaned in, those warm eyes earnest. Dark.

She held his gaze. 'It's all right, Eric, I don't need courting.'

He drew back, expression shocked. 'Not need courting? You are deluding yourself, you need more courting than most.'

'I do?'

'You've been over-protected. Rowena, I am not criticising your parents, they brought you up as they thought best. You are their only child and you are precious to them. However, you need to learn your value as a woman too.'

Rowena held her breath as she listened. Eric was wrong in his assumptions about her parents. She wasn't sure she was truly precious to them. To her mother, perhaps, but to her father? In her experience, her father treated her more as a commodity than a daughter—to him she was something to be traded to ensure that the family acres were passed into firm hands. She had rejected his first choice, Lord Gawain, and now she was presented with his second, a man he had trained himself.

Rowena shot Eric a sidelong glance. She couldn't deny that her father's second choice suited her far better than his first. Of course, it could simply be that this year she was ready to consider marriage. Last year, with Mathieu's death a scar on her soul, she most definitely had not.

Eric's handsome face was turned solicitously towards her, he was giving every sign that he was only thinking of her. However, Rowena was a realist and she knew otherwise. He was thinking about her inheritance. The inheritance someone like him—a foundling—could never aspire to unless he married Lady Rowena de Sainte-Colombe.

She sighed. It had to be wrong that she—a woman who had entered a convent convinced she must become a nun—wanted him to want her for herself. Yet so she did. He had said that he had always liked her and that went both ways. As a child, she had liked him very much. Heavens, she had dreamed about him! She knew him and trusted him and felt at ease with him. And that was important. She could do far worse than marry Sir Eric de Monfort. Except…she couldn't stop wondering whether Helvise's child was his. Eric was such a flirt. Would he always be so? Was he capable of fidelity?

'Why deny yourself the pleasure of being courted?' he was saying softly.

'Being courted is a pleasure, is it?'

'It certainly should be.'

Rowena thought of the maids at Jutigny; she thought of Helvise. 'Sir, you are an expert flirt. I am not certain I can take you seriously as a suitor.'

Eyes wide, he put his hand to his heart. 'My lady, what can you mean?'

'Your reputation precedes you. You enjoy women.'

A dark brow lifted. 'And that is a bad thing? I can see from your face you consider it so.'

'If you are to court me, there is something I would know first.'

'Aye?'

'Your views on fidelity.' Jerking her gaze away, Rowena stared at the smoke rising from the forge ahead and twisted the reins round her fingers. 'If we married, would you be a faithful husband?'

'You would want me to be?'

She nodded and her veil swirled about her. 'Do you think you could manage it?'

Eric blinked and stared at Rowena's profile. The answer flashed almost instantaneously through his mind. *Yes, I would be completely faithful.*

His gut knotted. The conviction behind that thought was unsettling. Eric did enjoy women and whilst he had hoped to marry some day, he'd never given much thought to what it meant when one promised one's wife fidelity. He shoved his misgivings aside. It wasn't as though his happiness would be resting entirely in Rowena's hands. There wasn't a woman on earth he would trust that far.

Doubtless the idea of fidelity unsettled him because he had never seriously considered marriage before this. Stepping into new territory was always daunting.

Rowena went on staring fixedly towards the forge, refusing to meet his gaze. As her veil danced in the breeze, he glimpsed a long twist of hair, bright as the sun.

He cleared his throat. Marriage unnerved him. Observation had shown him that many men found it a penance to remain faithful to their wives when the world was full of pretty women. None the less, it was flattering to know that Rowena wanted fidelity from him. He would be faithful. The thought settled deep in his mind. He would be faithful to Rowena. He could do it, he knew. It was disturbing. Unsettling. And yet...

We would belong together. There was a ball of tension in his gut and Eric was unable to identify its cause. Growing up at Jutigny, he had never felt as though he belonged. Even here in Monfort, in the manor that he had won through force of arms, he thought of himself as a steward, someone who was holding the land for the next incumbent.

'My lady, you may have my oath, if you marry me, I will be faithful to you.'

She turned her head, mouth going up at the side. 'It would be worth it I expect, for the lands I would bring you.'

'That is a cynical remark, but no matter.' He smiled. 'I see I will have to prove that I value you more highly than I value your inheritance.'

Her blue eyes held him. Captain stamped a hoof and Eric realised they were at a standstill, the horses must have drawn to a halt sometime since and he hadn't noticed. He held out his hand. 'Rowena, I should like to marry you and I will do my utmost to prove myself worthy of your trust.'

When she reached across and put out her gloved hand, his chest eased. He squeezed her fingers before releasing her and gestured down the road. 'Do you care to see the village?'

'Thank you.'

'I should warn you, it cannot compare to Provins.'

Eric rode with her through Monfort and all began well. The villagers must have heard of the arrival of Lady Rowena de Sainte-Colombe and were curious to see her. In the field strips, people paused in their work to lean on hoes and spades and watch their passing. Heads poked through shutters. Doors opened. Women carrying water from the stream paused to stare. Rowena nodded and smiled easily at them and Eric's heart warmed.

'You haven't changed. You are just as friendly as you were as a child,' he said.

She shrugged. 'On the whole, I like people.'

This from the woman who had intended to shut herself away in a convent?

They trotted past the smith, heading further down the path that led into the forest. Forget-me-nots the exact shade of her eyes flowered on the fringe of the track. Somewhere in the dappled shade, a woodpecker drummed. Eric smiled to himself, he couldn't have wished for a better day to show her his land.

'You would care to see the chase?'

'Certainly.' She was peering deep into the forest as the horses clopped steadily on and the trees closed about them. Oak, ash, beech…

'That's odd.' Her voice was puzzled.

'Hmm?'

'Someone's moving about, look, over there.'

Eric couldn't see anything unusual, just a shrub waving in the wind. 'It's probably a deer. We have good hunting, plenty of deer and quite a few boar.'

'And poachers?' She frowned across at him. 'Eric, I don't think it was a deer.'

Eric's skin prickled. As a warning it was far too little. It was also too late. Something whirred past him and buried itself in the trunk of a chestnut tree.

An arrow!

It had missed Rowena with barely an inch to

spare. Eric's insides felt as though they had dissolved. Time seemed to stop. That arrow had
almost hit her! He stared at the white fletchings
quivering in the trunk of the tree—they were as
pale as Rowena's face.

He had but one thought—get her to safety.
Whirling Captain round, he grabbed Rowena's
reins and spurred out of the chase. When they
reached the first of the cottages and he judged
they had put enough distance between her and
whoever had shot the arrow, he slowed the horses
to a walk.

'I can ride, Eric,' she said, voice shaking as
she disengaged her reins from his grasp. Her
hands were trembling and she glanced, wide-
eyed, over her shoulder. Her face looked drained,
her cheeks were white as snow. It had been so
close.

Gripped with cold rage and something else he
hadn't time to analyse, Eric focused on the forest
beyond the village. He must find whoever had
loosed that arrow. '*Mon Dieu*, you might have
been killed. Someone must be disciplined.' He
jerked his head in the direction of the manor
gates. 'I will get you inside and organise a search
party. I will find that archer.'

He heard her swallow, she was struggling
for composure, but her eyes were full of anxiety. 'Eric, it seems likely it was a poacher. He

will have realised his mistake, I don't think he's going to hang about in the chase for you to find him.'

'My lady, I cannot let this pass.' Lord Faramus had entrusted her to him and Eric wouldn't stand for her to be terrorised whilst in his care. Once he had her safely inside his manor, he would scour the forest for whoever had loosed that arrow. He set his jaw. 'Sadly our ride is over. I shall escort you to the stables and then I beg that you excuse me.'

Chapter Five

With Lily handed over to the care of a groom, Rowena trailed across the yard towards the hall. So much for her courtship, she thought wryly. Eric was bent on finding whoever had shot that arrow. Behind her, he was barking orders at his men. She paused at the top step. Hoofs clattered on the flagstones as men led out their horses; half-a-dozen foot soldiers were mustering by the gates; there was even a handful of archers. Well, she doubted they would find anyone. Any poacher worth his salt would be long gone.

As she stepped into the manor hall it occurred to her that her bedchamber window looked out over much of Monfort Chase. Naturally, she wouldn't be able to see it all, but she could see the path that trailed along the river past the village and the manor...

Upstairs, Rowena pulled the shutter wide and leaned out.

* * *

It was after noon before Rowena saw Eric again. By then she was sitting on a bench in a sheltered spot in the manor garden, sewing. Sewing always calmed her and after the shock of that near hit with the arrow—it had missed her by a whisker!—she needed to busy herself. She had found some linen and was efficiently running up a side seam when the click of the garden gate alerted her.

Thrusting the needle into the cloth, she folded up the linen to conceal what exactly she was making and smiled up at him. 'Any sight of the archer?'

Shaking his head, Eric crossed the grass and took his seat beside her. 'As you suspected, he was long gone. I have asked the villagers to report back to the manor if they see strangers in the chase.'

'I feel certain it was poachers,' she said.

'Most likely you are right.' Eric looked curiously at the bundle on her lap. 'What are you doing?'

'Sewing.' Rowena kept her hands on the linen and hoped she wasn't blushing. She was making Eric a shirt and she didn't want him to know what it was until it was finished. In Eric's absence she had prevailed upon Helvise to allow her to inspect the household linens. 'I hope you don't mind, but Helvise told me that the spare linen was kept in a coffer at the back of the minstrel's gallery. We have been tidying it. I was hoping to hem a cloth for the table, but there wasn't enough fabric.'

He gave her a wry smile. 'I don't expect there was. When the previous incumbent of Monfort left, he took most of the linens with him.' He glanced at the shirt and covered her hand with his. 'If it pleases you to sew, we can go into Provins and buy cloth. You did say you would need more clothes. And since it is my fault you arrived here without your belongings, I ought to make recompense.'

'My father is more at fault than you. He forced your hand.'

Eric grunted. His thumb was moving gently over her fingers, tracing their length. Slightly bemused, Rowena stared at it. Eric's touch had the strangest effect on her and she was not yet used to it. It made her short of breath, as though she'd been running. The cross at her breast trembled. She licked her lips, saw that he had noticed and felt her cheeks heat. Saints, now he would think she was begging for his kiss…

Thankfully, the breeze lifted her veil and toyed with a long wisp of hair, giving her an excuse to break eye contact with him as she made to tidy it.

His fingers tightened on hers. 'Leave it,' he said.

She shot him a glance. His gaze was dark, far too heated for comfort.

'I don't like being disordered.' Pursing her lips together, she fixed her gaze on a butterfly dancing past an apple tree and continued trying to free her hand.

'In my view you are not disordered enough. My lady, I like you very much as you are, but I am certain I would adore you if you allowed yourself to become a little more disordered.'

He was such a flirt. Rowena wondered if he even knew he was doing it. Then she caught herself up.

Of course he knew it. Eric had warned her he was going to court her and this was his way of doing it. It meant nothing. He wanted to win her so he could have her lands. He must remember that she'd liked him when she'd been a child, and obviously he was under the impression that she was attracted to him now she was a woman. Which she couldn't deny. Any woman with blood in her veins would find him attractive. Sir Eric de Monfort was heart-stoppingly handsome. So masculine. And the way he had of looking at her, his eyes seemed to smoulder, they seemed to say that she was the only woman in the world. Yes, Eric was undeniably attractive. She just wished he didn't know it. She also wished he hadn't twisted half the women of Champagne round his finger. Was one of them—Helvise—even now living under his roof?

Releasing her hand, Eric pushed her veil over her shoulder. His eyes narrowed and he subjected her to a glance so searching she felt it in her toes. Glancing towards the gate—no one was in sight—he stroked her cheek. Her stomach felt fluttery and her mouth dry. Rowena's breath hitched. It wasn't fair. The combination of glossy dark hair, green eyes and natural charm was well-nigh irresistible. And when he fixed her with another of those intense stares, she could almost feel she was the centre of his world. Did he know how compelling it was?

'Eric, please.' Her protest sounded weak, even to her own ears. She braced herself for what he might do next. *I must arm myself against him. I must resist. He is using his charm because he hopes to persuade me to his will. However, if we are to marry, I need to know that his methods won't change.* Leaving the convent for ever was a big step, she had to know she was making the right decision. She wasn't going to be bullied.

For now, that would be enough. It would be good to think that one day she might find love again, but Eric wasn't Mathieu. Eric had never shown the slightest inclination to form a deep bond with any woman. Mathieu had been gentle, he'd been kind and thoughtful. Her gaze skittered over Eric's wide shoulders, his strong arms. Mathieu had been a boy compared to Eric, but he had taught her something of great importance. Not all men dominated women by virtue of their muscles. Eric, as she herself knew, used charm. What would he do if he was crossed?

Eric tipped his head to one side. Her veil shivered as he slipped his fingers beneath it and found her plait. Slowly, he drew it out. It was an innocuous gesture, yet somehow it felt otherwise. The air between them seemed to sizzle in a way it had never done when she'd been with Mathieu. The glint in Eric's eyes and the tilt of his lips made it feel as though they were in his bedchamber and he was undressing her. Her body tightened. Her breath was flurried.

'Yes,' he murmured, smiling. 'And perhaps yet a little more disorder.' He pushed back her veil and his fingers slid into her hair. Stroking. Loosening her braid. Tempting her to surrender to feeling. The warmth of his body was a long caress against hers. He lowered his head and made her wait, his lips poised an inch from hers.

'You are a fiend,' Rowena said. It was that or groan in anticipation. Over the wall, the rooks cawed in the forest. She fancied she could hear the clanging of the smith's hammer on iron. She must be mistaken, for surely they were too far from the village to hear the smith.

'I would be more of a fiend, if you'd allow it,' he muttered. And kissed her.

Rowena kept very still. The instinct was there to take hold of those broad shoulders and cling. She had, as she remembered to her shame, done just that yesterday. She would not do it again. Eric was too sure of himself—far too much the flirt and she mustn't give in to him so easily. Not after yesterday.

So she held herself stiffly, allowing her lips to soften, just a little. They parted of their own volition and his tongue swept inside her mouth. She gasped and—so much for her resolution— found herself reaching for his shoulders. She could kiss him, surely? Thought faded. There was only Eric's scent—potent, masculine and oddly reassuring—and the warmth of his kiss.

He gave an appreciative murmur and the kiss drew out. Her veil was gone, it must be, for the wind was playing in her hair along with his fingers. Rowena no longer cared. The shirt she had been sewing for him fell to the grass and she pressed herself against him. A riot of wanton thoughts took her. She wanted to press her breasts to his chest. What would it feel like to lie naked with this man?

And still he kissed her. A heartbeat later she

was kissing him back. They were both very thorough. It wasn't the first time Rowena had been kissed so deeply, although it was the first time she had lost herself so completely. Mathieu had tried to kiss her in just such a way and she had pulled back, shocked. She'd been afraid of being discovered. Eric's kiss was overwhelming, it left no room for doubts.

This was why Eric was so popular with the castle maids.

Finally, when all Rowena could hear was the thumping of her heart, she managed to break free. Her cheeks felt as though they were on fire.

Eric's eyes gleamed. 'There,' he said, stroking her hair. 'As I suspected, you look so much better disordered. Truly adorable.'

'Really, Eric, you are worse than the wind.' Shifting along the bench, she retrieved the shirt, making sure she picked it up in such a way that he couldn't see what it was. She wanted to surprise him with it when it was finished. Eric's clothes, though of good quality, were very plain. Almost workmanlike, they could have been made for anyone. She wanted to make him something particular, something made especially for Sir Eric de Monfort. She set about tidying herself. 'My hairpins are missing. What did you do with my hairpins?'

'Can't say I remember.' He leaned back with

a grin, her veil clutched in his fist. 'And if I did, I wouldn't say. You needed disordering. I couldn't reach you before. I was beginning to worry I never would.'

'What do you mean?' He handed her the veil. 'Thank you.'

Rowena looked flustered. Good. With her cheeks as pink as her lips and her hair coming loose, she looked beautiful. And adorable. Exactly as Eric had known she would. She was pretending to be angry with him. At least he hoped she was pretending, Eric didn't like to think the anger was genuine. She had returned his kiss. His prim would-be nun was warming to him. Except that already she was rushing back into hiding. It was as if she had emerged briefly from a retreat and was racing back as quickly as she could. *She is hiding again. Why?*

'Rowena?'

'Mmm?'

'What happened to you?'

Blue eyes looked warily up at him as she adjusted the ties on her veil. 'What do you mean?'

'You're hard to reach and you weren't like this as a child. What happened?'

She frowned. 'Nothing happened. I grew up, I suppose.'

Eric looked thoughtfully at her. She'd been so open as a girl. The contrast between the happy girl he had known and this remote woman couldn't be more marked. 'Was it one too many clashes with your father? Is that what it was?'

She bit her lip and said nothing. Clearly, she had no wish to reply, but Eric couldn't simply drop the subject. There were too many questions. Too many inconsistencies. How had the young Rowena turned into the woman sitting next to him on the bench? A woman who shielded herself with a manner so aloof that she tightened her lips at the first hint of light-hearted banter. And yet, *mon Dieu*, she could kiss. When their tongues had touched, Eric had wanted to do nothing more than drag her from the bench and take her, right there on the grass.

How to reconcile the two Rowenas—the child from the past and the woman sitting next to him?

A shocking possibility flashed through his mind. Rowena had had a lover and was no longer innocent. She had lost her virginity and was terrified of being discovered. Was that it?

He studied her, she was already looking prim again. Almost severe. Her hair was scraped back out of sight; her veil was firmly in place. It would be highly unusual for a gently bred girl—a lady—to give herself to a man outside the bonds of marriage, but it did happen. Was this why she had refused Lord Gawain? She must have been afraid of what he might do when he found out.

'Rowena?'

Wide blue eyes lifted to his. All he could see in them was shyness and innocence, yet her kiss had been far from innocent, it had scorched him to his soul. 'Why did you refuse Lord Gawain? He's a personable fellow. And rich, since he inherited Meaux. Why didn't you marry him?'

'We agreed we didn't suit.'

Eric lifted a brow. 'It would have been an excellent match.' At least it would unless Rowena was already in love with someone else. In which case, her innate honesty would have made it impossible for her to marry Lord Gawain. Certain he was on the right track, Eric forged on. 'It was to have been a marriage of convenience, such as your father had always planned for you. It can't have surprised you. And Lord Gawain is not an unreasonable man, he would not have mistreated you. Think of the status you would have had as Countess of Meaux and one day of Sainte-Colombe.'

'I know.' She twisted the cloth on her lap. 'Eric, I couldn't marry him. Lord Gawain had a mistress and he loved her, he loved her so much that he asked to be released from our betrothal.' She shrugged. 'I simply agreed.'

'And retreat to the convent seemed like a good idea?'

She lifted her gaze and the bleakness in her eyes tugged at his heart. 'It did at the time.'

She went on twisting the linen on her lap. Eric didn't believe that Lord Gawain had asked to be released from his betrothal. However, the man was chivalrous to his core and if Lord Gawain discovered that Rowena was unwilling to marry him, he wouldn't have hesitated to take it upon himself to appear to have broken their agreement. Lord Gawain must have considered that Rowena was likely to bring her father's wrath down on her head by refusing his offer. He would have wanted to protect her.

Eric shook his head. Rowena had that effect on a man, she made him want to protect her.

Eric was certain he had solved the riddle that was Rowena. She had lost her virginity and was terrified of being discovered. Who could it have been? Well, it was clearly too soon to ask her that. She wasn't ready to answer. He sighed. He supposed he must be thankful she had become bored of playing the nun. And she did seem to be considering him as a husband. The thought of her being forced to marry Sir Breon made his skin crawl.

A blackbird was pecking about at the base of an apple tree. Eric watched it thoughtfully, all too conscious of the woman sitting next to him.

Unfortunately his conclusion, that Rowena had lost her innocence, only led to more questions.

If Rowena had a lover, where was he? Had he abandoned her? Was she in love with the man? It might explain why she was so skittish. Lord, the man must have been mad to have left her. If Rowena had lost her virginity, it might also explain why Lord Faramus had summoned Eric to Jutigny. Virgin brides were highly prized by noblemen who wanted to keep their bloodlines pure. A great lord would expect his young bride to be a virgin.

Icy fingers trailed down his back. Lord Faramus must have discovered that Rowena had lost her virginity. Eric's heart sank. *I am low-born. Lord Faramus has picked me out, not because he values me as a man of honour, but because he knows I have no bloodlines to speak of. I am not noble. I am no one. Count Faramus would not expect me to complain when I discovered my bride was not as innocent as she pretended. He offered Rowena to me because he considers her to be spoiled goods.*

An old memory surfaced.

Eric had been cornered in the Jutigny stables shortly after being taken in by Lady Barbara. Philip, the head groom, had been brushing mud from the flanks of the count's black stallion and Eric had been watching, fascinated. He was discovering he loved horses and he watched them whenever he could. That day, he must have made a noise for Philip turned.

'What are you doing?' Philip's scowl was dark.

'Just watching, sir.' Eric was so new to the castle that he was still hazy on the hierarchy. To be safe, he addressed all the men as though they were knights. The idea that he might unintentionally insult a knight gave him the chills.

Philip turned his back on him and went on grooming the stallion. 'Like looking at the horses, do you, little rat?'

The tone of Philip's voice was so cold, Eric hesitated before he replied. He was fast learning that not everyone in the castle was as welcoming as Lady Barbara. None the less, he replied truthfully, 'Yes, sir.'

Philip set the brush on the top of the stall and swung round. His face was full of malevolence and Eric shrank back, hitting his head on a bucket hanging from the hook.

'Well, looking is all a gutter rat like you will ever do.' The groom leaned over him, lip curling. 'If you're thinking you can work in my stable, think again.' He pointed at the door. 'Out. I'll have no gutter rats in here. Find work elsewhere. The kitchen is short of scullions.' His smile was vicious. 'And if they won't take you, you can clear out the midden.'

Eric pushed the memory away. Gutter rat hadn't been the worst insult that had been flung at him, but that first encounter with blind prejudice still had the power to sting. Fortunately, not everyone at Jutigny had behaved like the head groom. He'd made friends, Sir Macaire had been one of his most staunch supporters. And he liked to flatter himself that, foundling or not, he'd earned the respect of Lord Faramus.

However there was no escaping the fact that he was low-born. Lord Faramus must have summoned him to Jutigny for that very reason.

Swallowing down his bitterness—it was galling to discover that he was valued more for his low birth than for his achievements—Eric looked into the forget-me-not-blue of Rowena's eyes.

She gave him a shy, adorable smile. Eric couldn't help himself, he smiled back.

If he were honest he didn't care if Rowena wasn't as pure as she'd been painted. He had enjoyed her company once; he knew that at heart she was kind and generous. She was pretty. No, that didn't do her justice, she was stunning. A beauty and an heiress. And she was doing him the honour of considering him as her husband.

So what if her father had picked Eric out because he'd been a foundling? So what if Lord

Faramus believed someone like Eric would be less likely to cause trouble after she was bedded and her lack of innocence had been revealed? His gaze washed over her, lingering on her breasts before he realised what he was doing. It was hard not to think about bedding her and the longer he spent with her, the harder it became. He was really looking forward to the bedding.

Something clicked into place in his head. He wanted to win her. He would win her. Even if she wasn't the virgin he had thought her to be.

Rising, he held out his hand. 'If you wish it, my lady, we could ride into Provins this afternoon and visit the cloth market.'

She put her hand in his. 'Thank you, Eric, I should enjoy that.'

For Rowena the afternoon passed in a blur. Under her somewhat distracted direction, it quickly became plain that whilst Eric knew everything there was to know about horses and soldiering, he didn't know the first thing about fabrics. They bought yards of cream linen at the market in the Lower Town. Eric had insisted on bringing an escort with them and the men were soon staggering under great bolts of cloth.

'This one will make marvellous table linen,' Rowena said, fingering material on one of the stalls.

'What about that?' Eric asked, eyeing a bolt of red.

She shook her head and found herself examining the shape of his mouth rather than the quality of the cloth. The unsettled feeling was back in her belly. It was so strange. As they discussed the merits of one fabric over another her mind kept wandering. It seemed far more interested in watching the way Eric's mouth moved as he spoke, she had to keep forcing herself back to the job in hand. 'That red won't wash well,' she told him. 'See how open the weave is?' She pointed at another linen with a tighter weave. 'That is the better fabric. Or even this one.'

She shot another glance at his mouth—so fascinating—and tried not to think about how it had felt to kiss him. She wouldn't mind another kiss. Except of course they could hardly kiss in the middle of the market.

The stallholder was watching her, a knowing look in his eyes. Feeling herself flush, Rowena touched Eric's hand. Green eyes met hers, he was standing so close she could see the golden flecks in them. Warm fingers placed her hand on his arm. 'My lady?'

She drew him slightly aside and lowered her voice to a whisper. 'Does the world know I am staying at Monfort?'

'Your parents know, certainly. And I believe

Sir Macaire knows. The sisters at the convent too. I am not sure whether the world at large knows.'

Biting her lip, Rowena nodded.

'There's a problem?'

She shook her head. 'The merchant gave me such a strange look. I was wondering if he knows who I am.'

Eric's face seemed to freeze and under her hand she felt him go still. 'You do not wish to be seen with me.'

'No! Eric, please don't think that. It was just the way he looked at me. He thinks I am your *belle-amie*.'

'Would that you were,' he muttered.

'Eric!'

He smiled. 'My lady, you are my guest at your father's suggestion. Last night we observed the proprieties. If we were to be questioned, Helvise would vouch for us. As would everyone at Monfort. You need not fear for your reputation.'

They turned back to the cloth stall. Eric took Rowena's advice and they came away with several bolts of cloth—linens for undergarments and tablecloths. A lovely green wool for a gown for her. She tried to protest.

'Eric, I don't think you should buy fabric for me. Since we are back in Provins, we could quite easily stop off at the convent on the way back to Monfort and pick up my things.'

His mouth firmed. 'No.'

The vehemence of his response wrong-footed her. 'Why ever not?'

'The sisters won't let me go in with you, will they?'

'Not into the sleeping quarters, no.'

'Then you are not going back there.'

She frowned. He looked so concerned that she realised he must be thinking about her father's land. He was worrying about losing his prize. She found herself rushing to reassure him. 'Eric, I will come out again, I promise.'

'You are not going into that convent.'

Recognising finality in his eyes, Rowena shrugged. She wasn't about to start brawling in the market. 'Very well.'

His expression lightened. 'You will allow me to buy the green worsted?'

'If you wish.'

They bought threads and new needles.

'You ought to have that too,' Eric said, pointing as they walked past another cloth stall. 'The blue matches your father's colours.' He leaned in, mouth curving suggestively. 'And your eyes.'

'It cannot have escaped you that the blue is a match for your colours too,' Rowena said drily.

'In any case, it looks like samite—silk from the East.'

'You don't like samite?'

'You can't buy me that, it's far too costly. I have not yet given my formal agreement to our marriage.'

'So you will not allow me to dress you in blue?'

'Not yet. I am only allowing you to buy me the green fabric because I have to wear something and you will not permit me to collect my belongings from the convent.'

He heaved a great sigh. 'When we are married I will buy you the blue samite.' He gave her a little bow. 'Rowena, you will have to give me your agreement soon.' The golden flecks danced in his eyes. 'I shall pine away if you withhold it.'

Rowena bit her lip to keep in her smile, it seemed he couldn't stop flirting for longer than a moment. 'Eric, you don't have to court me all the time. We are meant to be buying fabric.'

'So? That doesn't mean we have to bore ourselves to death whilst we are doing it, does it? I enjoy wooing you.'

Her heart thumped. Truth be told, she liked it too. Far more than she imagined she would. She particularly liked the kissing part. Shooting a furtive glance at his mouth, she was sure there was another kiss for her there. Whenever she wanted. She only had to ask, Eric seemed determined to win her.

She had much to learn, of course. Thus far, each time they had kissed it had been at his instigation. What must she do to signal that she wanted another kiss?

He likes me disordered. Hmm…

Behind her, the bells of St Ayoul rang out the hour. She caught her breath. She'd last heard those bells just over a day ago. Her preliminary vows had been around the corner. And now she couldn't stop thinking about stealing another kiss from Eric?

When she'd fallen in love with Mathieu she surely hadn't spent so much time thinking about kisses. She and Mathieu had had to be discreet. Discretion had seemed important once, yet she was beginning not to care. Was it possible to have changed so much, so soon? She ought to be shocked, yet she wasn't. This was Eric, it wasn't as though he was a total stranger.

She peeped up at him, running her gaze over that thick brown hair, that strong profile. She must stop thinking about kissing him. 'It might be disappointing next time,' she murmured.

'What might?'

Her eyes went wide. Lord, she'd spoken aloud. He stopped walking and looked down at her, eyes puzzled. 'Disappointing, my lady? You are referring to the samite?'

'Never mind.'

'You have had enough of the market?'

'Thank you, yes.'

Eric sent half his men back to their horses with the cloth they had bought, and they left the market square with the rest of their escort trailing behind them. They were walking up the hill towards the Upper Town. At the other end of the street, the walls of Provins Castle reached to the sky. A memory pushed into Rowena's mind. The last time she had been there, she had mistakenly barged in on her betrothed when he had been with the woman he loved.

Lord Gawain had been bare-chested and Elise Chantier—she was now his countess—had been lying on the bed in such an abandoned manner it had been obvious what they had been doing. At the time, Rowena had almost died of mortification.

She walked steadily up the hill, her hand on Eric's arm. She loved the feel of him, the strong muscles, the warmth. Eric's muscles would be every bit as impressive as Lord Gawain's. There was no doubt of that.

She felt herself flush. Another church took up the peal and they continued up St Thibault's street with the sound of the bells drowning out the chatter of the townsfolk. As they walked, it dawned on her that she really need not take the veil. Her heart lifted. That time was behind her. She had been deluding herself to think that she might become a nun. Berthe had known it, as had her parents, but it had been Eric who had shown her a different and altogether more exciting future.

However, it was too soon to commit herself to him. Saints, only a day ago she was planning to take the veil. Even so, marriage to Eric was a real possibility. 'Eric?'

'Aye?'

She bumped her head against the top of his arm and said quietly, 'I am not certain about you and I, but I want you to know I will never become a nun.'

She knew immediately she had said the right thing. For even though it was broad day and they were standing in the middle of Provins and the proprieties ought to be observed, Eric did what she had been longing for him to do for the past hour. He swept her into his arms and kissed her. The townsfolk and Eric's men-at-arms were staring at them, grinning, and Rowena didn't care. It was a good kiss. And, like the kiss they had exchanged in the garden at Monfort, it was very thorough.

* * *

Eric's cavalcade turned off the main highway and on to the road for Monfort. The lowering sun striped the ridges and furrows of the fields with black shadows.

For the journey home, Eric had made sure that he and Rowena rode between two pairs of horse soldiers. The mules carrying the cloth lagged some way behind with another pair of horse soldiers. Eric wasn't expecting anything untoward to happen, but after that disturbing incident with the arrow in the chase, he couldn't be sure. All he knew was that he must keep Rowena safe.

She was frowning at some pewter-coloured clouds building up in the sky over the forest. 'It will rain soon,' she said. 'We are fortunate to have missed it.'

'Aye.' As they clopped long, Eric studied her, marvelling at the difference between the child he had known and the woman riding beside him. When had the pretty child metamorphosed into this beautiful woman? The changes, infinitely tiny, were impossible to identify. Petite as ever, Rowena hadn't gained much in inches. The curve of her nose and cheek seemed the same; she had the same long, sweeping eyelashes. Her blue eyes were immediately recognisable and yet she seemed a thousand times more lovely than she had as a girl.

Eric's chest ached with an emotion he couldn't pin down any more than he could identify the changes in this altered Rowena. Triumph? Pride that she was truly considering him—a foundling, for pity's sake—as a prospective husband? Perhaps even a touch of nerves, though why he should be nervous he had no idea. He was determined his courtship of her would be successful. He would win her. Rowena was going to be his wife.

Lady Rowena de Sainte-Colombe had yet to agree to marry him. She had, however, given him a shockingly public kiss in the middle of a Provins street. A kiss that had left them both extremely disordered. Admittedly, Rowena had tidied herself up quickly enough afterwards, the Rowena riding at his side was the aloof Rowena. Her veil was neatly tucked under her cloak, and try as he might, he couldn't get as much as a glimpse of a single golden tress.

He stifled a grin. He was looking forward to disordering her again quite soon—this evening perhaps, after they had eaten. His pulse thrummed with anticipation and he shifted in the saddle. Lord, the sooner she agreed to marry him, the better. Rowena might no longer be a virgin, but he intended to treat her with respect. When they bedded, it would be after they had spoken their marriage vows. Which had better be soon. Tension balled in his gut and he frowned as he tried to identify the cause. He felt uncertain, which was unlike him. Rowena must agree to marry him. He felt unnerved—another unfamiliar emotion, one he didn't care for. How was it that he could want her so much? It didn't make sense, not when they had not seen each other in years.

They rode through the village and were nearing the manor gate when Alard spurred up. 'Sir, behind us. The riders who followed us yesterday.'

Turning in the saddle, Eric found himself looking at the same group of riders that Lord Faramus had sent to keep an eye on his daughter. Frowning, he drew rein. The tension was back in his gut. The thought that Lord Faramus was continuing this surveillance didn't sit easily with him. The count must know he wouldn't hurt a hair on Rowena's head. Eric's birth might be questionable, but Lord Faramus had known him since he was practically an infant. For years, Eric had been labouring under the illusion that the count thought him trustworthy. Apparently not. He swore under his breath.

Rowena's harness jingled as she stopped at his side. 'Eric?'

He jerked his head back at the riders. The

party had grown, there were half a dozen of them today. 'Your father's watchdogs are back.'

She studied the horsemen, a small pleat in her brow. 'What are they doing?'

'Your father doesn't trust me.'

'That's nonsense, Eric, of course he trusts you.'

'Then why the watchdogs?'

The pleat in her brow deepened. 'Something's not right. Eric, those horses are all wrong.'

'Forget the horses, the point is that your father doesn't think much of my honour.'

Eyes earnest, she reached across and touched his arm. 'That's not true. Father has told me many times how proud he is to have trained you.'

'Then why the hell is he having us watched?' Eric scowled at the horsemen, shaking his head. He was angry the count didn't think it worth his while to honour their agreement. 'This is ridiculous, Count Faramus swore to give me a free hand. Either he trusts me or he doesn't.'

Unlike the previous day, the horsemen didn't seem inclined to keep distance between them, they approached at a steady trot.

Rowena gave him a gentle smile. 'Perhaps they bear a message.'

'Perhaps.' Eric sighed and kept his expression bland. The lead rider was wearing chain mail and the man at his side had a quiver full of arrows slung over his shoulder. His gaze sharpened. The arrows were fletched with white feathers. White feathers? Eric's stomach dropped.

The message these men bore was not from Rowena's father. Nor was it one that he wanted delivered. 'Alard!'

'Sir?'

'Get Lady Rowena inside the gates. *Move!*'

Eric reached for his shield and drew his sword. His mind raced as he homed in on the archer. Even as he watched, the man was reaching behind him, fitting an arrow to the bow.

Thank God Alard had been trained to respond instantly to his orders. Leather creaked, a spur chinked. Eric heard receding hoofbeats and Alard bawling at the guards to open the gate. Alard was taking Rowena into the manor. Behind the walls, she would be safe.

'Sergeant?'

'Sir?'

'Form a line. Shields at the ready?'

'Aye, sir.'

'Those men do not get past us.'

'Aye, sir.'

Chapter Six

Safe inside Eric's hall, Rowena's skirts dragged through the rushes as she paced up and down in front of the fire. Her heart was in her mouth and she wasn't quite sure why. If those horsemen answered to her father, why had Eric had her bundled inside so dramatically? What was happening out there? Who were those horsemen? Was Eric in danger?

'Alard?'

Eric's squire gave her a wary look. Rowena had let him see her displeasure at being manhandled in so disrespectful a manner. 'Yes, my lady?'

'I am going up to the solar,' she said.

'Then I must come with you.'

Her foot tapped. 'I don't see why. I shall be perfectly safe in the solar.'

The solar window overlooked the bailey and stable yard and it had occurred to Rowena that through it she would have a clear sight of what was happening outside.

Alard gave her a shrewd look. 'You wouldn't be thinking of looking out of the window up there, my lady?'

She stiffened. 'What business is it of yours if I am? I want to know what's happening.'

'There was an archer in that troop of horsemen.'

A chill draught fingered the back of Rowena's neck.

'His arrows were fletched with white feathers,' Alard went on. 'My lady, that window is well within range of an expert bowman and Sir Eric would string me up if anything happened to you. You had best remain here in the hall.'

'White feathers? Are you sure?'

'Yes, my lady.'

'Sir Eric told you what happened in the chase?'

'Yes, my lady, he did.'

She chewed her lip. 'The white fletchings could be just a coincidence, many arrows have white fletchings.'

'Be that as it may, Sir Eric wouldn't want to take the risk. My lady, you must stay here.'

Nodding, Rowena stared at the fire. 'If those men don't answer to my father, who are they?'

'I don't know. My lady, please don't concern yourself, Sir Eric will deal with them.'

Rowena's throat felt dry. She was trying to remain calm. It was her duty to hide her anxiety, it wouldn't do to undermine Alard's confidence in his knight. It was hard to hide her concern though, because it seemed that with every breath a new worry sneaked up on her. Thankfully Eric and his men outnumbered the strangers, but if they came to blows someone might get hurt—a carefully placed arrow could kill or maim even an armoured man. And Eric hadn't been wearing his chain mail for the trip to Provins, just his leather gambeson. An image of Eric, with an arrow—*no*!

Swallowing hard, she started pacing again. It made no sense. Why would a poacher want to draw attention to himself in such a way? 'If Eric doesn't hurry up, I shall kill him,' she muttered.

Alard gave her a weak smile. 'As you say, my lady.'

Even as Alard spoke, the hall door was pushed back and she heard the chink of spurs. Eric. Rowena let out a relieved sigh. There was no blood or any sign of any hurt, though he was breathing hard and there was a fine sheen of sweat on his brow. He thrust his gloves into his belt and strode to join her by the hearth.

'Eric, those men—they've gone?'

'Aye, they took to their heels swiftly enough

once you went inside. Chased them to the out-skirts of Provins where they disappeared.'

'Are they poachers?'

Dark-lashed green eyes bored into her. 'All you need to know is that they were not your fa-ther's men.'

'I had worked that out for myself. I kept try-ing to tell you the horses were wrong, but you wouldn't listen.'

He grimaced. 'My apologies, I should have heeded you.'

'Eric, horses have always interested me. I'm familiar with every last animal in my fa-ther's stable, but those—they were not familiar. At first I thought it possible Father must have bought new horses, but when Alard mentioned the bowman had white fletchings on his arrows, I thought of yesterday, of course.'

Eric's smile was tight. 'That man was no poacher.'

'Then who—?'

'Put him out of your mind, we have more important matters to attend to.' Her elbow was taken in a firm grip and she was steered in the direction of the stairwell. 'My lady, if you would accompany me upstairs. We will wait in the solar. Alard, find Sir Guy and ask him to join us. Then fetch Helvise and join us yourself.'

'Aye, sir.'

In the shadows of the stairwell, Rowena hung back. 'Eric? Who are we waiting for? What's happening?'

'I've sent for the village priest, Father Peter.' The grip on her elbow gentled. 'Rowena, I am sorry that it has to be done in such haste, but I will have you safe. We will marry today.'

She blinked. 'Marry? *Today?* Eric, I haven't given my consent.'

'You must.' His gaze was intent. 'Rowena, I beg you, we don't have time for all that. Marry me. Today. I need to make sure you are safe and I can best do that if you are my wife.'

Rowena's breath caught, the seriousness of his expression told her that Eric truly meant to marry her. Even as she was conscious of a tiny bubble of excitement rising inside her, she repressed it. Fresh from the convent, she wasn't ready to give her consent to marrying him. It was far too soon. She thought she'd have days, maybe weeks in which to decide. 'Today? You would marry me today?'

He gave her a soft smile and put his palm to her cheek. 'Aye.'

'Eric, it's far too soon.' She returned his smile, she trusted him. Eric was no tyrant. 'You won't force my agreement.'

'I am afraid that I must.'

Rowena stiffened. 'Eric?'

He grimaced. 'I must. Rowena, you will marry me today.'

'No.'

He looked as though she had slapped him across the face. 'Rowena, you don't dislike me. I swear I will care for you.'

'But my parents—I thought that if we did marry, they would witness our wedding. I'd hoped—'

'We can't delay.' Holding her fast by the hand, Eric towed her relentlessly up the stairs. 'You need fear nothing. The marriage will be legal and binding in every respect. Father Peter will be honoured to marry you and there will be witnesses.'

'Sir Guy, Helvise and Alard?'

'Exactly. We'll marry in the solar, come on.'

Rowena's head was in a whirl, there was too much to take in. One moment she was worrying that Eric was going to take serious hurt and the next he was dragging her upstairs for their wedding. In the solar he released her and looked down at her, mouth grim.

'Eric, why can't we wait for my parents to join us?'

He pushed back his hair. 'It is for your safety.' His chest heaved. 'Rowena, I didn't want to alarm you, but I believe the archer in the chase is the same man as the one who approached with those horsemen just now. And I believe you were his target.'

'Me?' Her jaw dropped. 'But why should anyone want to kill me? Why?' Even as Rowena spoke, the answer flashed through her mind. 'You think my cousin is responsible.'

Eric folded his arms across his chest. 'Who else?'

'Eric, it is true Sir Armand wants Father's land, but he wouldn't kill me for it!'

'Could you swear to that? Lord Faramus made it plain he loathes the man.' He gave her a rueful grin and stepped closer, so close that she had to tip her head back to look into his eyes. 'I blame myself. I had plans to make enquiries about Sir Armand, but some wench I know was taking up all my time. Demanding to be courted. Begging for my kisses.' He ran his fingers softly down her cheek.

'I did not beg!'

He grinned. 'You did, you know. In town, those big blue eyes were begging for a kiss all afternoon.'

Rowena had glanced at his mouth before she realised that he was trying to distract her from thinking about her cousin. And he was succeeding. Her heart warmed. Bless him, he didn't want her to worry. Pointedly, she took a step back. She needed to think.

'Sir Armand…' she breathed. 'He was trying to kill me.' It was horrible to contemplate, and yet all too plausible. Chillingly so.

'It would be dangerous to ignore the possibility that you are his target. Certainly he wants to prevent our marriage. He will not succeed. As my wife, you will be mine to protect. Rowena, your parents have given their blessing to our union. We marry today.'

Rowena heard footsteps, someone was hurrying up the stairs. Helvise entered, immediately followed by Sir Guy and Alard. Rowena stared at Eric, dazed by the speed of events.

'Father Peter is on his way, sir,' Alard said.

Eric took her hand. 'Well, Rowena,' he asked, his voice casual, relaxed. 'Will you have me for your husband?'

Strong fingers caressed her palm and her stomach swooped. The lines of tension about Eric's eyes and mouth told her that despite his relaxed manner, her answer mattered to him. That was no surprise, Eric was an ambitious man. He wanted her for her lands. And she wanted him because…because she wanted him. Yes, he was offering her an escape route after she had boxed herself into the convent, but that reason was fast becoming irrelevant. What she wanted now was Eric. She wanted him for himself. When he'd been a youth she had yearned for him, the man he had become was irresistible.

Rowena smiled up at him. 'Yes, Eric, I will.'

The lines in his face vanished and she was conscious of an ache, deep inside. Was it too much to hope that one day Eric would value her for herself? And that one day they might share the kind of love that she had imagined she might share with Mathieu?

'This way, my lady,' Helvise said, leading Rowena across the minstrel's gallery towards Eric's bedchamber. 'Sir Eric said that you are to share his bedchamber from now on. It is all prepared.'

Rowena nodded, glancing down into the hall below as she swept along the gallery. She hoped she looked calmer than she felt. Her wedding feast was coming to a close. She smiled quietly to herself and wondered what her mother would say when she learned of it. This was hardly the wedding feast Lady Barbara, Countess of Sainte-Colombe, would have expected for her daughter.

There had been no fanfare or entertainments. The minstrel's gallery had been empty and silent throughout. She and Eric hadn't been showered with dried rose petals and there had been no stuffed boar. Instead, the food had been honest rustic fare—half-a-dozen duck roasted to perfection, followed by apple pie. In short it had been nothing like the banquet her mother had told her she would have when she had been promised to Lord Gawain. Notwithstanding this, Rowena had enjoyed it very much. She might have been rushed into this marriage, but so far, she was enjoying it.

The evening had been refreshingly informal and it hadn't taken long for Rowena to overcome her shock at finding herself married with such speed. The atmosphere in Monfort hall was warm. Friendly. Eric's people liked him. They respected and trusted him. It was plain they enjoyed serving him.

At Monfort the household dined together, with everyone sharing a long trestle table. In honour of their knight's marriage, a servant had unearthed the white linen they had bought at the Provins market and spread it on the board. The cloth wasn't even hemmed. It hadn't mattered, everyone had been far too fascinated by their knight's hasty marriage to notice. Down the centre of the table, jugs of bluebells alternated with clusters of candles, a pretty touch that demonstrated the warmth with which Eric was held.

'I like the bluebells,' Rowena said.

Helvise smiled. 'I hoped you would. Sir Eric doesn't have any silver plate and they match his colours. I thought it would give it a festive look.'

Rowena nodded and they paused by the guardrail looking down into the hall. It made something of a contrast with the great halls at Jutigny and Sainte-Colombe. The rafters in her father's halls were hung with the colours of the Sainte-Colombe household knights, rank upon rank of them. Here, there were just two sets of colours—blue for Eric and purple for Sir Guy. At Jutigny and Sainte-Colombe, the whitewashed walls were hidden behind displays of ancient arms. The tapestries had been worked by her mother and grandmother. Here, all was simplicity. Eric's ancestry was unknown, there was no rusting weaponry. His forebears—whoever they might have been—were unlikely to have borne arms. Nor had his mother worked any tapestries for him.

Laughter floated up from below and Rowena's throat tightened. Eric might not have any family, but he had a great capacity for making friends. At his right hand, Sir Guy was refilling Eric's cup, the wine glowed ruby red in the candlelight. On his left, Alard was smiling at a comment from one of the maids. The pantry door swung wide, candle flames swayed and a slightly drunken roar of appreciation went up as the cook came through with yet another apple pie. It was the largest pie Rowena had seen. The air smelt of woodsmoke, roast meat and fruit.

They are like a family, Rowena realised. Eric has made his own family. She opened her mouth to say as much to Helvise and snapped it shut again. Helvise was staring at Eric with what could only be described as adoration. Rowena's heart dropped. 'Helvise?'

'My lady?'

'You love him,' Rowena said, in a hollow voice. 'You love Sir Eric.'

Helvise sent her a puzzled look. 'Sir Eric has been kind to me.' Her gaze sharpened and an expression of horror crossed her face. 'Oh, no, my lady, it is not as you think. Sir Eric and I— no, no, you are not to think that.'

Rowena couldn't help but glance at Helvise's belly. Folding her hands protectively over it, Helvise shook her head. 'My lady, I can see what you are thinking, and it is not true. You mustn't let such thoughts spoil your wedding night. My feelings for Sir Eric are simply those of a loyal retainer. Please, come this way.' Turning from the guardrail, Helvise led her into Eric's bedchamber.

Rowena trailed after her, praying that she could believe her. She wanted to believe her, she really didn't like the idea that Helvise and Eric might have been lovers. It shouldn't matter, Rowena had contracted this marriage for convenience, not love. She had been ready to leave the convent and marriage with a man for whom she could feel liking, if not affection, was her best option. At last she would be following her parents' wishes. They liked Eric as much as she did. And seeing him in the hall tonight, observing the way he commanded loyalty and affection from his retainers as well as obedience, made her see why he had risen so high in her father's service. When the time came, Eric de Monfort would be the best of stewards. The County of Sainte-Colombe would be in safe hands.

Pulse thumping, she went into his bedchamber. It was roomier than the one Rowena had been sharing with Helvise. The shutters were closed against the night; candles were glowing on wall sconces; a small fire crackled in the hearth. The bed was certainly large. Rowena's mouth went dry as she looked at it. Would Eric demand his husbandly rights? She felt ridiculously nervous. Much as she liked him, she wasn't ready for that. She had really only known him for a couple of days. Knowing him as a boy simply wasn't the same.

The oak headboard—it was plain and very masculine—looked new. The mattress and pillows were thick and the coverlet was turned down. On top of a heavy coffer, someone—Helvise most likely—had placed wine and pastries on a tray.

'My lady, I hope you don't mind,' Helvise said, 'I took the liberty of cutting up some of the sheeting you brought back from Provins to put on the bed. I didn't have time to hem it.'

'Thank you, Helvise.' Hoping Helvise couldn't see how nervous she was, Rowena forced a smile. 'We will certainly have yards of hemming to do later.'

'Miles of it, I should think,' Helvise said drily. She stepped forward, a line between her eyebrows. As she reached up to unpin Rowena's veil, her belly touched Rowena's hand. 'My lady, you mustn't be afraid. Sir Eric won't hurt you.'

Rowena took a deep breath, she had the uncomfortable feeling that Helvise was about to give her some motherly advice, and she wasn't sure she could take it from her. 'I don't suppose he will, Sir Eric is, as you say, a kind man.' *And he will not wish to alienate the wife who brings him so much in the way of land and prestige.*

Removing Rowena's veil, Helvise folded it and placed it carefully on a chest by the wall. 'I am glad that you have become his wife,' she said. 'Since Sir Eric took over Monfort he has often spoken of his time at Jutigny. He holds your family in great esteem.'

'That is good to hear.'

'My lady, did your mother explain—?' The

light shifted and Helvise broke off, flushing, Eric was in the doorway.

'Thank you for your help this evening, Helvise,' he said. 'I don't know what we would have done without you.'

Helvise dipped him a curtsy. 'It is my pleasure, sir. Will that be all?'

'Thank you, yes. Goodnight, Helvise.'

'Goodnight, sir.' Helvise left them, closing the door softly behind her.

'I thought you would prefer to forgo the bedding ceremony,' Eric said, lifting a brow.

Rowena grimaced. 'Bless you, I was dreading it. And thank you also for arriving when you did. I suspect that Helvise was about to educate me on what to expect from a husband in the marriage bed.'

Eric looked utterly bemused. 'Lady Rowena de Sainte-Colombe, you are a fraud to tease her so.'

Rowena stiffened. 'What do you mean?'

Walking up to her, Eric reached for her plait and untied the ribbon with uncommon care. 'I believe you, my sweet, are more experienced than you like to pretend.'

Rowena touched his hand. 'My experience, such as it is, is not large.'

'Is it not?' Eric smiled at her and gently unwound her braid.

Rowena gave him a startled look. 'You know about Mathieu,' she said. 'How?'

Eric shrugged and went on unwinding her hair. His touch was surprisingly delicate. 'I didn't know his name. However, it seemed likely that an aversion to Lord Gawain wasn't the only reason you secreted yourself away in that convent. There had to be more to it than that.'

'Not much more,' she said, frankly. A few stolen kisses didn't amount to much.

'What happened?'

She stared at Eric's neck. 'He was killed.'

Eric caught her by the chin, eyes intent. 'I recall that a squire of the same name was killed in a tavern brawl in Provins just over a year ago.'

'Yes, that was Mathieu.'

'I'm sorry. You loved him?' He released her chin. 'No, don't answer that, I have no right to ask. Of course you did. You loved him so much you couldn't bear the thought of marriage to Lord Gawain.'

Something in Eric's eyes tugged at her heart. 'Yes, I loved him. His death was devastating. In retrospect, I don't think we knew each other very well.' She held his gaze. 'He was the same age as me.'

'So he must have been about seventeen when he died.'

'Aye.'

'It is young. Poor lad.' He drew in a breath. 'So that is why you turned down the Count of Meaux.'

Something—a hint of vulnerability in the way he was looking at her—made Rowena interlace her fingers firmly with his. 'My father was furious, but I have no regrets.'

His face lightened. 'I am glad to hear it.' Taking her shoulders, he turned her to face away from him. She felt a warm kiss on her neck and those careful fingers began loosening the lacings at the back of her gown. As her gown started to fall away, another kiss was planted on her shoulder. 'Love is unreliable, in any case,' he went on, in that casual tone that she was coming to suspect meant he was hiding some unwanted feeling.

Smiling, she turned her head to look at him. 'You are the expert in that, I am sure.'

His fingers stilled. 'How do you come to that conclusion?'

She laughed. 'Eric, you lived at Jutigny for years. Every maidservant in the castle had eyes for you. As I recall, you made the most of it.' She paused. 'You had quite the reputation.'

'Did I?'

'You know you did.'

Eric stroked her gown from her shoulders, pushed her hair aside and another kiss was planted on her shoulder blade. Another little tug and her gown fell to the floor leaving her clad only in her convent shift. Thankfully, the fabric was thick, it hid her body from his gaze and she could see that he was studying her. Cheeks hot, Rowena stepped out of the gown and bent to pick it up.

He swallowed. 'Leave it,' he said hoarsely, and offered her his hand. 'Merciful heaven, Rowena, your hair—*you*—you are glorious.'

Heart in her mouth, Rowena slipped her fingers into his. Conscious of him looking her up and down, she sent him a shy smile. 'Eric, I am not sure I can do this.'

He gave her a quizzical look. 'Of course you can. An experienced woman like you.'

Rowena felt herself frown. What did he mean? He must be teasing her. 'I feel ridiculously nervous.'

Taking her by the waist, he pulled her close. 'No need, we shall do very well.' He nuzzled his way through her hair to her shoulder, and her body warmed as it had done each time they had kissed. Feeling herself weakening, she looped her arms about his neck.

'That's better,' he murmured, nibbling her ear.

Twisting her head, she kissed his neck.

'*Much* better.'

Whilst the sound of his voice in her ear weak-

ened her knees, it didn't make her any the less
nervous. 'Eric?'

'Mmm?'

'I don't feel I know you well enough.'

His head lifted. His eyes were black in the
candlelight. 'We've known each other for years.'

She thumped his chest. 'You know what I
mean, I've only been here two days.'

'*Mon Dieu*, is that how long it's been?' He
grinned. 'It feels like ten years.'

'Thank you, sir. You are charm itself.' She
curled her fingers into his tunic. 'Please, Eric,
can't we wait until we are better reacquainted?'

Smiling, he shook his head. 'Rowena, we shall
consummate our marriage tonight.'

Her pulse thudded. She searched his face and
sent up a swift prayer, that one day their marriage might come to be more than a marriage of
convenience. For both of them.

Cupping her face in his hands, Eric kissed her
nose. 'I don't want to lose you, there must be no
doubt that we are properly married. If you are
questioned, I want you to be able to swear that
we know each other in the full, Biblical sense.'
He pressed himself against her and she was in
no doubt but that he desired her. 'I want you, Rowena, and I will have you. Tonight.'

Rowena took a shaky breath and pushed doubt
behind her. Eric was her husband, her future

was with him. Her stomach was filled with butterflies, the sensation was unfamiliar and really quite pleasant. She knew it was desire. Her breasts felt heavy, as if they yearned for his touch. Whilst her mind might not be ready to bed with Eric, her body most definitely was. It was practically screaming at him to touch her. Everywhere.

She wasn't ignorant, her mother had warned her what to expect when she had become betrothed to Lord Gawain. Rowena knew it might hurt at first. She also knew—and hoped—the pain wouldn't last long. What she hadn't expected was this screaming desire. It felt as though she had a fever and it was frightening in its power. *Touch me, Eric. Touch me everywhere.* 'Very well.'

Eric caught Rowena's head in his hands and gave her a slow, possessive kiss. He wanted her to know without any doubt that he wasn't going to change his mind. They would become lovers tonight. His blood rushed through his veins. He nudged himself gently against her, took advantage of her sharp intake of breath when she realised what was pressing into her, and swept his tongue into her mouth. She tasted sweet. She smelt sweet. She was sweet. Insanely so. She drove him wild and all they were doing was kissing.

He listened to the small breathy gasps and edged her towards the bed, pulling back long enough to take in the rosy flush to her cheeks and the downswept eyelashes. He found her mouth once more and explored it. Much as he wanted her, he was afraid of rushing her. He should take it slowly. *We have the rest of our lives together.* The thought was new to him, it was both pleasing and humbling. He mustn't let his haste ruin everything.

He took her hand and placed it on his belt buckle. 'Undress me, if you please.' Lord, this was bad, he hadn't imagined how eager he would be. He hoped he didn't ruin things, he could barely speak.

Wide blue eyes gazed up at him. Her flush intensified. 'If you wish, my husband.'

My husband. Eric's heart lurched, he was moved beyond words. He'd never thought he'd be husband to a woman as precious and delicate as Lady Rowena de Sainte-Colombe.

He didn't understand how she did it, she gave every appearance of being completely innocent. It was extraordinarily beguiling, even though he was certain she had already had a lover in her Mathieu. Well, Eric knew a little about pleasing a woman and he would do his utmost to ensure it wouldn't be Mathieu's name she would be gasping tonight.

Small fingers undid his buckle and his belt fell to the floor with a clack. She looked uncertainly at him, reaching shyly for his tunic. 'This next?'

'Please.' Eric groaned, that teasing shyness would be his undoing, he was sure of it. He was almost bursting out of his braies.

Rowena took his tunic by the hem, lifted and gave a slight laugh. 'You are so tall, you must help me.'

In a flurry of movement, his tunic and shirt went the way of his belt. She bit her lip and looked at his chest, her hands suspended a few inches away from his flesh. Near enough for him to feel their heat. Her breath escaped in a sigh before she carefully set her palms against his skin. A *frisson* went through him.

'Eric…' she breathed.

His gut clenched, sweet and agonising.

Leaning forward, she pressed a kiss in the centre of his chest. She stroked his chest and shoulders, leaving a trail of sensation in her wake. Pausing to snuff out a couple of candles, Eric wound his arm about her waist and sat with her on the edge of the bed.

She didn't resist. Lit by the remaining candles and the fire glow, her eyes were enormous. Luminous and dark with desire. Nor did she resist as, with a rustle of linen and wool, several snatched kisses and a few nervous giggles on Rowena's part, he encouraged her to shed her shift.

His breath caught. She was perfectly formed. Compared to most women she was tiny, though there was nothing child-like about her body. Her breasts were high and small, her waist narrow. The line of her hips was entrancing. All was in perfect, womanly proportions. Eric placed his palm on her hip and swallowed hard as he caressed her. Her skin felt like silk. 'Rowena.' His voice sounded choked. 'The line of you, the curves. I am the most fortunate of men, you are quite lovely.'

Her cheeks were bright as poppies, but she was smiling encouragement, her expression gentle as she watched him learning his way about her body. Trusting. He stroked his hand slowly down her hip; he explored the length of her leg and as his hand worked slowly back to her breast, he savoured the softness of her skin. So smooth. Her eyes were dark. Inviting. In a rush of eagerness, he shed the rest of his clothes. Anchoring her against the pillows, he moved over her.

It shouldn't have hurt. It wasn't as though Eric was without experience, he knew his way around a woman's body. He took his time. He played and smiled and caressed. She caressed him back.

Their kisses scorched. Her touch scorched. He waited until he could feel that she was ready, in truth he waited until he could wait no more. Then he positioned himself over her, dotted a row of kisses along her neck and pushed. Her body closed about him. Bliss. He started to move when her gasp, high and shocked, penetrated the sensual haze.

Eric froze. 'Rowena?'

Small fingers gripped his shoulders. 'Be still. Please, Eric, give me a moment.'

'I hurt you?'

Her eyes were holding his, earnest and full of resolve. 'It will pass, I know.'

Her quiet laugh, slightly flustered, snapped something inside him. He made to withdraw.

Shaking her head, golden tresses flying every which way, she caught hold of his buttocks, holding him in her. 'No, Eric. Stay.'

Eric's breath was coming fast, she'd been a virgin. He had no idea how it had happened, but he'd misjudged her. She'd been innocent and he had hurt her. Lord, what had he done?

'*Mon Dieu*, Rowena, forgive me.' He nuzzled her cheek. 'I am an ignorant fool.'

She slid her fingers into his hair and kissed his mouth. 'There's nothing to forgive,' she murmured, pushing her hips ever so slightly against him. 'Everything is as it should be.'

Slowly, looking deeply into her eyes so he could be sure he gave her no more pain, Eric began to move.

Chapter Seven

'You were innocent, why didn't you tell me?' Eric asked, as he drew the covers over them. Rowena was nestled against his side with an arm about his waist, and he felt bad because she had not had her pleasure. He had been so appalled at having hurt her that he had rushed to the finish and quickly withdrawn. He felt nervous about touching her again. It was most odd, he never felt nervous with women. However, he'd never bedded his wife before. Thankfully, she was still cuddling him. She couldn't hate him. He hoped.

She lifted her head and he caught her fragrance—summer flowers. *Rowena.*

'You led me to believe you had a lover.'

Puzzled blue eyes searched his. 'No, I didn't.'

Eric cast his mind back, trying to recall exactly what she had said. 'You said that you and your squire—'

'His name was Mathieu de Lyon and he wasn't

my squire. I loved him, but we were never lovers.' She traced a circle on his belly and his stomach tightened. 'We were discretion itself. Mathieu said he respected me too much.'

Eric grimaced. 'I wish I'd known. I rushed you.'

'You thought I had given myself to Mathieu?'

'Aye.' Lifting her hand, he kissed her knuckles. 'Forgive me?'

'Of course.' She gave him one of her sweet smiles and Eric felt himself breathe more easily. 'Eric, you know it is not wise for an unmarried lady to make a gift of her body out of wedlock.'

'Naturally, I know that. However, it does happen.'

'Not in my case. Imagine what Father would say if I presented him with a child born out of wedlock.' She shuddered. 'In any case, I thought then I would marry and I wanted to save myself for my husband, for my wedding night.'

Eric ran his fingertips thoughtfully down a twisted strand of shining gold. Rowena belonged to him, she had never belonged to Mathieu de Lyon. The discovery made him feel different— proud and fiercely possessive. 'I thank you. I only regret that I hurt you.'

'It was nothing, a little pain is to be expected the first time. I am told there will be less pain the second time.'

Eric grunted and tucked her head against him and let the relief wash through him. They had both been rushed into this marriage. It was a pity he'd not had more time to prepare himself for the role of husband. Luckily, Rowena didn't seem to have taken against him for allowing desire to get the better of him. He frowned up at the ceiling, wanting to understand how he'd misjudged her so badly. It seemed he had been blinded by need for his delicate little wife.

She shifted her head and continued to draw disturbing circles on his belly. She ruffled the hair on his chest. Eric gritted his teeth and felt the slow throb of renewed desire. Rowena had been innocent. And whilst she was no longer a virgin, she remained inexperienced. She had no idea the effect her caresses had on him, if she did she would surely stop.

He let out a sigh and found himself wondering why Lord Faramus had chosen to give his precious heiress to a low-born knight. Whichever way you looked at it, the count must have hoped for a more auspicious alliance. Holy Mother, he'd had her betrothed to Count Gawain of Meaux! He put his hand over Rowena's, killing her tantalising—and innocent—caresses.

'Rowena?'

'Mmm?'

'Does your father know about your dalliance with de Lyon?'

'Certainly not. Mathieu was terrified of Father, so we kept it quiet. As far as I am aware, you are the only person who knows.'

Eric's heart swelled. Delight in her confession of trust warred with pride at the implication behind her words. He had not been chosen to shield an indiscretion. Her father wanted him for a son-in-law. Tucking her fingers under her chin, he tilted her face to his. 'So your father really did choose me for your husband.' He was met with another searching look.

'He summoned you to Jutigny, didn't he? He asked you to abduct me?'

'Aye.'

'Eric, Father chose you. He has always trusted you.' Taking his hand, she kissed his palm. 'Just as he trusts that you will care for his lands one day. And I have to tell you that I am glad that you were his choice.'

Overcome with conflicting emotions Eric couldn't begin to name, he smiled at Rowena—his wife—and tried to ignore the desire that was throbbing through his veins. He had been too rough with her tonight, he couldn't press his attentions on her again. She would need time to get used to him. He studied her gleaming hair; the curve of her cheek and nose; the colour of her lips. So pretty. He was surrounded by the scent of a summer meadow, a scent more intoxicating than any wine.

How long should he wait before approaching her again? A week?

Lord, that seemed far too long. A few days?

His heart ached. She ran her fingers over his skin with a sleepy murmur and he stifled a groan. Tomorrow. She would surely feel recovered by tomorrow.

Rowena was fascinated by Eric's chest. It was so broad and it was wonderful to be able to caress his skin and feel the shape of the muscles she had known lay underneath his tunic. She liked the slight abrasion of the chest hair that arrowed downwards. She wasn't sure, because she wasn't bold enough to slide her hand down, but a bump in the sheet hinted that he still desired her.

Smiling to herself, she explored a little further—the strength of his shoulder and arm; the width of his wrist; the warrior's hands, the palms slightly calloused from swordplay. As she explored, she learned that Eric was as pleasing to touch as he was to look upon. Her nipples tightened. Experimentally, she shifted against him, smiling as she heard the catch in his breath. Of all her father's knights, Eric was the finest. And now he was her husband. Linking fingers with him, she glanced at the sheet covering his belly and hummed softly under her breath. Their coupling hadn't been as painful as she'd expected and she'd been left feeling somewhat edgy. There had to be more to mating with a man than what had just passed between them. The way the Jutigny maidservants used to follow Eric with their eyes—yes, there was surely more...

'Eric?'

'Aye? Are you all right, shall I mull you some wine?'

His voice sounded croaky. Good. Pulling his hand to her mouth, she kissed it and listened with satisfaction to another sharp intake of breath. 'No wine, thank you. But there is something you can do.'

'Aye?'

'We ought to try consummating our marriage again.'

A large hand tipped up her head. 'I hurt you. You are a lady, you need to recover.'

'I am not made of Venetian glass. We need to be sure.'

He gave a strangled laugh. 'Rowena, there is no doubt. You are no longer a maid.' She grimaced and his eyes dropped to her mouth. 'Rowena?'

She shrugged. 'I confess to a certain curiosity. I am told it doesn't hurt the second time.'

'I couldn't say. I've never had a virgin before.'

'Well, so I was told. Eric, I am curious.' She lifted an eyebrow and kissed his cheek. 'And hungry to know more.'

His expression softened and a slow smile dawned. 'Hungry?' He gathered her close and a hand slid purposefully down her buttock. He pressed her to him. 'We can't have that.'

She placed another kiss on his cheek and then his fingers were tangling in her hair. His mouth met hers in a kiss that left her in no doubt that he was as hungry as she. They both moaned.

Butterflies awoke in Rowena's belly; her skin tingled at his lightest touch. And he did touch her lightly, for so strong a man Eric handled her gently. He turned her on her back, gently. He covered her breasts with kisses. Gently. He parted her legs. Gently. He touched her most secret place, with careful, knowing, gentle fingers.

The butterflies danced. Rowena found herself shifting against his hand. Moaning. Urging him on, quite shamelessly. Something lay just beyond reach and if only Eric would…

'Eric,' she breathed.

He shifted over her and then they were moving as one and what she was seeking seemed just a little closer.

'More.'

Gently, he bit her earlobe and reached between them. Touching her, stoking her hunger, feeding it, even as he urged her body to push against his. She moaned and his answering groan had the butterflies dancing and soaring. His touch had them swooping.

Rowena's heart pounded. She held on to Eric as though for dear life and the butterflies vanished in a blinding pulse of light that had her gasping his name. Eric buried his head in her neck and shuddered to completion. They lay there panting.

Holding her fast, Eric rolled on to his side and gave her a warm smile. 'Better?'

'Oh, yes.'

'No pain?'

'None.' Lips curving, she hugged him to her. It was extraordinary how safe she felt with this man. How much she trusted him. She truly felt content. 'Thank you, Eric. I knew there had to be more.'

'It was my pleasure, I assure you.'

Rowena nodded and sighed and rested her head against his beautiful chest. Eric understood how to make a woman desire him. More than that, he knew how to give pleasure as well as to take it. She was indeed fortunate, not all men understood women so well. And from what she had observed in Champagne as well as in Sainte-Colombe, most men never bothered to learn.

'Why the sigh?' A long finger touched her cheek. 'What's the matter?'

'Nothing.' Rowena pushed back her hair, noticed how disordered it was, and shook her head at him. 'Sir, you have made a dreadful tangle of my hair, it feels like a bird's nest.'

Reaching out, he ruffled her hair some more and gave her a lazy, sensual smile that had her longing for him all over again. 'You look perfect to me.'

At noon the next day Rowena was in the manor hall when she heard the clatter of what sounded like an army echoing around the manor courtyard.

Eric had set out for Jutigny when the sun had lifted over the horizon. By the sound of it, he had brought an entire troop back with him. Rowena hurried out of the hall and stood at the top of the steps.

The yard was alive with horsemen in full armour. Her father's colours hung from a lance and several of the riders dipped their heads at her in acknowledgement. Her eyes went straight to Eric, who dismounted and handed Captain's reins to Alard.

Taking the steps two at a time, Eric bowed over Rowena's hand and kissed it. 'Good morning, adored one.'

When Rowena felt the surreptitious touch of his tongue and—briefly—his teeth, her wits scattered. 'Eric, please, we are in company.' Feeling herself colour, she reclaimed her hand and hid it in her skirts. 'I see that you have spoken to my parents. You told them of our marriage?'

Straightening, he nodded, deftly unearthed her hand from her skirts, and walked with her towards the hall, swinging it at his side. 'Of course.'

'They were surprised?'

'A little.' Eric lowered his voice. 'However, when I explained the circumstances—what happened in the chase and later—they understood. They are anxious for your welfare and have charged me with suggesting that you return to Jutigny without delay.' He gestured at the troop. 'This escort is to ensure your safe arrival.'

Rowena bit her lip. 'You don't think I am safe here?'

Eric leaned a shoulder against the doorjamb. 'A manor like Monfort cannot compare with Jutigny. Jutigny is a fortress and Lord Faramus has ten times the men that I do.'

A horrible thought occurred to her and she gripped his hand. 'Eric, you are not sending me away, are you? You are coming too?'

An eyebrow lifted and she saw the golden

lights in his eyes. 'Try and stop me.' Leaning in, he planted a firm kiss on her mouth. He lingered and murmured, 'I missed you.'

One of the men let out a whoop. Another tittered.

Rowena's cheeks scorched and she drew her head back. He was such a tease and she really wasn't used to it. 'Eric, behave.'

Eric grinned. 'I am embarrassing you?'

'You know you are.'

'Pity.' He squeezed her fingers. 'You like it though.'

Rowena opened her mouth to deny it and closed it again. She wasn't going to lie, she did like having his attention. And the thought that Eric had missed her this morning was warming. She had certainly missed him, the bed had been cold and empty without him. 'You, sir, are an outrageous flirt.'

'De Lyon never flirted?' he asked quietly.

'Never.' Mathieu had been far too young and far too inexperienced, she realised. Claims which could not be levelled at her husband.

'What a fool.'

Rowena stared at her husband, her handsome, outrageous flirt of a husband with sudden insight. Mathieu and Eric couldn't be more opposite. Mathieu had been sensible. Serious.

Earnest. Innocent. Eric was amusing. Charming. A man of the world. And far too handsome.

Guilt rushed at her. This morning it was a struggle to recollect what Mathieu looked like. She had loved him so much yet now she couldn't recall his face? Heavens, how strange. If she had married Mathieu, she would have been bored to death in a month.

Marriage to Eric, on the other hand, would never be boring. There was so much to do. She would begin by strengthening the bond between them. Eric liked her, of course, and she liked him, but his feelings weren't fully engaged.

Rowena didn't view the lack of love as too large a drawback, many good marriages had been founded without love. Besides, not once had she seen Eric in love. He would never allow it. He might charm and cajole, but he never fell in love. Which meant that she must find some other way to strengthen the bond between them. If she succeeded, he would be less likely to turn to others for counsel or company. The thought of Eric taking his pleasure elsewhere made her feel distinctly queasy. When they got to Jutigny, she would ask her mother for advice.

Rowena would teach Eric to take comfort in her and her alone. Until that goal was achieved, she couldn't be sure that their marriage would succeed.

* * *

Sir Guy was to be given stewardship of Monfort Manor for the duration of Eric and Rowena's stay at Jutigny. Thus, some half an hour later, Rowena was mounted up in the bailey with her escort, listening with half an ear as Sir Guy stood at Eric's stirrup, listening to last-minute instructions.

'The smith is reliable,' Eric was saying. 'And he seems to have the ear of the villagers. Guy, I've instructed him to report straight to you if the strangers reappear. He has sworn to alert you to any unusual activity in the district. I needn't remind you that I would like to be told of anything, however trivial it might seem.'

'Never fear, man, if so much as a twig cracks in the chase, I will send word to Jutigny.'

Eric nodded. 'My thanks.'

Sir Guy glanced towards the hall where Helvise was waiting by the door, hands folded over her belly. 'Lord, I almost forgot, Helvise wanted to speak with you before you leave.'

Eric's saddle creaked as he gestured at Helvise to come forward and Rowena found herself watching his expression with uncommon interest. She was learning to read him, and she saw immediately that there was nothing to trouble her here. Any affection between Eric and Helvise was purely one-sided. Helvise was besotted with him and Eric simply liked the girl. Rowena felt herself relax, it was as though a weight had been lifted from her.

Eric smiled easily. 'There's a problem, Helvise?'

Helvise twisted her hands together. 'A minor one, sir. It's about the linens.'

'The linens?'

'Whilst you are away, would you like me to make a start on hemming the cloth you and Lady Rowena bought in the market?'

Eric looked utterly bemused. Rowena hid a smile. She understood that Helvise's question was but a ploy so that the girl could speak to him. And he had no idea.

'Saints, Helvise, domestic matters are in my wife's hands now, ask Lady Rowena about the linens.'

'Yes, sir.' Helvise's face seemed to slip, but she recovered quickly and lifted her gaze to Rowena. 'My lady, shall I make a start on the hemming?'

Rowena smiled. 'Please do. Helvise, I leave the domestic matters entirely in your hands. However, if you find yourself too busy, don't trouble yourself.' She let her gaze linger on Helvise's belly and lowered her voice. 'I hope to return to Monfort soon, but if I do not, I am sure you may apply to Sir Guy when your time comes.'

Sir Guy cleared his throat. 'Of course she may. Happy to help.'

Rowena nodded. 'I will also be asking my mother which of the local midwives she recommends. I shall send her to visit you.'

Helvise bowed her head. 'Thank you, my lady.'

'That was kind of you,' Eric said, as they guided their horses up the rise to the highway. 'I should have thought of it myself. It is Helvise's first child and she is bound to be worried. I have no deep knowledge of such matters, but judging by her size it looks as though her time will be soon.'

'I agree, I will speak to my mother as soon as we arrive. And if the babe surprises us, I am sure someone in the village will be able to help her.' Leaning forward, Rowena patted Lily's neck. They were hedged about by a double escort of her father's men as well as Eric's and they could surely hear what they were saying. She lowered her voice. 'Eric, you do know Helvise is in love with you?'

Eric gave her an impatient look. 'What nonsense.'

'I don't think so. Helvise is definitely in love with you.'

'In that case, Helvise is making a big mistake.'

'Eric, she's hurting.'

'You cannot lay that at my door, I did nothing to encourage her.' His gaze tracked the flight of a pair of swans heading for the river. 'The sooner Helvise learns that love is irrelevant, the happier she will be.'

Rowena blinked. 'Love is irrelevant? How can you say that?'

'Love won't help Helvise. Rowena, you've been listening to too many ballads. They lie. People are weakened by love. What use is that?' His smile was amused. 'Life is tough and the best marriages are those based on cool logic.'

Rowena sat stiffly in the saddle. Her life had been enriched by her love for Mathieu. Certainly it had brought her pain, but life without love was surely dull and cold. The longing to find love again was fierce inside her. She hoped to share it with Eric. 'You are thinking of our marriage?'

It cut her to the quick to hear Eric dismiss love so decisively. Since meeting him again, Rowena was beginning to realise that she had always been fond of him. It would be good to think that her fondness might be reciprocated. Eric was fond of her, he must be. He had been so kind in their wedding bed. He was simply shy of admitting it.

It came to her that if their marriage was to

be the true partnership that she was hoping for, she must tell him how she felt. She took a deep breath.

'Eric, you should know that to me our marriage is more than purely a business contract. I hold you in great esteem, I always have.'

He looked sharply at her. 'I feel the same. Rowena, I hold you in the highest regard.' His expression softened. 'And our compatibility in the bedchamber is a prize I had never looked for. But don't look for love from me, I cannot and will not love you.'

'Cannot?' Rowena frowned. Eric was deluding himself, he had to be. He had always been something of an enigma, but he must be capable of love. Already she'd seen evidence of the loyalty and affection that he was capable of rousing in others. She thought of their wedding feast, of the smiling faces around the table—Eric's tenants and retainers felt genuine warmth and affection for him. She thought of her mother, who all those years ago had gone out of her way to find a place in the Sainte-Colombe household for the lost little boy who had captured her heart. And then there were the maidservants whose faces lit up on seeing him. They wouldn't have idolised him like that if they hadn't felt his warmth.

Surely a man who inspired loyalty, even devotion, in the way Eric did, was capable of love?

I want him to truly love me. The thought caught Rowena by surprise, but it was suddenly clear that she wanted Eric's love more than she wanted her next breath. She didn't understand it, she should not need his love. As a wife, she was more than lucky to have him hold her in the highest regard. And to value her as a bedfellow.

High regard wasn't enough. She wanted love. She wanted passion.

'Love is a millstone, Rowena. It causes no end of trouble, not to mention pain.'

She gave him a keen look, her instincts were telling her that they were getting to the root of it. 'Pain?'

He nodded. 'You know this already, you don't need me to tell you. Think about it. Love got you retiring to a convent when you are clearly made for this world. A convent is the last place someone like you should spend your days. And you found yourself there simply because you fell in love with Mathieu de Lyon.'

'Eric, I was enriched by what I felt for Mathieu.'

'Enriched?' He sent her a look of exasperation. 'How can you say that? Love put you somewhere you had no place being. Rowena, you would have died if you'd stayed in that convent another day. Your parents knew that and, in your heart, so did you.'

'I can't deny that I am glad to be out of there.' She paused. If Eric linked love with pain, it made sense that he would want to be free of it. That explained why he had always steered clear of emotional ties. He charmed and he flirted, but he wasn't interested in anything more. Was he afraid of the pain he might feel?

This went back to his childhood. The little lost boy had found it hard to cope with what life had thrown him. That wasn't surprising. What was surprising was how successful Eric had become despite his past. And yet…

What if, locked deep inside him, that lost little boy remained? What if that child still mourned for his lost family, for his mother and father?

Was the lost little boy crying so loudly that Eric the man was being denied his full life? Holy Mother, didn't he realise that without love to pull him firmly into the world, he would always be standing outside the gate, looking in?

Rowena felt a chill wash over her. She was certain she had stumbled on the truth. This was why Eric was such a flirt. It might also explain why he kept women at arm's length.

'Well, it doesn't matter whether you believe

in love or not,' she said, firmly. 'Helvise loves you. Eric, it's obvious.'

Manoeuvring Captain close, Eric reached across and touched the back of her hand. 'Rowena, if you are imagining that Helvise and I—'

'I'm not. I admit it gave me pause, but not any more.'

'Dieu merci.'

With a quiet laugh, she leaned confidentially towards him. 'When I first came to Monfort and saw her affection for you, I did think the baby was yours.'

His eyes widened. 'Why didn't you say something?'

She shrugged. 'I am not certain. Your reputation certainly made me think.'

His expression was rueful. 'My reputation. Rowena, to my knowledge I have no children.'

'If you did, you would acknowledge them,' she said, on a sudden insight. Eric would never let a child suffer if he could help it.

Eric blinked. His eyes were very bright and she could see that her answer had both surprised and moved him. 'I would and I am glad that you understand that.' He cleared his throat. 'Rowena, when I won Monfort, the previous tenant, Sir Ralph de Honnecourt, left without making his farewells. In my belief he neglected his obligations. Helvise was in a desperate state. Hurt and frightened.'

'Sir Ralph is the father of her unborn child?'

'She has never admitted as much, but I believe so. On that first night Helvise crept into my bed-chamber.' Eric fixed his gaze on a cloud low on the horizon. Dark colour stained his cheekbones.

'She offered herself to you.'

'How did you know?'

'She was afraid you'd turn her out—she thought that if you bedded her, you might allow her to stay.'

'You have it exactly. I swore to her that she would always have a place at Monfort and that she didn't have to sleep with me to secure it.' Green eyes met hers. 'Rowena, I mean to honour that promise.'

'I feel for Helvise,' Rowena said, softly. 'It must be dreadful to be abandoned when you are in so vulnerable a state. As for Sir Ralph de Honnecourt—well, he can't have a chivalrous bone in his body.'

Eric grunted agreement.

The cavalcade had reached the main highway. Eric signalled to their escort and they spurred their horses into a canter. Guessing that Eric had her safety in mind—he wanted her inside her father's castle walls as soon as possible—Ro-

wena made no objection. It would give her time
to think.

As the miles rocked by, she glanced thoughtfully at him. His sympathy for Helvise wasn't
surprising. Rowena hadn't been born when Eric
had arrived at Jutigny. However, she'd heard the
tale so often, she knew it by heart.

It had been a snowy Christmas Eve and a
guard had found a small child shivering by the
gatehouse wall. Eric. The guard had summoned
Lady Barbara and she had swept Eric into the
castle where Eric had been fed and clothed. Lady
Barbara had insisted that Eric was accepted as
one of the household.

Rowena bit her lip and wondered how often he
thought back to the snowy night he'd been found
by the gatehouse. He'd been about six years of
age, so he must remember it. He would have
been cold and lonely and horribly confused. And
doubtless grieving for his family.

Rowena's mother had sent out search parties
to look for whoever had left him by the gate.
They had scoured the streets of both Jutigny and
Provins, but no one had ever been found. It was
as though Eric had materialised out of thin air.

'You are a kind man, Eric,' she murmured
over the hoofbeats.

'What's that?' Eric said.

Smiling, Rowena shook her head and they sped towards her father's castle.

Chapter Eight

As they rode up to the portcullis of Jutigny Castle, Eric tipped back his head. Masons were working on the overhead arch. Eric had seen them that morning, but there was more activity than there had been earlier. The air was full of the chinking of chisels and the banging of hammers. A spiky network of wooden scaffolding hung from the upper courses of the gatehouse walls and a hoist creaked as it turned, hauling a great block of stone in a sling to the top. Scaffolding groaned as men wove past each other, nimble as dancers with hods of mortar balanced on their shoulders.

Rowena followed his gaze. 'It looks as though Father has finally got round to setting our coat of arms on the front.'

Our coat of arms. Eric could scarcely believe it, he was no longer an outsider, by marrying Rowena he had become a Sainte-Colombe. He had a family. Finally, after all these years, he belonged.

Absently, Eric exchanged greetings with the guard. His head was full of the ramifications of his marriage as they trotted on to the drawbridge. Eric had imagined that he might have children one day, but he'd never thought to marry so high. Nor had he given any thought as to what it might be like to have a father-in-law and a mother-in-law. Luckily for him, Lord and Lady Sainte-Colombe weren't strangers. They knew him as well as anyone, which made their acceptance of him into their family something of an accolade.

A blistering oath from one of the workmen cut into his thoughts.

Lips twitching, Rowena raised an eyebrow at him and he held in a grin.

Another virulent oath floated down from above. 'Jesu, watch it!'

'Look out!'

The hoist was swinging alarmingly, a quick glance told Eric a rope had worked loose and the stone was slipping. He plunged into battle mode. Snatching Rowena's reins, he spurred through the arch and into the bailey.

They only just made it. The stone crashed on to the drawbridge, hitting the exact spot where they had been only moments ago. Wood cracked as the stone ripped through the slats and splashed into the moat.

No one spoke. A deadly chill settled on Eric's heart. Breathing ragged, he stared through the splintered wood to the wash in the moat beneath.

Rowena was chalk white. He watched her swallow.

Fighting an unnerving rush of panic, Eric put lightness into his tone. '*Mon Dieu*, that was careless.' There was no sense frightening Rowena more than she had already been frightened, but he was concerned, deeply concerned. A dark thought was taking shape at the back of his mind, turning the chill in his chest to ice. No—it couldn't be… Pushing it aside, he added, 'I shall have to speak to the master mason, you might have been killed. Come, let's get you into the solar, your mother will be waiting for you.'

The next half-hour passed in a flurry of smiles, hugs and greetings as he and Rowena were welcomed back to the castle. Sir Macaire welcomed them at the entrance to the hall, beaming like a beacon. Rowena's maid Berthe ran up, sniffling and smiling as she wiped away tears; maidservants lingered in passages and stairwells, chattering like sparrows about their marriage.

Eric hardly noticed. A dark thought had taken

root in his mind. After what had happened at
Monfort he couldn't help but think that the bro-
ken hoist had to be more than a coincidence. Did
Armand de Velay's reach extend *inside* Castle
Jutigny?

Finally, they reached the haven of the solar
and were alone with Lord and Lady Faramus.
Eric accepted a cup of wine from Lord Faramus
and stood with him before the solar fire. He was
unable to tear his gaze from Rowena who was
sitting in the window seat talking to her mother.
He heard Rowena ask Lady Barbara which mid-
wife would be the best to send over to Monfort
for Helvise, although he didn't hear the answer
because all he could think was that if Armand
de Velay's reach extended inside the castle, then
Rowena wasn't safe, even here. Lord, what was
he to do?

He couldn't let her out of his sight for a moment.

'I've spoken to the master mason, Daniel,'
Lord Faramus was saying. Eric forced himself
to pay attention. 'He can't fathom how that rope
worked loose, he checked the pulleys himself
this morning.'

'Would you say he's speaking the truth?'

Lord Faramus took a swallow of wine. 'No
question. Daniel is diligence itself, I can't imagine what went wrong. I've ordered him to fit a

new pulley and a stronger rope.' He looked at his daughter. 'Thank God Rowena wasn't hurt.'

Eric spoke softly. 'My lord, if you don't object, I should like to speak to Daniel myself.'

'By all means, but I don't think you will glean anything more.'

'None the less, I would like to speak to him.'

The count gave him a narrow look. 'What's in your mind, de Monfort?'

Eric made a dismissive movement and forced a smile. 'As you say, *mon seigneur*, most likely it was simply a regrettable accident.' He was reluctant to admit it with Rowena in earshot, but that falling stone had filled him with suspicions. Did Sir Armand have an ally at Jutigny? One who was prepared to kill so that Sir Armand could inherit the family holdings? He turned a shoulder on Rowena and lowered his voice. 'My lord, has Lady Rowena been involved in other accidents?'

Frowning, Lord Faramus poked a log with the toe of his boot. 'Lord, no, there's been nothing like that.'

'You are certain there was nothing before she entered the convent?'

'Nothing. And before you ask, if anything untoward had happened in the convent, the nuns would have informed me. There is only what happened today and the incidents at Monfort.

It's a pity we have no proof of who was behind them.'

Eric stared into the flames. 'We can't even say for certain that Lady Rowena was the intended victim, but it would be foolish to dismiss it as a possibility.' He grimaced. 'On the day I escorted your daughter to the manor I did mark riders following us, but I made the mistake of thinking you had ordered your men to keep an eye on us. If I had realised sooner that the strangers in the village were nothing to do with you, I would have been more wary and Lady Rowena might not have had that near miss in the chase.'

Eric's father-in-law made a sound of exasperation. 'Why would I send men after you? I trust you implicitly, de Monfort. Always have, always will.' He looked warmly at him. 'Thought you understood that. When you were knighted I let you choose colours that matched mine. Don't let every knight do that. Thought you understood.'

Eric's throat tightened. 'Thank you, *mon seigneur.*'

However, flattering though it was to have the confidence of the Count of Sainte-Colombe, Eric didn't feel any happier. Someone in Jutigny was trying to kill Rowena. 'My lord, I need to speak to you in confidence, it is a matter of some urgency.'

'It concerns my daughter?'

'Yes, my lord.'

Count Faramus set his cup on a side table with a snap and gestured to the door. 'We can talk in the chapel.'

'Thank you. My lord, I would feel happier if Sir Macaire attended the ladies while we are absent.'

Eric endured a searching glance from Rowena's father, who gave a brusque nod. 'Very well, de Monfort, if you think it necessary.'

When the solar door closed behind Eric and Rowena's father, Lady Barbara was quick to change the subject. She took Rowena's hand. 'You are happy with our choice of husband?'

'Yes, Mother.'

'And he is as kind to you now as he was when you were a child?'

'Yes, Mother.'

Lady Barbara's eyes bored into her. 'I hope that all is well in the bedchamber?'

'Mama!'

'Come, Rowena, there's no need to be coy with me.'

Rowena rolled her eyes. 'Yes, Mother, everything is fine.'

Lady Barbara leaned back into the cushions with a sigh. 'Thank goodness. I knew I was right about that boy. I knew that if anyone could persuade you round to marriage it would be

Eric.' She smiled. 'I always wanted a love match
for you.'

'Mama, you mustn't delude yourself, Eric and
I are not in love.'

'Not yet,' Lady Barbara said, softly. 'But you
will be.'

Rowena wasn't so sure. She grimaced. 'Mama,
I am fully aware that Papa manipulated us into
marriage.' When her mother would have spoken,
Rowena swept on. 'Papa relied on Eric's innate
sense of chivalry to force him to marry me.'

Lady Barbara's smile was complacent. 'That
is certainly true.'

'It wasn't fair on Eric.'

Her mother shrugged. 'I don't see him com-
plaining. God willing, Eric stands to be count
one day. And if all is well between the two of
you, I don't see the problem.'

Rowena twisted a cushion fringe between her
thumb and forefinger and tried to pin down her
sense of unease. 'I married him to save my pride.
And he did rush me.'

'Rowena, you needed to be rushed, you had
walled yourself in at St Mary's. Sir Eric helped
you escape.'

'Mama, I admit I was foolish going in there
in the first place. At the time it seemed to be my
only course.' She plucked at the fringe. 'I knew
the king would let me have my way and I played
on that. Forgive me?'

Her mother patted her hand. 'There's nothing to forgive. All is well, you can be happy with Eric.'

'Mother, it is *not* a love match.' Rowena jerked on a silken tassel. Her mother simply didn't understand. Eric had married her because he was a chivalrous man. And, as her mother had also pointed out, he had married her for dynastic reasons—the Sainte-Colombe acres loomed large in his mind. 'Not that I ever expected a love match, particularly after the disaster of my broken betrothal with Lord Gawain.' She took a deep breath and ignored a stab of…what? Longing? Whatever it was, it wasn't pleasant. 'Never mind, it is done. We are married and I shall have to get used to it.'

'I can see that marriage might take some adjusting to after life in a nunnery.'

'Aye. Mama, were you very angry when I entered the convent?'

'Far from it, I was heartily relieved.'

Rowena gaped. 'Mother?'

'Rowena, it was your father who promoted the match with Lord Gawain, not I. I always favoured Sir Eric.'

'You did?'

'Eric is like the son I never had. Incidentally, your father would never admit it, but I am certain he feels the same way. Unfortunately, a long-standing agreement with the family of one of his allies forced him to favour a match with Lord Gawain. With Lord Gawain's holdings in Meaux eventually being added to ours, it would have been the greatest of alliances. I couldn't argue with that.'

'But you weren't entirely in agreement?'

'No. And when you and Lord Gawain agreed to part, I realised a little time was necessary for your father to adjust.' She smiled. 'Also it occurred to me that you would need to come to terms with your broken betrothal. I knew you would be safe in the convent.'

'You're saying that Eric was always your choice?'

'Always. It simply took time for your father to come round to my way of thinking. It helped that he admires Sir Eric for rising through the ranks.' Gently, Lady Barbara removed Rowena's hand from the silken tassel. 'Don't do that, dear, it's unravelling and I was quite proud of it. It took me an age to make.'

Rowena frowned at the straggling threads and folded her hands on her lap. 'Sorry, Mama.'

It was something of a revelation to hear that her mother had considered Eric as a prospective bridegroom for some while, and it was even more of a revelation to discover that it had been her mother who had persuaded her father round to her way of thinking. Didn't her mother usually defer to her father? Rowena had always assumed so. In this case it seemed that she was mistaken.

Rowena's nails cut into her palms. Saints, in the rush to marry, she hadn't even thought about her godfather, the king. The king had approved her betrothal to Lord Gawain and after that had fallen apart he had been good enough to approve her choice of convent. What would the king do when he realised she had left St Mary's and married without his permission? Everything had happened so quickly, she hadn't even considered his reaction.

'Mama, what do you suppose the king will do when he learns I have married?'

Lady Barbara gave her a candid look. 'His Grace won't be best pleased. He asked to be informed of your progress in the convent, I believe he planned to attend your Profession Day. He will have to be told about your marriage, particularly since your father owes him fealty for his French lands. Ordinarily, the king would expect to give his consent to any marriage of his vassals' heirs, approving only of the alliances that further the interests of France. Ultimately, I am sure that His Grace will see, as we do, that marriage to Eric suits you better than convent life. And, most importantly, he will see that your father has chosen a man with the character to succeed him and hold his lands securely.'

'Eric will have to swear fealty to the king for our French lands,' Rowena said.

'Quite so.'

A scuffling sound drew their attention to the door.

'Whatever's that?' Lady Barbara asked.

'One of the servants?' Rising, Rowena went quietly to the door and opened it.

Sir Macaire was standing on the landing with his back to the door. He turned. 'My lady, all is well?'

'Thank you, yes.' Rowena brought her brows together. 'Sir Macaire, what are you doing out there?'

Sir Macaire cleared his throat, he looked decidedly uncomfortable. 'Your husband asked me to stay here in case…in case you should need anything.'

'He asked you to guard me.'

Lady Barbara came across. 'Very sensible too, given recent events. Sir Macaire, there is no need to stand outside like a sentry. Join us.' She gestured at the side table. 'Would you care for a drink?'

Giving Rowena a sheepish look, Sir Macaire strode in. 'Thank you, Countess, I'd enjoy a cup of ale.'

Lady Barbara poured him some ale and returned to the window seat.

Rowena shot a glance at Sir Macaire. 'Mama, is this necessary?'

'We can't be too careful.'

Ice trickled down Rowena's spine. Could Armand really be intending to kill her? Was his ambition so large that he would stoop to murder? 'You think that my cousin is behind the accident at the gatehouse?'

'It's hard to believe it. Even though I've never liked Sir Armand, he is the most God-fearing of men. Some would say dangerously so.'

'What do you mean?'

'He takes too much from his tenants, and most of his revenues end up in church coffers. His lands have been impoverished. Rowena, your father has no wish to see Sainte-Colombe treated in like manner.'

'Yes, I see that.'

Her mother patted her hand. 'Given Sir Armand's interest in the church, it is hard to imagine that he would wish you dead. None the less, Sir Eric is right to consider it. We shouldn't take any chances.'

'Surely I am safe in Jutigny?'

'I certainly hope so. None the less, I can't fault Eric for wanting to take extra care.'

Rowena stared at the floor. Events had swept

her along so swiftly, she'd not had time to think. The first incident in the chase had been easily dismissed. Poachers. The second incident had given her pause, but she and Eric had been married so swiftly afterwards, her head had been in a whirl. And then there had been their wedding feast and their first night as a married couple.

'And then in no time, we arrived here,' she murmured.

'What's that, dear?'

'I feel as though I've been swept away by a tidal wave.' Rowena rubbed her brow. A tidal wave that was Eric de Monfort. His seduction had overwhelmed her, pushing out all thought, including that most disturbing of realisations— her cousin could be trying to kill her. Armand might want her dead.

Rowena sat very straight. Surely she was safe in her father's solar?

'Mama, what would happen if Armand succeeded in killing me? Wouldn't he be the first to be suspected?'

Her mother's expression became pained. 'Don't think of it, dearest.'

'Mother, this must be faced. What would happen?'

'Your father and I would be desolate,' her mother whispered. 'Desolate.'

'And guilt would have to be proved.' Lost in

dark thoughts, Rowena fell silent. If she wasn't safe in Jutigny, where would she be safe?

Gripping Rowena firmly by the hand, Eric led her up the winding stairs of the south tower. For the sake of security, he had agreed with his father-in-law that the chamber at the top would be theirs. Guards were already posted at each of the lower levels—guards Lord Faramus swore were loyal and could never be bought. Eric had insisted that his own Sergeant Yder was in charge of them.

Eric's mind was racing in the way it usually did only in combat. He had gained a little peace of mind when Sir Macaire had volunteered to use the chamber below theirs until they were certain the danger to Rowena had passed. He had relaxed some more when Alard had agreed to sleep on the landing outside their door. Even so, worry gnawed at his insides. It was obvious that he and Rowena must remain in Jutigny for the time being, running away would solve nothing. Someone wanted Rowena dead and he had to catch them. If Armand de Velay was the guilty party, he had to be stopped.

The decision to stay at Jutigny had been the hardest that Eric had had to make, and he was praying he'd got it right. If any harm should come to Rowena he would never forgive himself, but Lord Faramus was immovable on this. Lord Faramus wanted proof of Armand de Velay's perfidy. He wanted to know that more than coincidence was at work here. With Rowena's agreement, she was to be used as bait.

Eric's jaw tightened. The count's ruthlessness concerned him, this was Rowena they were talking about. Eric wasn't used to having a wife to consider and the thought of her being put at risk was almost unbearable. But he had done what he could to ensure her safety. The tower bedchamber had once been used as a strong room, the oak door was inches thick. Then there were the guards at the lower levels; Sir Macaire; Alard…

Naturally, on their way up Rowena noticed the guards. As they passed the first and second floors, her expression became more and more pensive. They climbed higher. Rowena's veil floated out behind her, seeming to shiver with the swiftness of their climb. He wasn't looking forward to telling her that she was to become a prisoner in her father's castle.

At the top, the heavy door groaned as Eric pushed it open. The servants had been quick to respond to his orders. A large bed was already set up and they had shifted Rowena's belongings in from her usual chamber. There were a couple of coffers painted with blue-and-white swirls and, on a side table, an ivory comb and polished hand mirror. A damask cloak was draped over the bed, it was lined with fur. Eric's travelling chest was already in place, and Alard must have seen to it that his armour had been brought up— his shield was propped in a corner; his coat of mail hung on a pole. It gave him an odd pang to see Rowena's things and his stowed so closely together. There was no fireplace here, he noticed. He would have to arrange for braziers to be brought up. He didn't want her to be cold.

Rowena took a shaky breath. 'This is the chamber you have chosen?'

The door squeaked as he closed it, and Eric reminded himself to get someone to oil the hinges. 'Aye.'

'The window's so high and narrow all I can see is sky. What's wrong with my usual bedchamber?'

'Nothing. However, for the time being we ought to use this one. It's safer.'

'More easily guarded, you mean,' she said quietly. She drew her hand from his and wandered to the side table to pick up her mirror. 'I didn't think to see this again. Mirrors weren't permitted at the convent.'

Eric watched in silence as her gaze fell on his chain mail and travelling chest. He wished he could read her.

She raised her eyes to his, her face was strained. 'I am to be a prisoner.'

'Not exactly.' He grimaced. 'It's worse than that.'

'Worse?'

Stepping up to her, he covered her hands with his. Her fingers felt cold, softly he ran his thumb over them. 'With your agreement, Rowena, you are to force the assassin to show his hand. If Sir Armand is behind these incidents, we have to draw him out. And if he has an ally here in the castle, we have to uncloak them.'

She didn't respond at first. A draught from the window was playing across the back of his neck. Blue eyes gazed into his. A skein of golden hair lay across her breast.

'I am to be used as bait. With my agreement.'

'Rowena, it's the best way of catching him. You will be perfectly safe up here. As of this moment, the south tower is off-limits to all but a select few. The guards have been hand-picked by your father and myself, and they have orders never to leave their post unattended. Sir Macaire has taken the chamber below this one. Alard—'

'I thought that in marrying you I would regain some measure of freedom.' In the quiet of the tower room, her sigh was loud and her smile sad. 'Yet here I am. It seems that I have simply exchanged one form of prison for another.'

Eric's heart felt like lead. He reached for that bright twist of hair, winding it round his finger. 'Rowena, you are not really a prisoner. I don't want to confine you and I wouldn't dream of forcing you into agreeing. But you must see that this is the only way.'

'Is it?' She smiled. 'We could run away. We could leave all this behind us.' A wave of her hand encompassed the tower room, the castle and—Eric suspected—every last acre her father owned.

'Everything?'

'Everything.' She took a deep breath. 'We could ride out into the world and hide. We could step into new lives and become other people. There must be somewhere we can be safe.'

They could become other people? Mad though it was, Eric found himself actually considering her suggestion. For an instant. Firmly, he shook his head. He'd fought like a demon to win his spurs and marrying into Rowena's family was part of that. He was going to be steward of Sainte-Colombe, he wasn't about to toss that away. He was determined to prove himself worthy of the honour he'd been given—*two* honours—for having Rowena as his wife was just as much an honour as having the care of her father's lands.

'We can't walk away from our responsibilities here, it wouldn't work. How would we live? What would we do? And what about your parents? It would kill them.'

She sighed. 'You're right, of course. It wouldn't work.'

He looked intently at her. 'So you'll stay?'

'Yes, Eric, I'll stay. I'll act as bait.' Her expression lightened and she curled her fingers into his tunic. 'Only please tell me I don't have to stay in this tower the entire time.'

'No, no. You may wander freely within the castle if you promise you will let Sergeant Yder know your plans. He will ensure that two of the guards will accompany you.'

'I promise.'

'At all times. Rowena, there are to be no exceptions.'

An eyebrow shot up. 'What about when I need to go to the privy?'

'The guards will check before you enter and wait outside. Rowena, I will have your word on this.'

'You have it.'

'Good. Your mother can visit you up here at any time and you will have your maid.'

'What about riding?'

'Only with me.' Eric cupped her face with his hand and found himself saying something that he had never expected to say to any woman.

'Rowena, I will not lose you. I will guard you with my life. You are mine and you are precious to me.'

He gave her a slightly bemused smile, for what he'd just said had surprised him. Yet it was true, Rowena was precious to him. She was his wife. She was the greatest gift he had ever been given and he was going to cherish her.

She returned his smile and lightly touched his cheek. 'Thank you, Eric.'

When she tipped her face up in that way and looked at him through eyes that were soft with what looked very much like affection, she was irresistible. Eric slid his arms about her waist. Her mouth was close. Tempting. If he kissed her, the tightness in his belly—concern for her safety—would surely ease. The thought of her being hurt made him sick at heart.

Reaching up, Rowena ran her fingers through Eric's hair, pushing it back from his eyes so she could read him better. 'I've always liked the colour of your hair,' she murmured. 'The auburn streaks make it gleam. In summer they lighten beautifully.'

An eyebrow lifted. 'You like my hair?' He leaned in and nuzzled her cheek. A warm kiss landed on Rowena's ear. 'I am glad it meets with your approval.'

Rowena let her fingers sift through the dark

strands. It was very pleasurable, standing with Eric in the quiet of the south tower. It was…companionable. How strange. It looked as though her cousin was trying to kill her; she and Eric had not been married above a day, and yet she felt perfectly at ease with him. It felt as though they belonged together. Did he feel the same?

She smiled to herself, she knew better than to pose so serious a question. This was Sir Eric de Monfort, the strongest, most carefree champion-at-arms who had ever been born. He could seduce his way into the most reluctant of hearts and emerge entirely unscathed. He might tell her that she was precious to him, but he probably said similar things to all his women. Eric didn't have a heart to give. Or did he? Could the flirtatious manner simply be his way of keeping women at arm's length? Could it be one of the methods he used to avoid becoming truly involved? Well, things had changed. Eric was married, he wasn't going to find it easy to keep her at arm's length.

Squashing the impulse to hug him—she was afraid of revealing how much he was coming to mean to her—Rowena contented herself with stroking his hair, he seemed to like it and she was determined to use every means at hand to strengthen the bond between them. Down below, she could hear the tramp of soldiers' boots on the stairs; the distant buzz of conversation. She sighed with pure pleasure. Eric's hair was one of his best features, it was thick and shiny, soft as silk.

Rowena studied the gleaming auburn mixed in with the brown as she thought about the paradox that was her husband. She couldn't be the first woman to have admired his hair. Did he grow it long deliberately? Did he use it as part of his armoury in the war to win everyone's hearts? For that was what he tried to do. Eric wanted everyone to like him and, on a superficial level, everyone did. Women weren't the only people to respond positively to men who were tall and handsome. Men did too. They liked strong, personable leaders. His strength was reassuring, his men knew Eric wouldn't be afraid to lead in any charge.

I will guard you with my life. Her throat tightened. Did he know how seductive those words were?

Probably. Eric was very good at making people like him, and only now was Rowena realising why that was. The lost little boy had never felt as though he truly belonged. He had tried so long to make up for the charity he had received at her mother's hands that it had become a habit. He must know that it was no longer necessary, he had proved himself a thousand times.

Her father—not an easy man to impress—respected him. Her mother loved him. As did she.

Rowena's fingers stilled as the realisation sank in. She loved him, she loved Eric de Monfort. It wasn't possible. Not in a couple of days.

Except that it wasn't a couple of days. She had known him all her life. Had watched him at a distance for years.

Eric wanted people to like him. He wanted their love. It was just that he wasn't so sure about loving them back.

'Rowena, what's the matter?'

'Nothing.' She loved him. Saints, she loved a man who could charm the birds from the trees. Doubtless he always would. Did he have a heart? She burned to know. Would it ever be hers?

The young boy had grown into a sensitive man, a man who had learned to guard his feelings from an early age in order to thrive in a castle where he felt he had no real place. Rowena forced herself to look deep into his eyes. Eric had feelings, she was sure of it. They were hidden deep beneath that carefree, flirtatious armour. His eyes had darkened, he was watching her with the confident sensuality of a man who knew he would not be refused. Her husband.

He nudged his head against her hand. 'Why did you stop?' His green eyes were almost closed. 'I was enjoying that.'

Yes, Eric was the most sensual of men. Very well, she would use that knowledge. She would use his sensuality as a means of binding him to her. She would win his love.

Curling her fingers into his hair, she brought his head down for a brief kiss. His eyes closed completely, but not for long. As soon as she set her fingers to his belt they snapped open again. 'Rowena?'

She tipped her head to one side and smiled as she worked at the buckle. 'You are my husband, Eric.'

His mouth twitched. 'Hmm?' A large hand slid over her breast, gently kneading.

She edged him towards the bed. 'You put the servants to the trouble of assembling a bed for us up in this eyrie. The least we could do is try it out.'

Chapter Nine

Afterwards, they lay in each other's arms in the great bed. Rowena smiled to herself.

Eric shifted and kissed her shoulder. 'Why the smile?'

Rowena tightened her hold about his waist and nuzzled his cheek. It felt slightly bristly and very male. She liked it. She especially liked the discovery that Eric's sensuality extended beyond the act of love. Her husband took time to hold her, even now one hand was idly caressing her back, the other was toying with her hair. She might not have Eric de Monfort's love, but he was behaving as if he held her in affection. At the least it was companionable.

'I like lying with you like this,' she murmured.

'And I with you.' He sighed, and went on ruffling her hair. 'However, I can't stay long, your father is expecting me in the armoury.' He grimaced and released her. 'I should go.'

Rowena propped her head on her arm and watched him as he dressed. The play of light on his back muscles was endlessly fascinating; she loved studying the long lean length of his thigh, the curve of his buttock. When he had buckled his sword on over his tunic, he came to stand by the bed and his perfect male form—the wide shoulders, the narrow waist—was clearly silhouetted in the light streaming through the lancet.

'I will see you in the hall for supper,' he said. 'Don't forget, when you leave this chamber the guards are to accompany you. At all times.'

'Eric, I won't forget.'

'Good.' Picking up her hand, he bowed over it. 'I shall send Berthe up to attend you.'

Rowena sat on a three-legged stool, wincing as Berthe dragged a comb through her hair. Berthe had been tutting and fussing ever since she had walked into the bedchamber.

'Dear Lord, what has that man done with your hair? So many knots. Doesn't he realise how long it takes to comb them out?'

Rowena hid a smile and wondered what Berthe would say if she told her that Eric said she was adorable when she was a little dishevelled.

Berthe pulled at her hair and the tutting went on. 'Your hair was beautiful before Eric de Monfort got his hands on you. He has no notion of how to treat a lady. Men are all the same, they only care about bedding a woman.'

Rowena shrugged. She wasn't going to confess that Eric liked to lie in bed, simply holding her. That was private. She stared thoughtfully at a candlestick on a shelf in front of her. She had listened to enough gossip to know that whilst men rushed to enjoy the carnal aspects of marriage, it was a rare husband who simply enjoyed his wife's company as Eric seemed to enjoy hers. Eric had confessed he took pleasure in more than the actual bedding, he spent time cuddling her which must mean that the bond between them was strengthening. Eric was a loving man, she was sure of it. It was up to her to convince him of it.

She smiled to herself. Their shared delight in the physical joys of their union was a great boon, it would surely help her in her quest to win his heart.

Berthe's chest heaved. 'I suppose we should be grateful you still have your hair, it would have been chopped off if you'd been clothed as a novice. Are you happy with Sir Eric, my lady?'

The question was unexpected and, coming from her maid, verging on the impertinent. Picking up her hand mirror, Rowena angled it so she could see Berthe's face. 'Berthe?'

'I agree Sir Eric has great charm, but he's not exactly the match you might have expected.'

Rowena sat very still. 'What do you mean?'

'No one knows anything about his family. He's not noble, he might even come from peasant stock.' Slowly Berthe worked the comb through Rowena's hair. 'I know he has become a landed knight and has won himself a manor, but he's hardly Lord Gawain, is he?'

Rowena swung round so quickly her hair caught on the comb. Snatching it free, she took a couple of deep breaths to steady herself and put up her chin. 'Enough! Berthe, you are impertinent.'

Berthe's jaw sagged. 'My lady?'

'Count Faramus chose Sir Eric for me. It is not your place to question your lord's choice.'

Berthe looked at the floor. 'I'm sorry, my lady.'

'So you should be. Sir Eric is my husband and I for one am glad.'

'Yes, my lady.' Berthe lifted her gaze. 'I meant no disrespect, my lady. There's not a body in Jutigny who doesn't like and respect Sir Eric, it was just—'

'Berthe, you must appreciate that Father judges men by their character rather than their birth. The fact that Sir Eric's parentage is unknown is entirely irrelevant. His service as one of our household knights has always been exemplary.'

'Yes, my lady.' Berthe bit her lip. 'My lady, I am truly sorry to have offended you. I hope this doesn't mean you will put me to work in the laundry.'

'Don't be ridiculous, Berthe, of course I won't.'

Berthe gave her a strained smile. 'Thank you. I really am sorry, my lady. I didn't understand how it was between you.'

Rowena's parents had tried to instil a sense of fairness into her, her father in particular was fond of saying she must judge a man by his deeds and not by his trappings. Yet, shocking though Berthe's remarks were, they gave her new insight.

Were there others here in Jutigny who harboured similar doubts about Eric because of his humble birth? If so, it seemed likely that Eric had been running the gauntlet of prejudice for years. Did he perhaps come to expect it? From everyone? A man who expected to be treated poorly on account of his ancestry, or rather his lack of it, might find it hard to believe he was worthy of love. A lump formed in her throat.

Rowena had never heard so much as a whisper about Eric's family. Given his age when her mother had taken him under her wing, he must remember them. Yet he never spoke of his mother and father. Who were they? Did he never mention them because he feared that he might be judged, and all that he had worked for might be snatched away?

Does he think that poorly of us? Of me?

Realising that Berthe was looking expectantly at her, Rowena gestured at the blue-and-white coffer by the wall. 'I assume my old clothes are in that.'

'Aye, my lady, no one's touched them since you went to the abbey.'

'I've missed them.'

'I am not surprised.' With an air of relief, Berthe turned for the coffer. 'It will be good to see you in something brighter than those rags the sisters made you wear.'

'See if you can find the close-fitting rose brocade with the fur edging. I'll wear my silver girdle with the matching circlet.'

'The cream veil, my lady?'

'Please.' The rose gown was Rowena's favourite and she was curious to see Eric's reaction when she wore it. These past few days, he had only seen her in the drabbest of gowns. Rowena had never thought of herself as particularly vain, but she wanted Eric to see her in something a little more alluring. The rose gown had intricate lacings at the wrists and sides. The thought of

Eric struggling to unlace her was oddly stimulating.

Berthe shot her the strangest of glances and Rowena felt herself blush. For a wild moment, she fancied her maid could read her mind.

The bailey was full of shadow when the supper bell summoned Eric and Count Faramus from the gatehouse. As they crossed the yard, they were not alone—several knights had returned from patrol and they were emerging from the stables, bellowing orders over their shoulders as they headed to the fountain to wash.

'Check the shoe on that hind leg, Pierre.'

'Aye, sir.'

'And rub him down well.'

'Right away, sir.'

A maidservant flew out of the storehouse with a basket of eggs. She glanced at Lord Faramus and dipped into a curtsy.

'Good evening, my lord.'

'Good evening, Mary.'

Mary caught Eric's eyes and blushed. 'It is good to see you again, Sir Eric.'

Eric gave the girl a preoccupied nod. 'Good to see you too, Mary.'

As Mary hurried away in the direction of the cookhouse, Lord Faramus gave Eric a searching glance. 'Pretty girl, Mary,' he said.

Eric focused on Mary's retreating back. 'Oh, aye, she is that.'

'Something of a flirt, would you say?'

Eric was not so busy with his thoughts that he failed to notice the measuring look Lord Faramus was giving him. He stiffened. '*Mon seigneur*, Mary is, as you say, pretty. But if you are suggesting that I have eyes for her, you are very much mistaken.'

Lord Faramus lilted an eyebrow. 'Mary was known to have a *tendre* for you some years back.'

'That is in the past. In any case, it was quite innocent.'

Lord Faramus let out a bark of laughter and Eric felt his face heat. 'Innocent? The spring before you left Jutigny, you were seen lying with Mary in the meadows by the river.'

'Things are not always as they seem, my lord.' Eric remembered that spring when he and Mary had gone down to the meadows together to talk. It was oddly disturbing to realise that someone had been watching them and had reported back to Lord Faramus. There had been not much to see, in any event. Eric's friendship with Mary had been dictated mainly by fondness and liking, they had exchanged a mere handful of kisses. Mary made no demands on Eric and he had valued her for that.

'Meaning?'

'Whoever saw us in the meadows, misinterpreted what they saw,' Eric said firmly. 'Mary is no wanton. And even if she were, I can assure you that I shall never give your daughter cause to question my fidelity.'

'I am glad to hear it, de Monfort. Glad to hear it.' Lord Faramus clapped him on the shoulder. 'And there's no need to look daggers at me, a father likes to know he has made the right decision for his daughter.'

'My lord, you have my word I shall do my utmost not to disappoint either you or Lady Rowena.'

As Eric approached the hall steps at Lord Faramus's side, it came to him that his friendship with Mary must have been similar to Rowena's with her Mathieu—puppy love. Innocent but open to misinterpretation.

Realisation slammed into him. '*Mon Dieu*, I've been blind.'

Lord Faramus looked back. 'Eh?'

Thoughts flew through Eric's head, thoughts that brought goosebumps to the back of his neck. He struggled to order them. Rowena and Mathieu. Rowena had sworn that no one knew of her dalliance with de Lyon. She had told him their friendship had been innocent and Eric believed her, after all, she had been a virgin on their wedding night. Rowena's dalliance with the squire sounded very much like Eric's with Mary—childish, innocent and completely without passion.

Yet Mathieu de Lyon was dead.

What if someone had seen them together? Could Mathieu's death have been more than a random accident?

Eric stepped over the threshold and into the hall. *'Mon seigneur.'* Conscious of the rest of the household filing into the hall for supper, he kept his voice low. 'I hear that after I left your service, a young squire named Mathieu was fostered here.'

Lord Faramus didn't reply until he had reached the sideboard where cloths and a basin were laid out for them. He dipped his hands in the water and grunted. 'Bloody tragedy, what happened to him.'

'My lord, what did happen?'

'The boy was killed in a street brawl in Provins.' Lord Faramus shook his head and picked up a drying cloth.

'Oh?'

'De Lyon was in the wrong place at the wrong time. Like everyone here he had orders not to go alone after curfew. He had the ill fortune to choose the day of the brawl to disobey them. His body was found in a side street in town.'

'Did you discover what started the brawl?'

'Drunks, most likely. It took place in the market square in the lower town, by The Sun Inn.'

'The Sun?'

'The tavern by St Ayoul.' Lord Faramus tossed the cloth aside and gestured for Eric to take his turn at the basin. 'Count Henry's captain investigated the boy's death and he found nothing.'

'No one was brought to trial?'

'Unfortunately, no. It was a damn shame. Whilst the boy didn't have the build for a knight, he would have made a fine archer.'

A servant approached bearing wine on a tray. Lord Faramus reached for a cup. 'Mathieu de Lyon simply picked the wrong day to break curfew.'

Eric stared pensively at his father-in-law. Lord Faramus could be right, Mathieu's death might be a tragic case of the boy being in the wrong place at the wrong time. But the prickling at the back of his neck told him otherwise.

Mathieu de Lyon might have been murdered.

Murdered because he had been seen with Rowena? It was certainly possible. Mathieu could have been killed because someone had seen them together, someone who feared that they were about to become lovers and felt threatened by the possibility of an alliance between de Lyon's family and the Sainte-Colombe family.

Rowena seemed convinced that no one knew

about her infatuation with Mathieu. She had
to be wrong. Someone knew about their meet-
ings. And that someone could have been desperate to ensure Rowena's relationship with the
young squire proceeded no further. If Rowena
and Mathieu had married, there might soon have
been heirs. And who stood to lose if that happened?

Sir Armand de Velay.

Had de Velay engineered de Lyon's death?
If so, he was clever as the devil. Understanding
that Rowena's infatuation with Mathieu de Lyon
wasn't generally known, de Velay would also
have known there was little possibility of Mathieu's death being uncovered as murder. Who
would connect de Lyon's death with Rowena?

Thus, with Mathieu's death apparently an unfortunate accident, it wouldn't occur to anyone
that Rowena might be in danger herself.

What a blessing her betrothal to Lord Gawain
had been so short. What a blessing she had re-
treated to the convent. Eric shuddered to think
what might have happened otherwise.

Sir Armand was the obvious suspect. It was
hard to credit, Sir Armand's piety was legendary.
Yet it was possible. Someone in Jutigny could
be relaying messages to him. Eric dropped the
drying cloth by the basin. He must delve a little

deeper. Discreetly. If Sir Armand was his man, it would be hard to prove.

Eric took a cup of wine from the tray and started for the high table where, as Rowena's husband and future steward of the Sainte-Colombe acres, he had won the right to sit at his lord's right hand. Eric had questions for Lord Faramus and yet more questions for Rowena. However, the hall was filling fast—knights and soldiers; ladies, maids and children; the castle priest—all weaving in and out to secure their places at the long, cloth-clad tables. Servants darted hither and yon—doling out trencher after trencher; thumping platters on to the trestles. Eric sighed. With so many people in earshot, his questions would have to wait.

The door to the south tower opened and a man-at-arms came in—one of the men Eric had hand-picked to guard Rowena. The man held open the door, bowed, and Rowena appeared. She was followed closely by her maid and a second guard.

Eric's thoughts scattered. Rowena was clad in a dark-rose gown that hugged her every curve and would surely be the envy of every woman in Christendom. *Bon sang*, he was the most fortunate of men. Her veil was the colour of cream and held in place by a silver circlet that caught the light as she moved. A shimmering river of silk, the veil flowed down her back. The fabric was so fine that it barely concealed her hair, which had been bound with rose ribbons into a loose braid and hung over her breast. Rowena's tiny waist was encircled by a silver girdle that matched her circlet.

As her eyes met his, she sent him a shy smile and Eric found himself fighting for breath. He had married the most beautiful girl in all of creation. He hadn't realised he had set his cup down and moved to meet her until he was tucking that small hand into the crook of his elbow.

'I am glad to see you didn't forget the guards, my lady.'

Rowena smiled up at him and his chest ached. He covered her hand with his. 'Tonight your beauty outshines the sun,' he murmured and led her past Sir Breon to their place at the high table.

As Eric feared, there was no chance of talking discreetly to Rowena's father during supper. First potage was served and Sir Macaire claimed Lord Faramus's attention—something about a boundary dispute with a local merchant. Then a platter of roast pork was set on the table and Lady Barbara drew her husband into a heated discussion about a petition she had received from the convent that had lately housed their daughter. By the time Eric was slicing into a pear poached in red wine and honey he had given up. He would speak to Lord Faramus in the morning.

Not that he minded, attending to Rowena was distraction enough.

A page refilled the wine cup they were sharing and Eric handed it to her. It was hard to keep his eyes off her mouth. That shy smile was so beguiling. And that gown—Lord, it was cut so low that when she leaned towards him, he could see the rise and fall of her breasts.

'Do you care for a honey biscuit, my lady?'

'No, thank you.' Her veil danced as she shook her head. Her eyes sparkled in the candlelight, this evening they were the colour of the sky and infinitely fascinating, the deep blue seemed to draw him in so he couldn't look away.

Lifting a delicate hand, she hid a yawn. 'I confess I am a little tired, sir. Convent life was uneventful which is doubtless why I have found the change of these past few days exhausting.'

Rowena didn't look the least bit tired, Eric would swear that yawn was false. And she was biting her lip in a manner that suggested she was holding in a smile. Not to mention that the way she was leaning forward was tempting him almost beyond endurance. He wanted to snatch her into his arms and kiss her senseless. Yes, even here, in her father's great hall with her parents and her father's knights sitting scant feet away.

'Rowena…' His voice was choked. Rowena might have been innocent when they married, but she knew what she was doing. The sparkle in her eyes told him that she was deliberately trying to heat his blood. She was certainly succeeding. She gave another small yawn and her head came to rest against his shoulder. To an onlooker it would seem like a gesture of trust and affection, but Eric knew otherwise. The way that low neckline gaped made it an attempt at seduction. *She wants me.* Eric caught a glimpse of a rose-tipped breast and almost groaned aloud. He looked into her eyes and an eyebrow twitched. That shy, almost-smile was irresistible.

Time to surrender. He had given Berthe orders to have a brazier lit in their bedchamber, he hoped she had remembered. 'Tired, my lady?' Sliding an arm about his wife's tiny waist, Eric pushed the platter of pears aside with a sigh as false as Rowena's yawn. He turned to Count Faramus. 'My lord, with your permission, Rowena and I should like to retire.'

The faint glow of a brazier filled the bedchamber. *Good.*

Eric snatched up a taper, held it to a coal and lit the candle on a wall sconce. 'Come here, witch.'

'Witch?' With a swish of brocade skirts, she

came to his side. 'We haven't been married a week and already you are calling me witch?'

'You are a witch. Adorable. Enchanting. A witch. Your behaviour in the great hall...' Allowing his voice to tail off, he shook his head at her.

Her eyes softened. 'I shocked you,' she said, resting her hands against his chest.

He set his hands on her hips. 'Lord knows what your mother must have thought.'

'Mama thinks we're in love. She will excuse almost anything for that.'

'Love?' Eric felt his face freeze. 'That's not possible.'

'I know that,' she said lightly. 'You will have to forgive Mama, she has been listening to too many troubadours.'

Frowning, he lifted her hands from his chest and held them out, the better to examine her gown.

'Eric, what are you doing?'

'Looking for lacings.' He turned her about and couldn't see any opening at the back. 'It seems to be all of a piece, where the devil are they?'

He heard a soft laugh. 'At the wrist and sides.' Briefly, Rowena freed herself from his grasp, set the silver circlet on the shelf next to the candle and removed her veil.

Eric took her by the wrist and, leaning against the bedpost, pulled her to him. The lacings at the cuff were thin and fiddly. Naturally, in his eagerness his fingers turned into thumbs. As he wrestled with the fastenings, it seemed the chamber was filled with the heady fragrance of summer.

'This gown must have scandalised the nuns.'

The candlelight gleamed in her eyes. She huffed out a breath. 'I didn't take it to the convent.'

'I can't say I'm surprised.' Eric had finished one sleeve and loosened the side. He started on the other. 'Although perhaps the nuns wouldn't have worried if they had known what a trial it is to get you out of it.'

She laughed. 'It's not that easy getting into it. Berthe has to help.'

The second sleeve loosened, he moved on to the side lacings. 'Rowena?'

'Hmm?'

'I need to ask you about Mathieu de Lyon.'

'Yes?'

'You're quite certain no one saw you with him?'

'Quite sure. Why?' She touched his hand. 'You have heard something.'

'No. It is just an idea.'

She gripped his fingers. 'Tell me.'

'I'd rather not at this stage.' Eric couldn't tell her that he suspected de Lyon might have been murdered on her account. He had already had her put under guard and he didn't want to add to her worries. Leaning down, he pressed a kiss to her forehead. 'Rest assured, if I learn anything definite, I will tell you.'

Loosening the final lacing, Eric heaved a sigh of relief. 'Thank God. We shall have you free of this in no time.' Sliding his hands down her body, he caught hold of the rose brocade and pulled it from her.

When Rowena woke, pale light was filtering round the edges of the window shutter. She shivered, the brazier had gone out in the night and Eric had all the blanket. Pulling some of the covers back towards her, Rowena snuggled close. Eric was the best bed warmer.

He gave a murmur, opened sleepy eyes and smiled. 'It can't be morning already.'

They hadn't slept much last night.

'Not quite. I was cold. You, sir, are a blanket hog.'

A powerful arm wrapped round her. 'A blanket hog?' His eyes darkened. 'I can think of other ways of warming you, if you are agreeable?'

Afterwards, Eric rose and went to the jug and ewer to wash. He was completely naked and utterly unselfconscious. Rowena lay in bed, watching him. Admiring. He had such a beautiful body, but he was so much more to her than that. She was a lucky, lucky woman. If Eric had not agreed to her father's proposition…she shuddered. 'Eric, thank you for marrying me.'

He smiled and set the towel on the side table. 'It is no hardship, I assure you. I should be thanking you.' Moving back to the bed, he reached for her hand. As he kissed it, a dark eyebrow lifted. 'Marriage with you is greatly to my liking. I enjoy your company.'

She gave him a frank look. 'You're not alone in that. I too enjoy our time together, but I give you fair warning I want more from our marriage than that.'

'You mean children? I, too, hope we shall have children.'

A brief image of small children—a boy and a girl—with Eric's unusual eyes flashed into Rowena's mind. The pang of longing that followed was almost unbearable. Firmly, she ignored it. 'I wasn't referring to children. I think you should know that I intend to use our mutual enjoyment of each other's bodies to bind you to me.'

Expression puzzled, he turned and took his chausses down from a peg. 'Rowena, I am already bound to you, in marriage. What more can there be than that?'

'What about love?'

He froze. 'Love? You want my love?'

'Yes.'

Eric cleared his throat and she saw the muscles in his legs flex as he stepped into his chausses. His face was empty of all expression, he seemed to be at a loss for words. Then he cleared his throat a second time. 'I told you, you can't love me.'

His tone was flat. Firm. Uncompromising. Was he forbidding her to love him?

'Why not?'

'Rowena, you simply can't.'

He turned his back, leaving her to contemplate his wide shoulders. Something about the set of them told her that Eric was not ready to think about love. It was far too soon for her to pursue that line of thought. She held down a sigh. She would have to try another approach.

When Eric picked up his shirt, she saw her chance and flung back the bedcovers.

'Eric, I have something for you.' Winding a blanket about her, she padded over to her coffer. The hinge creaked as she held the lid open and drew out the shirt. 'I finished this yesterday just before the supper bell sounded. If you don't like it, you don't have to wear it.'

Handing the shirt to him, she held her breath. He shook it out and stared at it and Rowena's heart cramped at the bemused expression in his eyes. It was as though he had never set eyes on

a shirt before. 'This is what you began making
at Monfort?'

'Aye.'

'A shirt.' His voice was hoarse. 'For me.' He
stared silently at it, fingering the fabric, running
his forefinger along the tiny stitches at the neck.
A muscle flickered in his jaw.

He didn't like it. He was so silent. If he liked it
he would surely say something. 'Eric, you don't
have to wear it. It's nothing much, only an un-
dershirt.'

Rowena felt herself go still. She had never
seen him look quite like this. It came to her that
she had startled him. He looked vulnerable. Although, if she read him correctly, underneath
his surprise he was pleased. Deeply pleased. As
well as uncertain. She had made him a shirt and
he had no clue how to respond.

Her gut clenched. Surely this wasn't the first
time he'd been given a gift? Her mother had
given Eric clothes when he'd arrived at Jutigny
and he'd been issued with more as he grew older.
However, everything would have come from the
quartermaster. Thinking back, when they were
young Rowena could only remember Eric wearing standard issue. Likely he had started paying someone to make him clothes when he had
begun earning his knight's fee.

Even then his tunics had been plain. Straightforward. Like the man. Except that she was discovering that Eric de Monfort was nowhere near as straightforward as everyone supposed.

His head was bent over her work, he was examining at the initials she had embroidered on the front—'E' and 'R' entwined in blue-and-crimson silk.

He looked up, eyes hooded. 'This embroidery is very good. Excellent work. Rowena, I thank you. I have never had anything so fine.'

His forefinger traced over the blue 'R' and he bit his lip. Slowly, he shifted his finger over the crimson 'E'. 'I like the way you've worked our initials.'

'You are my husband.' She shrugged. 'I saw the pattern in my head and thought they would look pretty intertwined.'

Green eyes bored into hers. His face was unreadable. Then, snatching up his tunic and sword belt, he strode out. The door thumped shut.

Rowena sank on to the edge of the bed, the blanket clutched to her breast. She closed her eyes. Her gift—likely the first that had been fashioned especially for him—had angered him and she wasn't quite sure why. It was obvious he was pleased at becoming part of the family. She felt sure that her gift had touched him. Was that the trouble? He didn't know how to respond.

Opening her eyes, she stared at the door. She

could no longer hear his footsteps, he must be downstairs with Alard already. At least he had taken the shirt with him. Would he wear it? She had no idea. Clearly, winning Eric's heart wasn't going to be as easy as she had hoped. She would have to take it one step at a time.

Chapter Ten

A man on a mission—in truth a man on *two* missions—Eric stalked into the bailey, his cloak flapping at his heels. His squire was waiting for him near the gatehouse.

The horses were already saddled and tethered to a ring in the wall and Alard was leaning against his horse's withers, knuckling sleep from his eyes. On seeing Eric, Alard straightened and pulled Captain's reins from the ring.

Eric dragged on his gloves and took the reins. 'My thanks.'

When he and Alard were mounted, Alard looked at him. 'Where are we going, sir?'

'Provins. The cloth market.'

Alard stared. 'Again?'

Eric felt his face heat. 'I made a promise and I must fulfil it.'

That bolt of blue samite lingered in his mind's eye. That was his first mission. Rowena had admired it and now they were married he intended to buy her a length to make a gown. Admittedly, he hadn't expected to be doing this quite so soon.

Leather creaked as they heeled the horses into a walk. The sky was overcast, the colour of pewter, and the wind was coming from the north. It would rain later. Absently Eric rubbed his chest. Rowena's gift lay beneath his gambeson and tunic, next to his skin. He had finished dressing in a chamber beneath theirs and when he had pulled on her shirt, he'd had a lump in his throat the size of a gull's egg. It seemed ridiculous to be moved by so small a thing. He was married and his wife had made him a shirt.

It was not an uncommon thing for Rowena to have done, wives made clothes for their husbands every day. Yet somehow her gift had wrong-footed him. The fabric she had unearthed from the Monfort linen chest was soft against his skin, the stitches tiny. Perfect. Never in his life had he owned anything so fine, the stuff he usually got the seamstress to sew for him was coarser and the stitches heavier.

It felt strange wearing something Rowena had made for him. He liked it even though it unsettled him. Had Rowena's mind been on him while she had been setting those tiny stitches? Before she had given it to him, she had said something

about wanting his love, even though he had
warned her not to expect it from him. Had she
been thinking about love when she had sewn his
shirt? He would never love her, he would never
love any woman.

As they left Castle Jutigny behind them and
joined the road to Provins, Eric grimaced. His
response to her gift left much to be desired. She
must think she had married the most surly of
men; she must think that he disliked the shirt
when the opposite was true. Eric had been struggling to frame some sort of a decent response
even as he noticed that the delicate stitching of
the red and the blue was more than just a pretty
pattern. It was their initials, interwoven. The
knowledge had floored him. He'd been utterly
stunned.

What had he done to deserve her? Lady Rowena of Sainte-Colombe had married him under
duress. It was obvious she'd been mourning Mathieu de Lyon when she'd entered the convent.
She'd been forced to marry Eric, and yet she was
behaving in every way as though he were her
choice. Eric wasn't her equal. He had become a
knight but there was no escaping that a foundling could never be her social equal. *Mon Dieu*,
she hadn't the first clue about his background.

Eric stared blindly at Captain's ears as he remembered the gentle expression in her eyes as

he had traced his finger over their initials, as he had understood what they symbolised. We are united, those initials seemed to say.

Rowena's wholehearted acceptance of him made no sense. It puzzled him. Eric told himself not to dwell on it. It shouldn't matter. What did matter was that he was delighted with his bride and whilst he could never love her, she would always have his affection. He would do his best to make certain she never regretted their marriage, the blue samite was hers.

As for his second mission, Lord Faramus had mentioned that Mathieu de Lyon had died near The Sun. The Sun wasn't an inn Eric was familiar with, but it wouldn't hurt to make enquiries, someone might remember what had happened that night.

'Alard?'

'Sir?'

'Have you ever been into The Sun? It's by the market in the Lower Town, near St Ayoul.'

'I know the place, sir, but I've never been inside.'

'Dommage.' Pity.

Alard was looking at him, eyes wide with curiosity. 'I understand it's a rough place—a while back one of the Jutigny squires was attacked in the alley nearby. He was found dead later.'

Eric grunted. 'So I heard.' He wasn't about to

confess—even to Alard—that the squire's death was haunting him, drawing him to The Sun. Clearly, Rowena had loved the boy. *Bon sang*, in mourning the loss of him, she had turned down Lord Gawain de Meaux.

The idea that Mathieu de Lyon had meant so much to Rowena didn't sit well with him. However, worse than that was the suspicion that the boy's death might have had something to do with his relationship with Rowena. The suspicion that someone had wanted de Lyon out of the way because of his closeness to Rowena was becoming stronger by the day. As was Eric's fear that Rowena wasn't safe even in her father's castle.

It was imperative that Eric learn how—and why—Mathieu de Lyon had died.

Of course, there might not be a connection between Mathieu's death and Rowena. Unfortunately, Eric's instincts were screaming otherwise and he couldn't rest until he had answers.

And if he was wrong? If he discovered that Mathieu's death had indeed been an unfortunate coincidence as Lord Faramus believed? Then there would be no harm done. In any case, it might help Rowena if Mathieu's killer was found and brought to trial. Eric couldn't shake the thought that her love for the boy remained strong.

If Eric got justice for de Lyon, if he brought

his killer to trial, it might give her ease. Whatever the cause of Mathieu de Lyon's death, the boy deserved justice. And for Rowena's sake, the least Eric could do was try and discover who had killed him.

It wasn't long before Eric was standing at the cloth merchant's stall as the merchant unclipped his shears from his belt. 'How much did you say you would like, sir?'

'Lord, I don't know in yards and inches, just make sure there's plenty to make a gown for a lady.'

With great reverence, the merchant rolled out the silk so it lay like a river of blue across the cutting board. 'I assume it is for the lady who accompanied you the other day—the petite lady with fair hair?'

'Yes, she's my wife. Don't stint on the length, I must be sure there's enough.'

'Very good, sir.'

The shears crunched through the cloth and the merchant looked up, eyes bright and expectant. 'You'd like ribbons to match—to adorn your lady's hair?' He waved at a tray of ribbons in every colour of the rainbow.

Eric looked helplessly at the tray. He was out of his depth buying cloth, never mind ribbons. Recalling that Rowena's hair was, often as not, bound in ribbons made from the same stuff as her gowns, he decided that a different ribbon or two wasn't a bad idea.

'I'll take a couple of the blue ones, thank you. And the cream with the silver threads. And that black and gold.' A rose-coloured ribbon caught his eye, he knew she liked rose. 'And that rose.'

'Very good, sir.'

Wrapping the blue samite and ribbons in a scrap of plain sheeting, the merchant handed the bundle over and Eric gave him his coins.

Alard was waiting with the horses a few paces away. Whilst Eric had been at the stall, dozens more people had poured into the market square, it was now so crowded they were having to squeeze past each other. Over everyone's heads, Eric caught sight of a flash of yellow—a signboard emblazoned with a bright yellow sun.

Stowing the cloth and ribbons in his saddle-bag, Eric led Captain through the press towards the tavern. Alard followed. They were almost across the square when Eric saw a chestnut gelding tethered under the makeshift awning that must pass as a stable here. Eric stopped mid-stride and a prickle of unease tickled the back of his neck.

'Alard?' he said softly.

'Sir?'

Eric stepped out of the flow of traffic and

motioned his squire to the side so they stood a little way off from the inn. It could be a coincidence, though he doubted it. He jerked his head towards the chestnut gelding tethered with the other horses. 'Do you know that animal?'

'The chestnut gelding? That's Sir Breon's horse.'

Eric studied it. Logically, there was no reason on earth why Sir Breon shouldn't choose to take refreshment at The Sun. It could be mere chance that had brought the man here. Unfortunately, Eric didn't think it was any such thing. He was debating whether to go in or not when a couple of yards from the stable area a side door opened and Sir Breon himself emerged.

With a grimace, Eric ducked his head behind Captain and prayed Alard would follow his lead. Luckily Alard was a bright lad and Sir Breon didn't see either of them. He was listening intently to his companion—a tall, swarthy man with a sharp face and a nose as thin as a blade. Eric hadn't seen him before.

'My thanks, Breon, I won't forget this,' the man said.

Sir Breon muttered something Eric couldn't catch. His companion clapped him on the shoulder and clicked his fingers at a gap-toothed urchin. 'Our horses, boy.'

'At once, sir.'

When the two men had mounted and spurred up the hill, Eric straightened. Digging into his purse for a penny, he urged Captain under the awning, caught the urchin's eye and held the penny aloft. 'This is yours, my lad, if you can tell me the names of those men who headed towards the Upper Town.'

Of course Eric knew Sir Breon, but it might be useful to know whether he was going by his real name when he came to The Sun.

The boy's eyes lit up and he looked hungrily at the penny. 'That's easy, sir. The man on the chestnut was born in Provins, his name is Sir Breon.'

'And his companion?'

'Sergeant Gildas, sir.'

'The sergeant works for the Provins guard?'

'I don't think so, sir.'

One of Count Henry of Champagne's castles stood in the Upper Town. This sergeant could well work for Count Henry. 'Perhaps he rides for Count Henry?'

'I don't think so.' The boy's gaze never shifted from the silver coin. 'I don't think he comes from hereabouts.'

Interesting. Eric took a step closer. 'But you would swear he's a sergeant and that his name is Gildas?'

'So I heard, I'm sorry I don't know anything

more.' The boy's face brightened. 'One of the girls inside might be able to help you, sir.'

'My thanks, you've been most helpful.' Silver gleamed as it spun through the air.

'Thank you, sir!'

'Come, Alard.' Eric waved at the side door. 'I could use some ale, how about you?'

Alard grinned. Leaving the horses with the urchin, they went inside.

Despite its poor reputation, The Sun's proximity to the market guaranteed that most of the scarred benches were full. Spotting a space at a small table under a smoke-blackened beam, Eric secured a place and ordered ale.

The man next to him—a merchant by the look of him—was eating, spooning up grey broth as though he hadn't eaten in a month. Judging by the smell it was mutton-and-barley stew, though it was hard to see any meat in there. The merchant was sweating profusely and a sour odour wrinkled Eric's nostrils. Eric's stomach turned. *Mon Dieu*, the man smelt worse than the stew.

The girl who arrived with the ale was a welcome distraction, she was young with brown eyes and hair. A certain innocence in her expression told him that she hadn't been working at The Sun for long.

Eric smiled at her. 'Was that Sergeant Gildas I saw leaving?'

'Aye, sir.'

'*Dommage*. Pity. I was hoping to speak to him. Do you know where I might find him? Does he live nearby?'

'Not that I know of, sir. He's a regular customer though, so he must come to Provins often.'

Eric smiled encouragingly. 'Oh?'

'I've seen him here a number of times, he and Sir Breon are firm friends.' She focused thoughtfully on Eric's ale cup. 'Last time Sergeant Gildas was here, someone else was with him. I believe he was a knight like Sir Breon. Certainly the sergeant deferred to him.'

Eric held his breath. 'I don't suppose you caught the other knight's name?'

Slowly, the girl shook her head. 'I am sorry, sir, I can't remember.'

Another customer waved for service. 'Over here, wench.'

As the girl moved off, she glanced back at Eric. 'I'll let you know if it comes to me before you leave.'

'My thanks.'

Later, as they made their way to the door, the girl ran up. 'Sir, I've found out the name of the knight who met with Sergeant Gildas and Sir Breon. He was called Sir Armand.'

A chill swept Eric head to toe. 'Sir Armand de Velay?'

'That's it.' She pointed at another serving girl. 'Marguerite has worked here longer than me, she knew his name.'

'Bless you.' Eric slipped a *pourboire* into her hand. 'Here, share this with Marguerite.'

'Thank you, sir.' Smiling, the girl dipped into a curtsy.

Eric spurred towards the Provins gate and the Jutigny road with his heart in his mouth and a squire who had as many questions as he did.

'Sir Armand de Velay is a relation of Lord Faramus, is he not?' Alard asked.

'A distant cousin.' Eric's understanding was that Sir Armand hadn't exactly been on visiting terms with the family. 'They are not close, in all my years at Jutigny, I've never so much as glimpsed the man.'

'I wonder how Sir Breon knows him.'

Eric shot his squire a grim look. That was the question that was uppermost in his mind too. However, Sir Armand could have met Sir Breon anywhere. At a tournament, in Paris, anywhere. Who was to say that Sir Armand hadn't visited Jutigny after Eric had won his manor and left the count's service? To an onlooker, it would seem perfectly natural. Rowena was the count's heiress and should Rowena die childless, Sir Armand would inherit the County of Sainte-Colombe.

Gripped by anxiety, Eric urged Captain into a trot. Why the devil had Sir Breon taken to meeting de Velay's sergeant at regular intervals? He had a bad feeling about this, a very bad feeling. When he had woken that morning, Eric had intended to go straight to Lord Faramus. He wanted the count's opinion on Sir Armand's character. Was de Velay the type of man who would resort to murder to achieve his ambitions?

Lord, what a fool he was. Rowena's gift of the shirt had distracted him. The blue samite had leapt into his mind and all he could think was that he must get it for her. In his eagerness, he'd decided to speak to her father later.

Eric clenched his fist. With the guard he had set about her, he was reasonably confident that she was safe. None the less, his mouth was dry and his heart was thumping. He had to get back to Jutigny. He must see her. At once.

'Alard, what do you know of Sir Armand?'

'Other than that his life is said to be an endless round of pilgrimages and penances, not much. He's said to be God-fearing, high-minded and full of piety.'

Which was about as much and as little as Eric himself knew. They cleared the outskirts and gave the spur to the horses. Eric would relax when he had seen for himself that Rowena was safe. He'd been deluding himself, he realised.

He'd told himself that a knight like Sir Armand, one with a reputation for being pious and high-minded, wouldn't stoop to murder. He'd been careless. Worse than careless.

He couldn't stop thinking about Mathieu de Lyon's death so close to The Sun—a tavern frequented by Sir Armand's sergeant. A sergeant who often met with Sir Breon there. Why, Sergeant Gildas was probably one of the horsemen who had trailed after Eric when he and Rowena had made their way from St Mary's to Monfort. He might even be that archer.

As the fields of Champagne flowed past, Eric's suspicions multiplied. Why the devil had Sir Breon been meeting with Armand's sergeant? Had they been talking about Rowena? Was Sir Breon responsible for the rope on that hoist snapping the day Rowena crossed the drawbridge? Sir Breon had known when Rowena was due to arrive.

Sir Breon was in on this, he had to be. Had the man lost all honour? As one of Count Faramus's most long-serving knights, Sir Breon had sworn the knightly oath to protect the weak and uphold the law. He ought to have his lord's best interests at heart and that must include Rowena's welfare.

Eric had never warmed to Sir Breon, all he

seemed to care about was money. Even so, he had never dreamed that Sir Breon might make an attempt on Rowena's life. Doubtless he was being well paid for his perfidy.

And who would have thought that a man as pious as Sir Armand would sully his hands with anything so grim?

'Blast it, there's no proof,' Eric muttered, gritting his teeth. Despite the lack of evidence, he was certain Sir Armand wanted Rowena dead. At the least, Sir Breon had to be feeding information to Sir Armand. Sir Breon must be in de Velay's pay.

They pounded past a stand of oak trees with Eric ignoring the curious looks Alard was giving him. It wasn't going to be easy to persuade Lord Faramus that his longest-serving knight had to go. All he had was a bucketload of suspicion. Furthermore, de Velay's reputation for piety would make Eric's convictions appear even more outlandish.

Perhaps a religious man like Sir Armand thought nothing of paying others to do his dirty work. Aye, that fitted. In working hand-in-glove with Sir Breon, de Velay was relying on a man whose piety extended not to the worship of God, but to the worship of money.

Sir Breon must go.

* * *

Eric strode into Jutigny great hall. No Rowena. Her father was there though, sharing a cup of ale with Sir Macaire. Both men were smiling.

Telling himself that they wouldn't be smiling if something had happened to Rowena, Eric strode over. '*Mon seigneur*, do you know where I might find Rowena?'

'She rode out to the abbey.'

Eric hoped he looked calmer than he felt. He needed to see with his own eyes that she was safe. 'She took a full escort, I hope?'

'Indeed she did. De Monfort, I don't know what you told Sergeant Yder, but he insisted she took four men-at-arms as well as a couple of grooms.'

'That's good to hear.' Nodding briefly at Sir Macaire, Eric looked earnestly at Rowena's father. 'My lord, I need to speak to you most urgently.'

Lord Faramus gave him a searching glance and gestured to a side door. 'The chapel?'

'If you please.'

In the chapel Eric closed the door and joined Lord Faramus on the cushioned wall bench. He told him everything he had seen and heard at The Sun—making mention of Sir Breon, Sergeant Gildas and Sir Armand.

The count's face grew hard.

Eric also mentioned his suspicions concerning Mathieu de Lyon's murder, but he was careful to skate over the nature of Rowena's relationship with the boy, saying merely that they had felt some affection for each other and perhaps that was why the boy had been attacked.

For once, Count Faramus seemed speechless. He looked utterly dazed, shaking his head and pulling at his whiskers, as though he couldn't believe his ears.

'In short, my lord,' Eric said, in conclusion, 'it is my belief that Sir Breon is in the pay of your cousin. Furthermore, I believe he will know who murdered that squire.'

'Sir Breon's been with me for years.'

Eric braced himself for a hard fight. 'You think I have misjudged matters?'

Lord Faramus swore under his breath and then, abruptly, his shoulders sagged. He seemed to have aged a decade in a moment. 'Sadly, I don't. Although it seems incredible that a feeble-minded man like my cousin, a man who is practically a monk, would stoop to try and kill Rowena.'

'My lord, we can't take any chances, Sir Breon has to go. If he doesn't, Rowena and I shall leave.'

'Lord, I don't want that.' The count scrubbed his face and stared at a wooden statue of the

Madonna and child. 'We'll have to be careful with what we say.'

'Agreed. I doubt we'll get a confession out of Sir Breon until we confront him with firm proof. We need evidence as to what happened to de Lyon and until we find it, it would be best if Sir Breon wasn't alerted to the fact that we are looking into the boy's death. Once we have our evidence, it should be easier to point the finger at your cousin regarding the other incidents at Monfort and the gatehouse.'

Count Faramus stroked his moustache and gave a thin smile. 'De Monfort, I think we've just received word that a steward in one of my minor manors—let us say Sir Gareth—yes, Sir Gareth Dubois has fallen gravely ill. Sir Breon has long had an eye on the office of steward, he will be honoured to step into his shoes. Be so good as to fetch me a scribe. I need to send word to Sir Gareth.'

Eric raised an eyebrow. 'A scribe, my lord? Is that wise?'

His father-in-law blinked. 'Devil take it, you're right, we must be discreet. Forget the scribe. Fetch a quill and parchment. I'll dictate and you can write—your hand is neater than mine. We shall send the letter immediately so it's well on its way before Sir Breon leaves.'

'Very good, my lord.'

'You'll find parchment in the trunk behind the dais. My joints are on fire today, I'd be glad if you would fetch it. Once the letter is dispatched to Dubois, we shall give Sir Breon his new orders.'

Rowena had suffered from too much coddling all day, and by the time she guided Lily across the drawbridge and back into the Jutigny bailey she was at screaming point.

If she had thought the day had started badly with a phalanx of guards following her when she went down to break her fast, it had soon got worse. When she'd ridden out to the abbey to visit Novice Amélie, her entourage had bunched up around her, riding so close that it was nigh on impossible for poor Lily to break into a trot, never mind a canter. And now, even though she was once again safely within her father's walls she couldn't simply hand Lily over to the groom, no, she must wait for her guards to dismount. Sergeant Yder insisted on crossing the bailey with her and personally escorting her inside.

In the great hall, Sir Macaire was taking his ease on one of the benches on the top table.

Rowena caught his eye. 'Excuse me, sir, is my husband about?' At least when she was in Eric's company, the guards gave her some peace.

'Aye, my lady, he's in conference with your father.'

She nodded. 'Very well, I shall join them.'

A pained expression crossed Sir Macaire's face. He cleared his throat. 'My apologies, Lady Rowena, but Sir Eric gave particular instructions. They are not to be disturbed.'

Rowena felt herself frown. 'Surely that does not apply in my case?'

'I am afraid so, my lady. No one is to join them.'

'Very well.' Rowena spoke through clenched teeth, even as curiosity rose within her. What could be so secret that Eric didn't want her in on the discussions? If it touched upon what had happened at the gatehouse then she was directly involved. She had a right to know what was happening and Eric should not be keeping her at bay.

She blew out a breath. Eric was turning out to be just as patronising as her father. Rowena had married Eric, hoping she had left all that behind her. Her father had never let her in on his plans for her, the first she had learned of her betrothal to Lord Gawain had been when she'd been presented to him as his fiancée. Lord Faramus hadn't bothered to consult her until the ink was dry on the betrothal contract.

Eric, I thought you were different. Had she misjudged him? Rowena had remembered the boy he had been and thought the man would be cast in the same mould. Apparently not. Did prestige turn men's heads? Did command of their men lead them to believe they could command their wives in like manner?

Rowena bit her tongue—it wouldn't do to let Sir Macaire see how disappointed she was—and stalked towards the south-tower stairwell. Sergeant Yder kept as close as her shadow. When Eric deigned to speak to her, she would make it plain that she wasn't going to be kept in the dark. Her memory rang with echoes of that husky voice as he had set about wooing her. He had said she was adorable. Adorable? Huh! She would show him adorable. The next time she saw him, he was going to have to learn that if he wanted an adorable wife, he was going to have to earn it.

He must stop patronising her, he must allow her into his mind as well as his bed. Clearly, her belief that carnal intercourse would bind him to her had been entirely wrong.

The time had come for different tactics. And, since she wanted privacy for what she had to say to him, she wasn't going to wait for him here in the hall. She would meet him on her own terms.

She paused at the foot of the stairs. 'Sergeant, I am retiring to my bedchamber for a while. If

Sir Eric asks for me, would you tell him where to find me?'

'Of course, *ma dame*.'

'And if he is still in conference when the time comes for supper, would you be so good as to ask Berthe to bring my supper up on a tray?'

'Yes, my lady.'

'Thank you.' She hesitated. 'If I give you my word I will not leave the tower, will you and your men be content to remain at your posts in the lower chamber?'

'If that is your wish, my lady.'

Rowena climbed up the tower. Her keepers followed her and then, true to the sergeant's word, they fell back after the first twist in the stairs. She continued up to the bedchamber on her own. The shutter was open wide enough for her to see the grey clouds outside.

Saints, she hated being hemmed in like this. Eric didn't know her very well if he thought she could stand it for long. To her mind, however, what was far, far worse, was that Eric had barred her from taking part in his conference with her father.

Outside, a pigeon fluttered past, it probably had a roost on the watch point on the tower roof.

Her head throbbed, it felt as though it was banded in iron. Rubbing her forehead, Rowena

slowly unpinned her veil. She needed to get out,
yet here she was, a prisoner in her father's castle.

She dropped her veil on to the bed as another
pigeon's shadow briefly darkened the chamber.
It too was heading for the freedom of the roof.
Freedom. Rowena stared at the narrow strip of
sky visible through the window. In the past, she
had enjoyed going up to the watch point. Were
there guards up there now?

Moving to the door, she lifted the latch and
stepped on to the landing. When she reached the
door at the top, she slid back the heavy iron bolt,
pushed the door wide and stepped on to the bat-
tlements. Behind her, the door shut with a clang,
briefly startling the pigeons from their perches.
There were no guards. She let out a relieved sigh.

Up here, the wind was fresh. A flurry of rain
had left its mark, the walkway was dotted with
puddles. Above, the clouds shifted slowly to
the south. The pigeons settled. Rowena leaned
against a merlon and peered through the cre-
nel. Her father was down by the stables, talking earnestly to Sir Breon. Sir Breon's squire
was there too, heaving a saddlebag on to Sir
Breon's chestnut gelding. They were too far away
for Rowena to read their expressions, however
she did see Sir Breon clasp her father's arm as
though in farewell.

Sir Breon was leaving? His squire ducked into

the stable, brought out his own horse and started loading that with even more baggage. Judging by the amount, they would be gone some time.

How strange. No one had mentioned anything about Sir Breon leaving.

Behind her, the door clanged and she almost leaped out of her skin.

Chapter Eleven

'Eric! You startled me.'

Eric's fists were clenched and his brow furrowed—as he looked her up and down, his brow cleared. 'My apologies. I was concerned when you weren't in the bedchamber.' His mouth twitched into a charming smile and Rowena steeled herself to resist it. 'Thought you'd given me the slip.'

She narrowed her eyes on him. 'As if I could. Eric, it's intolerable, they watch me all the time.'

Reaching for her, he pulled her up against him. Before she could object, he had dropped a kiss on her nose.

'Eric, I don't like it. It makes me feel like a felon.'

'It's for your safety.'

'I've had enough. Furthermore, I want you to tell me—' A clatter of hoofbeats cut off her words, Sir Breon and his squire were riding across the drawbridge. She gripped Eric's arm. 'Sir Breon's leaving?'

Eric's eyes were hooded. 'I believe he is. Sir Gareth Dubois needs his assistance.'

'Oh?'

'Dubois has taken ill.'

'And Sir Breon is to take over?'

'For a time.'

Thoughtfully, Rowena watched the retreating horses trot into the street and out of sight behind the castle wall. 'I wouldn't have thought Sir Breon had the patience necessary to make a steward. There's something you're not telling me.'

Strong fingers covered hers. 'Far from it. Dubois is ill and Sir Breon has been despatched to lend a hand.'

Eric's green eyes were wide, his expression far too bland. 'Eric, I'm not a child. You've learned something about Sir Breon and you've had him sent away.'

Eric said nothing, his face was so shielded, what he was thinking was anyone's guess.

Rowena stepped back, forcing him to release her. She made her voice hard. 'Eric, I agreed to marry you because I have always liked you. However, I have to tell you that I have no wish for a husband who keeps things from me. Furthermore, you wilfully undermine my authority.'

His eyebrows snapped together. 'How so?'

'You gave orders not to let me in on your conference with Father. I know you have discovered something, something concerning Sir Breon. Tell me what it is.'

'Rowena, you will have to trust me.' He offered her his hand and she simply looked at it.

'Eric, I did trust you.' Her voice cracked. 'I believed you were different. I thought we could have a true marriage.' Her eyes misted and she blinked rapidly, she refused to let him see her weakness—she wanted him to be different.

He stepped up to her, the wind was ruffling his hair. 'Rowena, we will have a true marriage.'

'Will we? You refuse to love me. You hedge me about with guards. You ban me from attending discussions with my father. You tell me nothing. What next, Eric? What next?'

Taking her by the wrist, he hauled her against him. Refusing to meet his gaze, she stared at his tunic and heard him swallow. His chest heaved in a great sigh.

'Very well. Rowena, I didn't want to worry you, but today I learned something which led me to conclude that Sir Breon may have been involved in the accident with the hoist. There is no proof, so until I can discover more there is little we can do. In the meantime, your father agrees there is reason for concern. He has removed Sir Breon from play here by posting him elsewhere.'

'Sir Breon knows you suspect him?'

'No.' Eric shoved his hair out of his eyes. 'Your father believes you will be safer if Sir Breon is kept ignorant of our suspicions. The main point is that Sir Breon has gone, which leaves me free to continue investigations in Provins unhindered.' His mouth went up at one corner. 'You will be doubtless glad to hear that as a result of this your escort has been reduced. Henceforth, Sergeant Yder and a guard and groom will accompany you if you leave Jutigny.'

Resting her head briefly on Eric's tunic, Rowena let out a breath. 'Thank you. I confess having a pack of watchdogs at my heels was driving me mad.'

Gentle fingers tipped her face up. He gave her a brief kiss and a wry smile. 'I never would have guessed. Come, I have something for you.'

Back in the bedchamber, Rowena ran her fingers over the blue samite spread across the foot of the bed. It was sumptuous, gorgeous stuff, fit for a queen. 'It's lovely, Eric, thank you.' She met his gaze. 'And a whole length, it must have cost a fortune.'

'I wanted to thank you for the shirt.' His cheeks darkened and he shrugged. 'In any case,

we married too soon. I hadn't finished courting you.'

'Eric, I am your wife, you don't have to woo
me.'

He held her gaze, eyes steady. 'I promised you
that cloth after we wed and it was my pleasure
to get it for you.' He stepped closer and reached
out to cup her cheek with his palm. 'Just as it is
my pleasure to court you.'

Then his arms came round her and Rowena
forgot everything save the warmth of being held
by Eric.

Days slipped by and nothing seemed to
change. Rowena and Eric had not lost their compatibility in the bedchamber, yet they were no
closer. Rowena began to lose hope, sometimes
she caught herself thinking that perhaps Eric had
been right, perhaps he didn't have a heart to give.
Apart from their time in bed, she saw him less
and less. Under the guise of making enquiries,
he rode into Provins almost every day.

One evening in the early summer, Eric returned with a message from Monfort. As they
climbed the stairs to their tower room, he looked
back at her. 'Sir Guy tells me that Helvise has
been delivered of a baby boy.'

'The child is well?'

'He's thriving, apparently.'

'Does he have a name?'

'James.'

Eric held open their chamber door for her and Rowena was no sooner inside than he set about removing her circlet and veil. His eagerness for her body hadn't diminished. Nor, she thought wryly, had her eagerness for his. Resting her hands pensively on his chest, Rowena watched his mouth as he set about removing her belt. In a moment he would kiss her and she would kiss him back and their blood would heat and she would, for a time, forget that the distance between them remained.

'A healthy baby,' she heard herself murmur. 'What a joy.' If she and Eric had a baby, would it bring them closer? If she gave him a child, would she win his love?

Rowena had taken Eric's warning concerning Sir Breon seriously. She heeded his advice concerning the guards and never went anywhere on her own. However, as the weeks slipped by and nothing untoward happened, she began to hope that the danger must be over.

Removing Sir Breon from Jutigny seemed to have done the trick. Summer came and went and there were no unfortunate accidents. The days passed in a blur.

At night, there was Eric—his warmth next to hers in bed and the never-ending joy of his body joining with hers. Neither of them mentioned love. In the day, Rowena helped her mother review supplies in the cellar. She went to the solar and made inroads into the mountain of mending that seemed to be part of life in every castle. On her rides she heard skylarks singing as they soared over the fields and vines; she watched butterflies hovering over purple thistles.

Then, almost before she could blink, the thistles had turned to thistledown and were drifting across the road. It was September already. The hedgerow grasses were brown and dry. And still there had been no accidents.

By the time the swallows were flying south for the winter, Rowena felt relaxed enough to think she no longer needed a guard. Only the realisation that she would be going against Eric's wishes prevented her from dismissing them. She ached to believe that his insistence on an escort was a sign of his deep and abiding affection. Practically, it seemed far more likely that he was protecting his interests.

It wouldn't do for him to lose her before she had given him an heir. Eric needed an heir to secure his interests in her father's county. If she proved barren, Sir Armand would doubtless be mightily relieved.

By the summer's end, there was no sign of Rowena quickening with child. And it wasn't for the lack of trying. When Eric was with her he was as attentive a husband as she could wish. They made love often. The walls of their eyrie echoed with moans and sighs almost every night. Eric was careful with her, he handled her gently and apparently with great affection. Despite all this, Rowena knew she was no closer to winning his heart, he guarded it too well.

One morning, Rowena woke to a definite chill in the air. As usual Eric was up before her and she was alone. The bed felt cold. Shivering, she huddled under the covers until Berthe came in.

'Good morning, my lady. Shall I plait your hair?'

'Please.' Rowena grabbed her shawl. As she padded over to the stool, her breath made mist in the air. 'Berthe, do you know if Sir Eric went into Provins this morning?'

'I believe so, my lady.'

'Again?' Rowena scowled at a flower painted on to the plaster. She had painted the flower herself and it was slightly crooked, she would have to redo it.

Since Eric was adamant they had to live up in the tower, she had decided to make the most of it. To that end, the top of her coffer was littered with paint brushes, pots of pigment and rags. She was eager to get back to work. It wasn't as

easy as she had imagined, yet despite the difficulties she enjoyed making up patterns to put
on the walls. If she worked quickly, she hoped
to complete a section of the frieze by the time
Eric came back tonight.

Was it necessary that he spent so much time
in Provins? All she had been able to get out of
him was that he was pursuing enquiries for her
father. Berthe might have heard something, it
was possible that Alard had talked. Craning her
neck, she looked Berthe in the eye. 'Where does
Sir Eric go when he rides into Provins, Berthe?
Have you heard?'

Berthe gave her a sideways glance. 'I hear he
spends much of his time in one of the taverns,
my lady.'

'Which one?'

'The Sun.'

'Where is that, exactly?'

'In Provins Lower Town, in the square in
front of St Ayoul.'

'I see.' Berthe had finished her plait. Rising,
Rowena went over to the pigments and selected
a brush.

'Aren't you going down to break your fast,
my lady?'

'In a moment, I just want to try something.'
Rowena dipped her brush into the pigment—red
ochre—and carefully placed five dots to repre-

sent petals on the walls. Squinting critically at it, she tried out another flower before setting the brush aside once more. Yes, that was better. She smiled. 'Berthe?'

'My lady?'

'After breakfast, I shall finish that section of frieze and then I am riding into Provins.'

Berthe looked warily at her. 'You're not going to that inn, my lady?'

'Why not? It's just an inn, isn't it?'

Berthe pulled a face. 'It's far too shabby for a lady. Sir Eric would not like to see you there, I am sure.'

A cold fist clenched in Rowena's belly. Until that moment she'd never thought to question Eric's repeated visits to Provins. Berthe's reaction gave her pause. 'It…it's not a whorehouse, is it?'

'Not that I know of. It's known to be a mite rough. And dirty, or so I've heard. You shouldn't be thinking of going there.' Berthe touched her arm. 'I shouldn't have told you about the place, Sir Eric will be most displeased if he knew. Please, my lady, don't tell him it was I who mentioned it.'

'Relax, Berthe, I won't breathe a word.' Crossing to the ewer, Rowena washed her hands. 'Whilst I am breaking my fast, would you please tell Sergeant Yder that we will be riding into

town and that I shall require the usual escort.'
Seeing that Berthe's expression was one of intense disapproval, she inched her chin up. 'I'm only riding past it.'

'I should certainly hope so, my lady.'

December arrived in a whirl of wind and rain. Rowena was ready to tear her hair out, she didn't seem to be any further forward in her quest to win her husband's love.

Her investigations into The Sun had led nowhere, save to confirm that her husband had become one of the tavern's most regular customers. The inn was, as Berthe had said, not very reputable, but it could have been worse, it wasn't a brothel. Rowena had also learned that Eric spent hours at the garrison in Provins Castle, closeted with Count Henry's captain.

When Eric joined her in their bedchamber at night he was in the habit of parrying most of her questions. It was a habit she was determined to break, he was keeping things from her, she was sure. Luckily, Eric wasn't as close as her father. Rowena was coming to see that if she pressed him, she could usually get some sort of a response from him. It was hard work though.

Rowena would sit up in bed, fluff the pillows and lean back, arms folded across her chest as

Eric disrobed. 'Did you go the castle garrison today?'

'Aye.' Tossing her one of his charming smiles, Eric hung his cloak on a wall peg.

'You spoke to Count Henry's captain?'

'Mmm.' He added a few coals to the brazier and rubbed his hands together. 'It's freezing out, I wouldn't be surprised to see snow soon.'

'Eric, what exactly do you do all day?'

He shot her a startled look. 'I told you. Rowena, I am working to protect your interests.'

'And that means days spent in that tavern, does it?' Whatever Eric was doing in Provins seemed to have become an obsession. It occurred to her that a change of scene might break the cycle. 'I would like to return to Monfort.'

His mouth firmed. 'That's not possible, I'm afraid.'

'We could see Helvise and baby James. And I am sure Sir Guy has matters to discuss with you.'

Peeling off his clothes, he shrugged. 'Guy sends regular reports. All is well at Monfort.'

'Eric—'

'I am sorry, my love, we must stay here for the time being.'

Rowena forgot to breathe. Love. Eric had just called her his love.

Oblivious of how he had stunned her, Eric

lifted the bedcovers and slid into bed. A muscled arm encircled her waist. He picked up a strand of her hair and wound it round his fingers.

Rowena's throat felt tight. She wasn't sure he realised what he had said—he had used an endearment for the first time. He had called her my love. Telling herself not to read too much into it, it was a few moments before she noticed that he was letting her in on his thoughts too.

'Beloved, what I am doing in Provins isn't easy. Your father is relying on me to prove your cousin's involvement in a plot to deprive you of your inheritance. We can't simply charge in spewing accusations every which way. Without proof we would lose credibility. Sir Armand is clever and Sir Breon's departure from Jutigny, however carefully managed, will have told him that our suspicions have been raised. He will be alert to danger and we must be circumspect. This business requires patience and diligence. I have made friends in that tavern and that cannot be done overnight. It takes time to build trust.' Brushing her hair aside, he pressed a kiss to her shoulder. 'Sir Armand will reveal his true colours eventually, of that I am sure.'

'And then we may go to Monfort?'

'If that is your wish.' His gaze fell on her mouth and his expression softened in a way that told her he was about to kiss her. 'Meanwhile, my love, I want us to stay together. However, you may visit Monfort whenever you like. Sergeant Yder will be happy to escort you there and back.'

There it was again. My love. Finally, after all these months, she had hope.

Sliding her hand into his dark hair, happier than she had been in an age, Rowena guided his mouth to hers.

It grew colder, it was almost Christmas and at Jutigny the castle kitchens were preparing for the Christmas feast.

Geese were plucked, hams smoked and costly spices—cinnamon, cloves, nutmeg—were ordered from the merchants and stowed under lock and key. Parties of squires were sent out to find likely patches of ivy to hang in the great hall. Bets were laid as to which page would win the prize for finding the holly bush with the most red berries. It was too soon to actually cut the greenery, that wouldn't happen until just before Christmas. The scent of mulled wine filled the air.

Winter set in. It was unseasonably cold. In the garden, a patch of teasels was covered in hoar frost. Puddles were crisp with frost and cracked underfoot. Fingers and noses went red, then blue. Teeth ached, and clouds of breath wreathed the heads of the guards on the wall walk. It was so cold, Rowena stuck her head out of the bed covers one morning and found herself thinking twice about going out for a ride. Her head felt as though it was shrinking. Eric, naturally, was long gone, his half of the bed was empty and his cloak was no longer on its peg.

She sighed. Doubtless he was in Provins again. Well, she couldn't fault him for his diligence, although it would have been nice to wake up with him for once, instead of to an empty and cheerless bed. She stared at the empty peg and, smiling, got out of bed and went to open her coffer to find her sewing. She knew exactly how she was going to spend her morning and it didn't involve going out into the bitter cold.

She was making Eric a gift of a cloak for Christmas and, apart from sewing on the fastening, it was almost finished. If she missed her ride, it could be done by this afternoon. Shivering, she pulled it out. The fabric was a deep green, an English weave that matched the colour of his eyes, and she'd lined it with fur which hadn't been easy. Her fingers were pricked to bits. He had better like it, she thought, as she fished about in the bottom of her coffer for the silver fastening. A swirl of silver, cunningly wrought so it would split in two, she'd found it in a silversmith's in town. The clasp was Celtic in design. It was reminiscent of the illuminated letters in her mother's gospel. As children learning to read, she and Eric had pored over that Bible together, more fascinated by the illustrations than by the words. Would he remember? When she had finished the hem, she would sew on the fastening. The cloak was finished by noon with the fastening securely in place. Rowena returned the cloak to her coffer and went down to the hall to see if her mother needed help in the storeroom. When the supper bell sounded, the hall soon filled. There was no sign of Eric.

Ordinarily, Rowena wouldn't worry, Eric could look after himself. But in a few days it would be Christmas Eve and something was niggling away at the back of her mind. A worry she couldn't quite place.

Christmas Eve. Eric.

Frowning, Rowena found herself looking at Mary, one of the maidservants whose name had in the past been linked with that of her husband. She thought about Eric's reputation as a young man, about the way he flirted with everyone. Mercifully, she'd seen no sign of that since their marriage.

Soon it would be Christmas Eve. There it was again, that unpleasant little niggle. Something was wrong, she was sure of it.

Rowena waited until they were clearing the

boards just in case he should appear. Then, seeing no sign of him, she went over to Mary.

'Mary, do you have a moment?'

Mary dipped into a curtsy. *'Ma dame?'*

Rowena drew Mary to one side, she felt
slightly embarrassed—this could be awkward.
She didn't want Mary to be offended, she must
hope Mary understood her concern. She kept
her voice low. 'Mary, I understand you knew
my husband before our marriage. Before he won
his manor.'

Colour tinged Mary's cheeks. 'We were good
friends, my lady.'

Nodding, Rowena schooled her face into neu-
trality. 'Mary, I have a faint recollection that one
year around Christmastide, Eric disappeared. I
was very young and don't remember much about
it. Do you know what happened?'

'No, my lady. Save to say that it was generally known that Eric—sorry, my lady—*Sir* Eric
often took himself off around Christmas.' Mary
jerked her head towards the main entrance. 'Particularly if it was snowing.'

'So it didn't happen just the once?'

'No, my lady.' Mary came closer. 'I did wonder if he was remembering his past. The time
Lady Barbara fetched him in from the cold.'

Rowena reached for Mary's hand and

squeezed it. 'Thank you, Mary. I too had that thought. You've been most helpful.'

Turning to go, Mary hesitated. 'Lady Rowena?' Her face was crimson. 'Sir Eric and I— we were only ever friends. Truly, my lady, we were never lovers.'

'Thank you, Mary.' Rowena smiled. Mary's tone was so earnest, she could not help but believe her. Lightly, she touched her hand again. 'Thank you, indeed.'

Rowena stood unmoving while about her the boards were taken up and stacked by the hall walls. She thought about her husband and his habit of quietly taking himself off around Christmas.

Biting her lip, she looked towards the door. It was snowing tonight, just as it had been when he'd been a boy. Eric was surely remembering. Was he mourning his lost past? Mourning the loss of his parents?

Eric was such a vibrant, confident man, it was hard to imagine him dwelling on his past, yet that must be what he was doing. Her chest ached. She found herself staring at a pair of hounds curled together in front of the fire. Those particular hounds had come from the same litter and they were inseparable, one of them rested its head on the other's belly, never questioning for a moment the other dog's acceptance of it.

Realisation slammed into her. Eric didn't expect to be loved. In his youth, her mother and father had shown him as much favour as they could, given he was not their child. They'd been obliged to treat him no better, nor worse, than the noblemen's boys they had fostered. If anything, her father had been sterner with Eric than with the other pages and squires, as though his unknown parentage meant that his right to bear arms had to be tested more severely.

Eric wanted to be loved. It was one of the reasons that he teased and flirted; it was why he strove to be an honourable knight. He wanted people to like him, but not for one moment did he take it for granted. He couldn't. Those early years had scarred him and nothing that had followed—not her mother's acceptance, nor him winning knighthood, nor marrying her—nothing had healed him.

Eric carried invisible scars. Scars from wounds that were buried so deep inside, it was possible that even he did not realise they had not yet healed.

The hall door opened and an icy blast cut through the air. A sentry strode in, stamping snow from his boots. Eric was out there somewhere, hurting and alone, because the abandoned little boy that he had once been had never truly healed.

Whisking round, Rowena hurried to the tower stairwell. She needed to find him. However confident Eric might appear, she wanted him to know how much he meant to her. If he understood that, perhaps he might bring himself to love her. She didn't know if it would work, but she had to try. As she picked up her skirts and hurried past the guardroom, she poked her head through the door and caught the attention of one of the men.

'Alain, would you please find Sergeant Yder?'

'My lady?'

'Ask him to saddle Lily, will you?'

The guard's jaw dropped. 'You're going out? At this hour? My lady, night is drawing on. It's snowing.'

Rowena put steel in her voice. 'Find Sergeant Yder.'

Then she continued up to the bedchamber to find her cloak and boots and the cloak she had made for Eric. He might have need of it tonight.

Chapter Twelve

Waving for Marguerite, Eric lifted an eyebrow at Alard. The boy was slumped on the rickety bench beside him, head thrown back against grimy plaster, snoring gently. Bored to death, Eric thought, and no wonder. All week there had been whispers that de Velay's sergeant had been seen in town. As a result, Eric and Alard had been haunting The Sun, hoping that even if they weren't lucky enough to see de Velay's man for themselves, they might hear something. Anything. Eric was desperate for Rowena to have the comfort of knowing that Mathieu de Lyon's killers would be brought to justice. Sadly, that didn't look as though it was going to happen any time soon.

Eric had written to Gareth Dubois asking him if he knew of any communication between Sir Breon and Sir Armand. Sir Gareth swore there'd been nothing. Sir Gareth might have been fooled. Eric wasn't. Something was going on. Without telling Dubois, Eric had sent men to pose as grooms and inveigle their way into Gareth's manor. Other than one or two rumours, the men hadn't learned much.

Armand de Velay was said to be in Paris, visiting a shrine built to house a fragment of the True Cross. That fitted with the man's supposed piety, but Eric would swear de Velay's little pilgrimage was a cover for something far more sinister. De Velay wasn't going to allow Sainte-Colombe to slip through his fingers.

Eric gave a weary sigh and closed his ears on a gale of laughter that rose from a bench by the farthest wall, where some early Christmas celebrations were getting a little out of hand. All he had were loose ends. It was very frustrating. The lack of progress had doomed him and his squire to sit at this greasy table for hour upon wearisome hour while about them the townsfolk got merrier and merrier. In truth, Eric and Alard had been here so long they were doubtless seen as part of the furniture. He'd had enough. He would have a last warming drink and head back to Jutigny.

Marguerite came up. 'Sir?'

'A mug of that mulled wine, if you please.'

Another roar went up from the table at the end and Marguerite glanced at Alard, sleeping through the noise with the blithe innocence of youth. 'And for your squire, sir?'

'Please. It might help him wake and we'll be leaving shortly. I assume it's still snowing out?'

'Aye, sir. It's turned into a real blizzard.'

Wonderful.

While Marguerite went for the wine, Eric listened to Alard's snoring and allowed his thoughts free rein. He was certain that Mathieu de Lyon had been murdered on the orders of Armand de Velay and he'd thought that by now he'd have proof. *Mon Dieu*, he had hoped to solve this riddle months ago.

The uncertainty and, more importantly, the *worry* about Rowena was driving him insane. Was their life together to be marred for ever by fear that de Velay could strike at any moment? It was intolerable. Eric wanted—needed—to know that she was safe.

If it wasn't for Rowena and the warmth they shared in bed, Eric's mood would have been dark indeed. He felt closer to Rowena than he had to any woman, and that too brought its difficulties. He felt guilty about the way they had married; he felt conflicted. On the face of it, Rowena seemed content, so why on earth did he feel so uncomfortable? Why?

She had needed his help and, with her father's blessing, he'd given it. She brought him great joy, equally she brought him worry. That was the curse of it. The stress. He'd had no idea that being married would make a man worry so.

She was kind and sweet, like her mother. His lips twitched. She had spirit too, at times she could be a real termagant, just like her father. Eric liked all those traits, he always had. He'd just never thought to marry her.

The door opened and two men stamped in, the hoods of their cloaks capped with snow. Making a beeline for the serving hatch, they squeezed past Eric's table.

'It's bitter enough to freeze your eyeballs,' one of the men muttered, sleeving snow from his eyelashes. The other man grunted agreement.

Indeed, the cold was coming off them in waves and as Eric tracked their progress towards the wine kegs his mind did a strange thing. It whisked him back to that Christmas Eve when his mother had towed him through the dark and the snow towards the light of the Jutigny gate-house. His fingers curled into a fist. Hell burn it, did this have to happen *every* year? Why couldn't he forget?

'Attract the guards, Eric,' his mother had said, nodding towards the flare of the torches. 'They'll take you in.'

'Mama, I'm cold. I want to go home.'

His mother had bent down to give him a tight

hug before nudging him on to the drawbridge. 'The guards will help you. Ask for Lady Barbara.' Then she had turned and walked away. She hadn't looked back.

That night, the cold had bitten through to Eric's bones. Tears had frozen as soon as he had shed them. He'd turned to ice. The sky had wept snow.

'Mama? *Mama!*'

A shadow fell over him and Eric was dragged back to the present, the mulled wine had arrived. He stared blankly at the steaming cups and drew in a shuddering breath.

'My thanks, Marguerite.' His voice was so hoarse he didn't recognise it, he must be thirstier than he thought. He picked up the cup and inhaled the rich scents of Christmas. Cinnamon. Cloves. Bay. His stomach cramped. Holy Mother, he loathed Christmas.

A howl went up from the far table.

Eric dug Alard in the ribs. 'Drink up, lad, we're leaving.' Lifting his cup, he drank deep. He would learn nothing more tonight, not with half the town lost in a fog of ale and spiced wine.

The door opened again, admitting a flurry of snow. The candles guttered. Eric stared into his cup, vaguely hearing the complaints.

'Mercy, what a gale.'

'For pity's sake, shut the door!'

He caught a softly murmured apology and the door clacked shut. The candles flickered and someone pushed past the table.

A hand touched his shoulder. 'Eric, are you all right?'

Rowena? Here? Stomach lurching, he jumped to his feet. She was stripping off her gloves. Her cloak was covered in snow and her face was pinched with cold.

'Jesu, Rowena, what's happened?'

'Nothing.' She gave him one of her gentle smiles and, removing her cloak, allowed him to take it from her. He draped it over the end of the bench. 'I am glad you're here though, I wouldn't have wanted to scour the town for you.'

Out of the corner of his eye, Eric noticed Sergeant Yder and some of the Jutigny men claiming a table on the other side of the fire. Nodding an acknowledgement at the sergeant—praise the Lord she had brought her escort—Eric turned back to Rowena. 'Something must have happened at Jutigny. Lord Faramus?'

'Father is fine. I was worried about you.'

Eric blinked, her words didn't seem to make sense. 'You worried about me?' No one had worried about him in years.

He was met with another gentle smile. 'I missed you, too.' A shiver went through her. 'It's freezing out and I didn't like to think of you out in the cold. Particularly so near Christmas.'

He stared blankly at her. 'I was about to come home, we can ride back together.' He gestured at the wine. 'We ought to leave soon in case the snowstorm worsens. Would you care for some mulled wine first? It will warm you.'

'I'd love some, thank you. I've been curious about this place, I've ridden past it a few times.'

'You have?'

Nodding, Rowena settled on the bench and he sat next to her, drawing her snug against him while she looked about her.

Catching Marguerite's eye, Eric handed her Rowena's cloak to hang near the fire and ordered more wine. He drew in a breath. 'Rowena, apart from the fact that it's freezing out and you might catch your death, you know you shouldn't be here. Your father wouldn't approve.'

Her eyes danced. 'Aye, Berthe did try to tell me. But since I brought Sergeant Yder with me, I felt sure you wouldn't mind.' She leaned her head against his shoulder in a way that was becoming achingly familiar and gave a small sigh. 'It's almost Christmas, you see. I didn't want you to be on your own, I knew you'd be upset.'

Eric opened his mouth to tell her that he was nothing of the sort and that she ought to take more care of herself, when it occurred to him that she was right. He wasn't feeling quite himself. It was nothing he couldn't handle, of course, but he had been dwelling on the past. He'd been trying not to notice the inexplicable bursts of raw pain that cut across his thoughts every so often, he pushed them aside as he always did. Christmas often had a bad effect on him, particularly when it snowed. 'I am not upset.'

'Liar,' she said, rubbing her cheek against his arm and linking her fingers with his. 'It's Christmas and it's snowing. Tell me.'

He looked down at her. Her silver circlet winked in the candlelight, it was slightly crooked—she must have dislodged it when removing her cloak. He straightened it and as he did so blue eyes met his.

'I didn't think you knew about Christmas,' he said, quietly. 'You weren't born the year your mother took me in.'

'Eric, how many years have you been a friend? I knew.'

Marguerite set another cup of wine on the table and Rowena murmured her thanks. While she sipped, Eric watched her. He liked watching her. In the few months they'd been together Rowena's features had become dear to his heart. He adored the elegant line of her hand holding the cup. He adored her slender wrist, the line of her nose and brow and the rosy tint to her cheek. He especially adored the slight bow in her top lip. He hid a smile. In truth, her mouth drove him wild. Whenever he looked at it, he felt bound to try and tease it into a smile. Her mouth lured him, it made him want to touch it, to press his mouth to hers and kiss her senseless. Rowena was the most desirable of women. He would want her until the end of time. She made him feel things he'd never thought to feel about any woman. Witness the way he worried about her. The idea that she had been concerned about him too had caught him entirely by surprise.

Lord, it didn't seem possible. He had long known that Rowena was a caring woman, yet the idea that she might worry about him enough to bring her out on a night like this was unbearably touching. It shouldn't be a surprise. Wives and husbands looked out for each other. It was in their interests to do so.

In the deepest depths of his memory something shifted, something from so far back in his past he could barely grasp it. His father, Simon. Lord, they must have put something in the wine. Eric hadn't been able to conjure his father's face in years, yet all at once there he was. He could see him in his mind, clear as day.

Sadly, Eric wasn't remembering his father in his prime, he was seeing him as he had last seen him, breathing his last on his deathbed. His father had held out his hand and his once-strong arm had been stick thin. His face had been so wasted by disease that he was barely recognisable, eyes stared out of sunken sockets. His father had looked exhausted, only his voice had been the same.

'Listen, Eric,' his father had whispered. 'Listen well.'

Eric had clung to his father's hand.

'My son, I shall shortly be leaving and I won't be coming back. I ask you one thing. One thing. Will you do it?'

Eric had been so small he had barely understood what his father had been asking, none the less he had nodded.

His father had given him a slight smile and, small though he had been, Eric had understood that the smile had used nearly all of his father's reserves. 'When I am gone, look after your mother. Love her and look after her. Understand?'

'Yes, Papa.'

Eric stared blindly at his lovely, adorable wife and felt something crack inside. His father had loved his mother unreservedly, there had been no self-interest. He swallowed. 'I failed my father,' he said.

Large eyes intent on his, Rowena set her cup on the table. 'In what way?'

Eric stared at a split in a wooden beam, he had never spoken of this to anyone and it was a battle to get the words out. 'Father was ill. Before he died, he asked me to look after my mother. It was the one thing he asked me to do. The one thing, and I failed him.'

Under cover of the table, Rowena laid her hand on his thigh. 'How old were you when he died?'

'Three, I think, I cannot be certain.' He rubbed his forehead. 'My memory plays tricks with time.'

She stared at him for the space of a few heart-beats and he felt her hand, gently rubbing up and down on his thigh. The gesture wasn't sensual, it was soothing—she was offering him comfort. Unfortunately, it seemed to have the opposite effect. Eric's eyes prickled and for a moment he felt as he had done all those years ago, when his mother had left him at the castle gate. He felt as though he'd been stabbed in the guts.

Her veil shifted. 'Eric, a child of three cannot be responsible for his mother's welfare. It should be the other way around.'

'Oddly, when your mother brought me into the hall, she said the very same thing.'

Rowena's eyes glistened and she bit her lip, and Eric knew she understood what he *wasn't* saying. That he had loved his mother, and had tried in his childish way to do his best for her, and she had still abandoned him. 'Mother told me she guessed you were around six years of age when you came to Jutigny. By that reckoning your father would have been dead for some years.'

'Aye.'

'Eric, if you can remember that conversation with your father, you must remember what happened after his death.'

He looked at her, all twisted inside. Everything was a jumble, a painful jumble. 'I hate Christmas.'

'Eric, you don't have to tell me if you don't wish to.' She gave him a gentle smile. 'But I think it would help you to talk about it to someone.'

His throat felt parched. Taking a sip of wine, he found more words. 'I would rather talk to you than anyone, but this is hardly the place.'

'Later then?'

'Perhaps.' Eric lifted her hand to his lips. 'If I talk to anyone, my love, it would be to you.'

She leaned into him and gave a soft murmur and he could see by the light in her eyes that something he said had pleased her. He squeezed her fingers.

She flinched and drew her hand from his.

'Rowena?'

'It's nothing, my fingers are sore. Too much sewing, I'm afraid.'

Recapturing her hand, he turned it over and examined her fingers. The tips of her fingers looked raw. 'No thimble?'

'I used a thimble.'

'What the devil were you sewing, chain mail?'

Her smile peeped out and her eyes danced. 'A gift for my husband.'

Gently, he rubbed the pad of his thumb over her fingers. 'No shirt would have done that.'

'No, indeed. This was quite a challenge. Would you care to see it?'

He lifted his brows. 'You brought it with you?'

'Yes, I was going to give it to you on Christmas Day but, given the weather, I thought you needed it sooner rather than later.'

Rowena raised her hand, which must have been a signal she'd arranged earlier, for Sergeant Yder immediately rose and came across. Placing a bundle in her hands, he nodded at Eric and withdrew.

'Here you are,' she said and handed it to him.

It was heavy. A green worsted bundle that had been tied with silver ribbon to keep it together. Conscious of blue eyes watching his every move, Eric kept a smile on his face and untied the ribbon. A cloak unrolled, a fur-lined cloak with a silver fastening.

He shook it out and looked at it. It was a fine English wool, the weave tight and strong. Warm. The fur was soft as silk, he'd never be cold again. For the second time that evening, his eyes stung. '*Mon Dieu*, Rowena, it's fit for a prince.' He cleared his throat. 'It must have taken you hours.'

She laughed. 'Weeks, actually. You'd better make the most of it, I doubt I shall make another like it.'

'It must have been such a penance sewing through fur.' Reaching for her, he pulled her against him and kissed her cheek. '*Merci mille fois*—a thousand thanks. I never had anything half so fine.'

Blue eyes smiled up at him. 'I hoped you'd like it.'

'Indeed I do.'

Her mouth curved. It was so tempting, Eric didn't bother to resist. Lowering his head, he kissed her again. Properly. The cloying smell of spices—of Christmas, of pain—faded and he was surrounded by the fresh scent of summer. Rowena. Just Rowena. He drew the kiss out until a choking laugh from Alard recalled him to his senses.

Across the inn, the Jutigny guards looked highly amused.

A man on a nearby table snorted and made a

crude gesture with his fingers. 'There's a mattress upstairs.'

A girl tittered.

Eric sighed. His emotions might be all in a tangle, but his desires certainly weren't. He was aching for her. Again. Always. Sliding his hand round her neck, he leaned in again and froze. Some words were hovering on the tip of his tongue. Words he'd never thought to say to any woman. Words that couldn't be true. *I love you.* He closed his mouth. No, he didn't. He couldn't love her. He was fond of her. He felt affection. He adored every inch of her body.

I do not love her. There wasn't room in his life for love. Love was a trap, once caught in its toils it would unman you. He would never love anyone.

Love turned to hate. Eric had seen for himself, many times. Holy Virgin, he'd experienced it. His parents had taught him that love was the most cruel of masters. Fathers died. Mothers ran off when offered the chance of a better life. Love let you down. Eric would never love anyone, especially not Rowena, he was far too fond of her to love her.

'Eric?' Her eyes, soft and dark and welcoming, searched his.

Pressing a quick kiss to a prettily flushed cheek, he straightened and gave her a crooked smile. 'We should leave soon, my lady. You are at risk of being gravely disordered if you look at me like that. And tempted though I am to continue in this vein, this tavern is not the place for what I have in mind.'

Outside, it was dark and bitingly cold. Snow stung Rowena's face the instant she crossed the threshold, she caught her breath with the chill of it.

Eric grimaced as he swung on to Captain's back. His silver cloak pin glinted and Rowena's heart warmed. He was wearing the fur-lined cloak and he looked well in it, in truth, he was as handsome as a prince.

'I don't want you riding to Jutigny in this, my love,' Eric said. 'You'll freeze to death.'

Behind them, Rowena's guard was mounting up. The tavern's shutters must be cracked, for light flickered through them, striping the snow with yellow. 'Perhaps we might stay at the inn, after all.'

'I am not having my wife sleeping at The Sun. There's only a common chamber and there won't be proper beds. Bed bugs. Fleas and Lord knows what else.' He heeled Captain into a walk. 'I'll be glad to see the back of the place, I shan't be returning.'

'Oh?'

He shrugged. 'My enquiries weren't leading anywhere, but I had been trying for some discretion. Your arrival this evening with half the Jutigny guard has put paid to all that. I'll try another tack.'

Rowena felt her jaw drop. 'Oh, Eric, I am sorry, I didn't realise.' She fiddled with her gloves. 'I had to know you were all right.'

'It is of no moment, I appreciate your concern and I have other ideas.' Reaching out, he squeezed her hand. 'Put The Sun out of your mind. Count Henry's palace is only up the hill, we'll seek shelter there. The palace steward owes me a favour, he'll be happy to give us house-room.'

Shivering, Rowena nodded her agreement and shrank into her hood. 'It's certainly bitter.' She was nothing but goosebumps.

It was only a short ride from the market square to Count Henry's palace, yet it seemed to take for ever. Snow crunched beneath the horses' hoofs. Above them the wind howled, hurling snow out of a black sky. As they neared the palace gates, Rowena knew that staying in Provins was the right decision. The gatehouse torches lit up drifts of wind-sculpted snow, the approach road was a dazzling sea of white. Everything was frozen and even breathing was a painful business, Rowena's chest ached.

Not that she regretted coming out on such a bitter night. On the contrary, she felt as though she was on the point of making a breakthrough. Much as he had tried to hide it, Eric had been miserable when she'd arrived. He'd been dwelling on his past. As she suspected, he remembered more about his early life than he'd ever admitted. Tonight she was determined to get him to open up to her.

They drew rein at the gatehouse and, while they waited for the guards to admit them, Rowena made a vow to herself. By tomorrow morning, Eric's childhood would no longer be festering inside him.

Eric touched her arm. 'Rowena?'

'Aye?'

'Lady Barbara will be concerned when you don't return home. Yet the weather's so filthy I am reluctant to send a man back with a message.'

'I didn't tell Mama where I was going, she thinks I retired to our bedchamber, so I don't think a message is necessary. Berthe knew where I was going, of course. She also knows Sergeant Yder escorted me. If Mama speaks to Berthe she will be able to tell her that by now I am with you.'

The tramp of booted feet announced the arrival of Sir Perceval de Logres, Count Henry's palace steward, and in no time at all Rowena and Eric were ushered into the warm splendour of the great hall. Shortly after that they were shown into a candlelit bedchamber at the end of a long gallery overlooking the hall. The candlelight revealed a bedchamber smaller than the tower chamber at Jutigny. Their breath misted in the air. Most importantly, embers were glowing in a fireplace set in the outer wall.

Rowena headed straight for the fire, dropped a couple of logs on to the glow and stirred it back to life. Eric bolted the door.

Though small, the room was richly appointed. The terracotta hearth tiles were patterned with yellow birds and the bedchamber walls were panelled with brightly painted wood.

Eric was studying the bed, a slight frown in his brow. It wasn't large for a man of his height, but it was a relief to see a pile of fleecy-looking blankets. Rowena went over to him, wrapped her arms about his waist and smiled. 'The cold goes deep. I am blessed to have you to help warm the bed.'

He kissed the top of her head and they undressed quickly, laying their cloaks on top of the covers for extra warmth. Then they slipped beneath the sheets and into each other's arms.

Rowena waited until they had settled before framing Eric's face with her hands. She looked deep into his eyes. 'Well?'

'Well what?'

'Will you tell me what happened after your father died?'

Eric's gaze focused on something behind her and Rowena held in a sigh.

'Eric, I would feel honoured if you could tell me.' She smoothed back his hair and kept her voice calm. Much as she burned for him to trust her enough to open up to her, she wasn't going to push him. 'But if you can't tell me yet, I can wait.'

His arms tightened about her. 'No, it's all right, it probably is time you learned the truth.' His lips twisted. 'Or as much of it as I know. I don't know it all. After my father died, Mother—'

A loud knocking cut off the rest of Eric's words. The door latch rattled. 'De Monfort, open up! *De Monfort!*'

Swearing softly under his breath, Eric tossed the bedcovers aside and reached for his cloak. 'Hold your horses, I'm coming.' He threw back the bolt and opened the door.

Sir Perceval stood on the threshold, lantern in hand. He blinked sheepishly at them. 'I am sorry to disturb you, Sir Eric, my lady. I think you might need to know that a couple of envoys have just ridden in from Paris. They are bound for Jutigny. Like you, they decided to break their journey here because of the storm.'

Sir Perceval's tone was so serious, the hairs rose on the back of Rowena's neck. She bolted upright, holding the blankets to her neck. 'Envoys from Paris? What is it, sir?'

Stepping into the chamber, Sir Perceval glanced down the corridor in what could only be described as a furtive manner. Firmly, he closed the door. 'The envoys bear messages from the king.'

'It's nigh on midnight, de Logres, can't this wait?' Eric said, moving to stand next to the bed. 'You can tell the envoys that Lady Rowena and I shall accompany them to Jutigny in the morning.'

With a grimace, Sir Perceval cleared his throat. 'De Monfort, there's more, you'd best brace yourself.'

In the short silence that followed, Eric folded his arms across his chest. 'Go on.'

'The king's men hold a summons for Lord Faramus to appear at the Paris court. They also hold an arrest warrant.'

Rowena gasped. 'An arrest warrant? For whom?'

Sir Perceval shifted uncomfortably and spots of colour appeared on his cheeks. 'For your husband, *ma dame*. King Louis has summoned Sir

Eric de Monfort to answer charges of abducting his goddaughter Lady Rowena. The king was of the understanding that Lady Rowena should have taken her vows at St Mary's Abbey. De Monfort, you are accused of forcing Lady Rowena into marriage.'

A shiver ran down Rowena's spine. 'Father promised he would write to the king, he said that he would explain everything!' She caught Eric's gaze. 'I had to beg the king to get into the convent in the first place.'

'I remember.'

'I knew the king would be upset by my change of heart,' Rowena said. Her head was beginning to pound. 'Father promised me he would make it right with him.'

Eric grimaced. 'It looks as though he has forgotten.' He turned back to Sir Perceval. 'Goodnight, de Logres. You have my thanks for bringing this news.'

Sir Perceval's eyebrows rose. 'You're going back to bed?'

Eric's face grew hard. 'Well, I'm certainly not running away, if that is what you're suggesting. This must be faced. I suggest we get a good night's sleep. Did you inform the king's men that I am in the palace?'

Hand on the latch, Sir Perceval shifted. 'Not

as yet.' He smiled. 'Thought I should warn you first.'

'My thanks for the thought. However, it might be best if you let them know I am lodged here tonight.'

'What will you do?'

'On the morrow I shall escort the envoys to Jutigny with my lady. When the envoys have spoken to Lord Faramus, we can take it from there.'

'Very well, de Monfort, if you're certain?'

'Quite certain.'

Sir Perceval nodded and went out. Eric bolted the door behind him.

Rowena watched him calmly—how could he be so calm?—join her in bed.

Firelight flickered over his face as he gripped her hand. 'Listen, my love, I don't know why Lord Faramus delayed writing to the king, but it looks as though someone has been busy in Paris.'

'Sir Armand.'

'Exactly. Rowena, it's important you must do exactly as I say, I may be in Paris for a while.'

She frowned. 'I'm coming with you.'

'No, my love, you are not.'

'I'm your wife! My place is at your side.'

'Not this time, it isn't,' Eric said, curtly.

Rowena's breath stopped. What was happening here? One moment Eric seemed poised to open his heart to her and the next he was acting the tyrant? 'You sound just like Father.'

Green eyes narrowed. 'Listen, Rowena—'

Her fists clenched. 'Listen, Rowena? I won't. I'm coming to Paris.'

'Rowena. My love.' Taking her by the arms, Eric leaned his forehead against hers. 'You can't come with me. I must go to court and hear these charges. And whilst I am gone I want—*need*—to know you are safe. You're not coming within spitting distance of Armand de Velay, I've heard he's in Paris. You will remain at Jutigny with Lady Barbara. Rowena, you will give me your word that you will not leave the castle precincts.'

'I will do no such thing!'

'Yes, you will. Only if you stay in the castle can I be assured that your father's household knights and Sergeant Yder will see to your safety. With luck, the king will come round to our view and I shall be back at Jutigny before you know it.'

Chapter Thirteen

The Christmas festivities were no excuse for Lord Faramus and Eric to delay setting out for Paris, one couldn't put off a summons from the king. Particularly when the summons mentioned that the king had never heard of one Sir Eric de Monfort and demanded proof of his honour and integrity. The men left the next morning.

Thus, by the time Christmas Eve arrived a somewhat diminished household attended the customary mass. The mood was subdued. Clouds of incense filled the chapel; the sound of chanting echoed round the vaults and out into the corridors. After the service, when the last of the incense was but a faint curl of smoke, the congregation filed out for their breakfast, leaving Rowena and her mother alone on the wall bench.

Rowena wasn't hungry. Since Eric had left Jutigny she had hardly slept. Her nerves were on edge—she missed him. She feared for him and she could think of nothing else but when they might be together again.

'Mother, I distinctly remember Father promising he would write to the king to inform him of our marriage months ago. Why didn't he?'

Lady Barbara sighed. 'He was waiting.'

'Waiting for what?'

Lady Barbara looked mournfully at the chapel floor.

Rowena twisted her hands together. 'Why did Father delay? He must have known it would anger the king.'

'The lands your father holds from the king are not significant, my love,' Lady Barbara murmured. 'The bulk of our holdings lie in Sainte-Colombe.'

'Well, the king obviously thinks our French lands are important, else he wouldn't have sent his summons. For heaven's sake, Mama, Eric is under arrest!'

Her mother shook her head. 'Not for long, I am sure. Rowena, you surely heard your father swearing he would bear witness to Sir Eric's character?'

Rowena nodded and her mother covered her hands with hers.

'Dearest, try not to fret. Your father will convince the king that Eric is the most suitable of stewards and the king will accept him. The king needs loyal men he can rely on.'

'It might have been better if Father had sent word to the king as soon as we married. King Louis is a religious man and all this time he has been believing that I was serving God in the convent.'

'Your father thought the king would accept your marriage more readily if the succession was assured. He was waiting until he knew that you were with child.' Her mother resumed her contemplation of the floor. 'Dearest, we chose Eric not only because of his sense of honour, but also because of his reputation. We thought that if anyone could win you over it would be Eric.'

'Are you telling me you chose him for his charm?'

Her mother gave her a troubled look. 'Eric was chosen first and foremost for his capabilities. He is the most honourable of men.' Her expression lightened. 'Although I have to admit we did recall your fondness for him when you were young. Your father and I knew that if anyone could get you out of the convent, it would be Eric. We also knew that if anyone could get you into the marriage bed it was likely to be him. He does, as you say, have charisma. We thought— hoped—a grandchild would soon be on the way.

You see, dear, it occurred to your father that Eric might need a child to bolster his claim.'

Rowena stiffened. 'You mean because of his birth or, rather, lack of it.'

Her mother made a helpless gesture. 'Rowena, your father and I are, like you, aware of Eric's admirable qualities.' She smiled. 'He grew up here, after all. However, you must understand that the world may not see him as we do.'

Rowena spoke through gritted teeth. 'Mama, Eric needs nothing to bolster his claim. He is more honourable than most knights of my acquaintance.'

'Of course he is. Be easy, Rowena, your father will ensure that the king knows this. There will be no annulment.'

Rowena's heart dropped. 'Annulment? What annulment?' Panicky thoughts flew this way and that. What was her mother saying? Eric had gone to Paris to discuss annulling their marriage? Why had no one mentioned this? 'The king is thinking of annulling our marriage? He can't do that!'

Her mother grimaced. 'I am afraid that he can. Vassals of the king should not marry without his permission. However, it won't come to that. Your father will support Eric's claim and he will offer proof of Eric's character.' She smiled.

'It's not hard to find, after all. You have no need to worry.'

Rowena jumped to her feet. She couldn't believe what she was hearing. The king was considering annulling her marriage. 'No need? There is every need. Mother, I am going to pack, I shall leave for Paris at first light. The king must be made to see that I want this marriage.'

'Eric told you to remain here.'

Rowena lifted her chin. 'Loving and obeying are not always the same thing. My place is at his side.'

'Is it? Rowena, your father agrees with Eric, you and I should remain here. Remember, they have your welfare in mind. In any case, I am sure that by the time the Twelfth Night festivities are under way, Eric and your father will be home and this dreadful business will be behind us.'

Rowena found her gaze flickering guiltily towards the cross on the altar. Something her mother had said had given her an idea. And may God forgive her because she was about to lie, and in God's house too.

Looking her mother straight in the eye, she laid a hand on her belly. 'Mama, there's something I must tell you. I haven't mentioned it to anyone—it is too early to be certain—but I believe I might be with child.'

Her mother gave her a hard look. 'Rowena,

you wouldn't make up something like this, would you?'

'*Mother!*'

Her mother narrowed her eyes. 'I am sorry, Rowena, I don't believe you.'

Rowena felt her shoulders sag, she had always been an appalling liar and her mother knew her as well as anyone. If she couldn't convince her mother, what hope had she of convincing the king?

'Rowena, you can't be thinking of lying to the king. You, who professed to the world that you wanted to be a nun!'

'If it prevents the king from calling for an annulment to our marriage, it will be worth it.'

'And when you produce no child?'

'I can say that I miscarried.'

'Rowena, this is madness.'

'Mama, I can't lose him, I won't.'

Her mother's face softened and she reached for her hand. 'You love him.'

'Of course I love him, I've loved him for months.' She paused. 'Years probably, although the way I love him has changed somewhat.'

A delighted smile lit her mother's eyes. 'I knew Eric was right for you.'

'Mother, I don't care what you say, I'm going to Paris.'

'Very well.' Lady Barbara got to her feet and

shook out her skirts. 'If you insist on going to Paris—against your husband's orders I might add—I shall go with you.'

Rowena's brow creased in confusion. 'What about your husband's orders? Didn't Father command you to stay here?'

Her mother's eyes danced. 'I'll let you in on a secret, dearest. I agree with you, loving and obeying are not the same thing.'

Rowena's jaw went slack, never in a thousand years had she expected her mother to say such a thing. 'You always agree with Father.'

'Do I?' Her mother lifted her shoulders. 'Perhaps I simply appear to. Be that as it may, we shall both go to Paris. Only hear me well, Rowena. When we get there, you will not be misleading the king in any way. Agreed?'

'Yes, Mama.'

Lady Barbara picked up her skirts and turned to the door. 'Come along, dear, I think we will pack more efficiently if we break our fast first.'

A sharp draught picked up the edge of Rowena's veil. Someone was marching down the chapel corridor. It was Sergeant Yder.

'Lady Rowena, may I speak with you?'

'Of course, sergeant.'

'Two townsfolk have arrived at the gatehouse with a message for Sir Eric. When I told them he was away with Lord Faramus they insisted on speaking to you. They won't say anything, my lady, except directly to you.'

'Bring them here, if you please.'

'At once, my lady.'

Rowena and her mother returned to the wall bench and shortly afterwards the sergeant returned with two nervous-looking women. They hovered with linked arms in the chapel doorway.

Rowena rose. 'Come in, please.'

Rowena recognised one woman from The Sun. The other was much younger, about twelve years of age. A similarity between them led Rowena to suspect that they were mother and daughter. The girl's face was very round and something about her made Rowena suspect that she might be simple in nature. She had pretty grey eyes which travelled wonderingly over the embroidered altar cloth, the gold cross and the brass candlesticks.

'Lady Rowena.' The older woman dropped into an awkward curtsy. 'Lady Barbara.'

'How may we help?'

'We've come because we heard Sir Eric had been called to Paris.'

'Heavens, word does get around,' Lady Barbara murmured.

'Yes, my lady. My name is Marguerite, I work at a tavern in the Lower Town.'

'I believe I saw you there a few days ago,' Rowena said.

'That's right, my lady. Your husband has been a regular customer of late and I can't help but notice that there's less trouble when he's around. We all like him.'

'I am glad to hear it.'

'My lady, we know your husband comes to our tavern because of what happened to that Jutigny squire. We know he wants justice for the boy. I hope you won't take this amiss—I like your husband and I respect him. When I heard he had been summoned to speak to the king, I knew I could no longer keep silent. I know of a witness to the squire's death.'

Rowena's pulse jumped and she fought to stay calm. A witness? Was her cousin's involvement in Mathieu's death about to be confirmed? Her gaze shifted to the young girl.

'My lady, this is my daughter, Cécile,' Marguerite said, slipping an arm about her daughter's waist.

Rowena took a step forward. 'She saw what happened that night?'

'Aye. Forgive us for not speaking out earlier. Cécile isn't like other girls, I was trying to protect her. I'm not confident she can cope with being cross-questioned.'

'Thank you, Marguerite,' Rowena said.

Pleased at the steadiness in her voice, she smiled at Cécile. 'Cécile, I'd love to talk to you, would that be all right?'

Marguerite tugged at her daughter's hand. 'Cécile, this is the lady I was telling you about, Lady Rowena. Will you talk to her?'

'Yes, *mama*.'

Rowena ushered Cécile to the wall bench. 'Please, take a seat.'

Paris. The bridge across to the Île de France, the *petit pont*, was shiny with ice crystals as Lady Barbara, Lady Rowena and their entourage rode across. Horses skidded; merchants leading pack animals slipped and swore. The margins of the Seine were rimed with hoar frost, the waters fretted by a December wind that blustered along the river with such force that white horses frothed and foamed on the surface.

'Shall we seek lodgings at the palace?' Lady Barbara murmured, staring anxiously at the ruffled waters flowing beneath the bridge.

Flexing fingers that were stiff with cold, Rowena pulled her hood more closely about her. 'Given our arrival is unlooked for, I am reluctant to presume on the king's hospitality. Sergeant Yder will find us lodgings.'

On the eastern arm of the island, the cathedral of Notre-Dame towered over the other churches, its crisp new stonework showed white through a complicated tracery of scaffolding. On the western arm, the walls of the Palais de la Cité rose sheer out of the windswept river.

The Île de France wasn't large, none the less, the sun was sinking by the time Sergeant Yder had secured lodgings for them in the merchants' quarter near the palace. Once there, Rowena barely had time to wash and change into her blue samite gown before Sergeant Yder was again knocking at the door.

'Come in, Sergeant.'

'My lady, the palace steward tells me that the king is spending the day in the Ecclesiastical City behind Notre-Dame. It is Holy Innocents' Day, you see. Sir Eric and Lord Faramus are to meet with the king after attending a special mass.'

Rowena snatched up her cloak. 'Lead on, Sergeant.'

When Lady Rowena de Sainte-Colombe and her mother, Lady Barbara, arrived at the Ecclesiastical City the mass had ended. On this part of the Île de France, the main streets had been swept clear of snow. They were directed around one side of the cathedral to a stone building whose entrance was guarded by the burliest monk Rowena had ever seen. A deep scar cut across his face, and Rowena knew without being told that this man had been a mercenary before he had entered the cloisters. His breath fogged the air.

'Excuse me, Brother.' Rowena dipped into a curtsy. 'This lady is the Countess Barbara de Sainte-Colombe. I am her daughter, Lady Rowena.'

'How may I help you?'

'I understand that my father, Count Faramus de Sainte-Colombe, is meeting my godfather, the king, here. My husband, Sir Eric de Monfort, should be with them. We apologise for our tardiness, but we should like to join them.'

The monk folded his arms across his chest, and Rowena sensed that this man did not take well to being importuned by a woman.

'My lady, I have no orders from His Grace about your arrival.'

'Brother, we realise our arrival is unexpected and we apologise, but it is vital we speak to the king.'

'You say King Louis is your godfather?'

'Indeed he is.' Rowena clasped her hands together and hoped she looked suitably meek. Suitably prayerful. She *was* prayerful, she was praying that the monk had not heard how she had married Eric to escape the cloisters. 'Brother, I believe I have a right to be present at this conference. It is my marriage they are discussing. Please show us the way.'

The conference chamber wasn't large. The king was sitting on a vast gilded chair resplendent with red cushions. Rowena was disturbed to see he looked as though he was sitting in judgement. She was aware of others in the chamber— her father and a handful of clerics and knights including, unfortunately, her cousin Sir Armand. Rowena smothered a groan. With her cousin present it was hard to see her way forward.

Her gaze was drawn to Eric. His eyes widened as she walked in and his expression seemed to soften as he inclined his head at her. 'My lady.'

Rowena threw him a quick smile. With King Louis present, there was no time for more. Anger burned in her breast. It shouldn't be Eric who was being questioned here, it should be Sir Armand. Her cousin should be made to answer for his actions and it looked as though she was going to have to persuade the king to arrest him. Praying for strength, Rowena focused on Eric and wondered what had already passed between him and the king.

Eric was standing in the light of a narrow lancet and she couldn't help but see that he wasn't armed. However, they were in a holy city and none of the other knights was bearing arms either. No one was under restraint. Yet.

Walking up to the king, Rowena lowered her head and sank into her deepest curtsy. 'Your Grace, I beg you to forgive the intrusion, but I had to come.'

'Lady Rowena.'

The king's voice was questioning, as if he doubted the identity of the person kneeling before him. That didn't seem like a good omen and Rowena dare not look up. Not yet. She stared at the king's red leather boots and the gilded claw feet of his chair and prayed that he would soften towards her.

A white hand reached out, a ruby ring flashed as the king tilted her face up. 'Lady Rowena, you may rise.'

Rowena straightened. 'Thank you, Sire.'

The king's eyebrow lifted as he looked pointedly at her clothes. 'I have to say you have astounded me. I thought to see you next in the garb of a nun and here you are, a married lady.'

'Your Grace, I—'

The king cut her off with a wave of his hand. 'My lady, when we last corresponded you wrote most eloquently of your desire to take the veil. I was aware of your father's displeasure—he was most anxious that you should marry—yet you insisted your calling was genuine. *Ma dame*, both your father and the man you currently call your husband insist that you are content in your marriage. You have made a fool of your king.'

The words *the man you currently call your husband* sounded like the death knell of her marriage. Rowena lowered her gaze to the king's red boots. 'Your Grace, that was never my intent. I can only apologise. I—'

Footsteps approached and another pair of boots walked into the edge of Rowena's line of sight. She caught the swirl of a green, fur-lined cloak.

'Your Grace.' Eric's voice was low. Calm. 'I beg you to understand, Lady Rowena is not to blame. She is content now—'

'Yes, I am,' she put in quickly. 'Very content.'

Eric took firm hold of her hand. 'Rowena, if you would allow me. Your Grace, I abducted her. It is my fault that she did not become a novice, that she did not take the veil.'

More footsteps tramped up and Rowena saw a third pair of boots. Her father.

'My liege, as we have explained, Eric was my household knight before he won the manor at Monfort. He abducted Rowena at my instigation. I am wholly to blame.'

'No husband, you are not.' Lady Barbara spoke from the doorway. 'If you recall, we chose Eric for our daughter together.'

Lord Faramus harrumphed. 'Woman, be silent.'

'I will not.' Lady Barbara's skirts swept the tiles as she came up and sank into a curtsy. 'Your Grace, I am as much to blame as my husband or Sir Eric.'

A slow handclap began. Sir Armand, standing among a group of knights and clerics in front of a large wooden cross, curled his lip. Arrogance in his every line, he bowed at the king. 'My liege, this show of family solidarity, whilst touching, smacks of self-interest. It does not excuse them for arranging a marriage without your consent. In my view, your best course would be to confiscate their entire French estate.'

The king tapped his forefinger on the arm of his chair. 'Sir Armand, as far as I am aware you are not a member of my council.'

'No, my liege.' Some of Sir Armand's arrogance fell away. Even so, it was plain from his manner that no mention had thus far been made of Eric's suspicions regarding Sir Armand's involvement in Mathieu's death, nor indeed in the incidents at Monfort and at the Jutigny gatehouse.

The king's fingers drummed the gilded arm of his throne. 'Yet you presume to offer advice?'

'No, no, of course, my liege, I presume nothing.' A tight smile appeared and Sir Armand made a show of crossing himself as he bowed his head at the cross on the wall. 'I do, however, feel obliged to point out that should Count Faramus's French lands be placed into the care of a loyal relation, one known to have the interests of France at heart, a substantial donation would be made to aid the completion of Notre-Dame.'

The king's gaze shifted thoughtfully from Sir Armand to her father and then to Rowena and Eric. In the silence that fell, Rowena heard her father smother a groan. Saints, she felt like groaning herself. Devil that he was, Sir Armand knew his king.

His king's weakness was his piety, everyone knew that. Why, when Lord Gawain had negotiated the breaking of her betrothal, he had given a large donation to the king's favourite monastery. Currently, the project dearest to the king's heart was the completion of the cathedral at the heart of his kingdom.

Winding her fingers more tightly with Eric's, Rowena realised she could wait no longer. King Louis must be made to see Sir Armand in his true colours.

Her heart bumped about in her breast. 'Your Grace, may I crave a moment's speech with my husband? There is something I wish to tell him.'

'Granted.'

No one moved, everyone was watching them,

including Sir Armand. Rowena's heart sank. She had to tell Eric that the witness he had long been seeking had come forward, but how could she do that with Sir Armand's gaze boring into her back?

Her cheeks warmed. 'Your Grace, I had hoped to speak privately to my husband.'

The king's lips firmed. 'I am sorry, my lady, my patience is wearing thin. I will resolve the matter of this marriage without further delay. We will hear what you have to say to him, then I will make my decision.'

'In that case, Your Grace, I should like to suggest that you summon your guard.'

The king blinked. 'My lady?'

Drawing strength from Eric's presence at her side, Rowena held her ground. 'Your Grace, until you summon the guard I can say no more. What I have to say touches on more than my marriage.'

After the briefest of hesitations, King Louis snapped his fingers, exchanging nods with one of the knights. The knight slipped from the chamber. Lines formed around Sir Armand's eyes. Rowena heard the clump of boots marching across stone flags and the murmur of voices. Shadows shifted in the street outside and after a brief space the knight reappeared.

'The guards are in place, my liege.'

The king looked down his nose at his goddaughter. His forefinger tapped on the arm of his throne. 'Continue, if you please.'

Taking a deep breath, Rowena launched in. 'Your Grace, I came to Paris with two aims in mind, the most personal being to fight for my marriage. The second aim is also related to my marriage and I beg you to bear with me. It involves gaining justice for a terrible wrong.' She clasped her hands together. 'Will you hear me, Your Grace? Do I have your permission to begin?'

'Please continue.'

'I shall start with my marriage. When Sir Eric removed me from the convent, I confess I was extremely startled. However, Sir Eric did not have to force me to go with him.' A pleat formed in the king's brow. Rowena pressed on. 'I made no objection, Your Grace, partly because I knew Sir Eric would never harm me. As you may recall, he was brought up at Jutigny and I knew him well. The other reason that I made no objection was because I was starting to see that entering the convent might have been a grave mistake. I had gone into St Mary's because I had known that I could not marry Lord Gawain. Further, I needed time to think of a way to become reconciled with my parents. I wanted them to forgive me for writing to you and pleading to become

a nun. I was also concerned that you, my godfather, would naturally be disappointed in me.

'Your Grace, when I went into the convent I
honestly believed my reluctance to marry Lord
Gawain meant that I had a calling. My days in
St Mary's began to prove me wrong. When Sir
Eric came to abduct me—'

'My lady, abduction is not the act of an honourable man,' the king said, severely.

Rowena stepped forward. 'It was done with
honourable intentions.'

'Explain, if you please. I have heard something of this from Lord Faramus, your version
of events would interest me.'

'When Sir Eric took me from the abbey, he
was acting at the request of my father. He was
acting to save me from…from a marriage I could
never have stomached, not if I lived to be a thousand. In short, Sir Eric committed a dishonourable act with honourable intentions. He did not
force me. On the contrary, he granted me space
to decide what to do next. Sir Eric gave me a
choice, Your Grace, that is why I went with him.'

The king's eyes flickered to Eric and back
again. 'In short, you trusted him.'

'I would trust Sir Eric with my life.' She
glanced at Eric and smiled. 'Your Grace, he is
the most honourable of knights.'

'His family are unknown,' the king said, resting his chin on his hand as he looked at her, eyes curious. 'His father might be a murderer.'

Rowena tried not to look at her cousin. 'Having noble forebears is no guarantee of honourable behaviour. Your Grace, I know Sir Eric. I have always liked him and in the months since our marriage I have come to love him. I am proud to be his wife and could wish for no other husband.'

Releasing Eric's arm, Rowena sank to her knees. 'I beg you to forgive us for marrying without your consent. I beg you to allow our marriage to stand. I beg you not to call for an annulment.'

Peeping up, Rowena saw the king scratch his chin. His eyes were thoughtful and she rather thought a smile was forming.

'And the other reason for giving us the pleasure of your company, my lady?' Leaning forward, the king gestured for her to rise. 'You mentioned justice. A wrong that needs righting.'

Rowena's throat felt dry, she could feel Sir Armand's gaze burning into her back. Praying that the guards in the street were ready for anything, she turned to Eric. 'Sir, I have to tell you that yesterday the person you have been searching for in Provins came forward.'

Green eyes searched hers. 'The witness?'

'Aye.'

'Have you brought him to Paris?' Eric asked.

Rowena grimaced. Out of the tail of her eye she could see that her cousin was hanging on their every word. 'The witness is a she and I'm sorry, it wasn't possible to bring her. She… she's not well enough to travel.' *Nor is she well enough to bear witness,* Rowena thought, but she couldn't say that. It would undermine their case.

Sir Armand edged closer, Rowena could feel his breath stirring her veil. She was suddenly very afraid of what her cousin might do to Cécile if he discovered she was their witness. She certainly wasn't about to mention actual names.

Eric studied her. She could see he understood that she had more to say, he knew she was constrained by Sir Armand's presence.

The king made a sound of exasperation. 'Lady Rowena, must you speak in riddles? Tell us plainly—what witness? Witness to what?'

'Rowena, I think it best if I take it from here,' Eric said. 'Forgive me, my love, but I must betray your confidence. Your Grace, shortly before Lady Rowena's betrothal to Count Gawain, one of the Jutigny squires, Mathieu de Lyon, was killed in Provins. His death was believed to be an accident—the result of a drunken brawl outside a tavern. Since I met Lady Rowena again—'

'Since you abducted her and prevented her from following her true calling, you mean,' Sir

Armand got in. He was white about the mouth and his hands were opening and closing, opening and closing. He looked as though he could bolt for the door. Either that or strangle Eric. 'That has to be blasphemy of some kind.'

'Sir Armand, you are ridiculous.' Eric shook his head and continued. 'Your Grace, shortly after Lady Rowena left the abbey and returned to Jutigny, I came to see that the squire's death might not have been an accident. Lady Rowena and Mathieu de Lyon had been close friends. Certain incidents took place that led me to believe Rowena's life was in danger.'

The king's eyes widened. 'Lady Rowena was attacked?'

Briefly, Eric explained about the near miss with the arrow in the chase and the troop of horsemen who had threatened to attack outside Monfort.

Sir Armand huffed. 'Who would possibly want to kill my cousin?'

'Someone who had reason to kill her because he was afraid she might marry and bear a child,' Eric said quietly. 'Your Grace, after these incidents, Lady Rowena and I married and returned to Jutigny. Almost immediately there was an accident at the castle gatehouse—one in which both Lady Rowena and I might have been killed. That was when I became seriously concerned.'

'Sir, it is you who are ridiculous.' Sir Armand laughed. 'This fairy tale about Lady Rowena's life being in danger is nothing but a fabrication. A fabrication designed to show yourself in a good light.' Sir Armand inclined his head at the king. 'Sire, you cannot believe a word Sir Eric is saying. All he cares about is keeping the land that Lady Rowena brings him.'

Eric sank to his knees and the green cloak pooled about him. 'Your Grace, I acknowledge my birth is questionable, but I swear to you that if you ratify our marriage there will be no happier man alive. Lady Rowena is very dear to me.'

'You love her?' the king asked.

'With all my heart.'

Tears stung at the back of Rowena's eyes. Eric sounded so sincere and she ached to believe him. Unfortunately, it was obvious he had realised that the king was fond of her, and was saying what he thought the king wanted him to say. In truth, Eric was fighting for her father's land and the status that came with marriage to her. He couldn't wait to become steward of Sainte-Colombe.

Eric laid his hand on his heart. 'Marriage to your goddaughter has given me all I have longed for. A beautiful wife and a family I hold dear.'

'Rise, de Monfort.' The king paused thoughtfully. 'I hear you have been making improvements at your manor since you won it.'

Eric's face was startled. 'Your Grace?'

'I made enquiries before this hearing.' The king smiled. 'It's important to get the measure of a man if you are coming to a judgement about him. Diligent stewards are worth their weight in gold. However, at present that is by the by. I should like you to tell me more about the death of this Jutigny squire and his connection with my goddaughter.'

'Your Grace, I suspect the boy was killed because of his friendship with Lady Rowena.'

Sir Armand snorted. 'I've never heard such an unlikely tale in my life. A squire? Killed because of his friendship with Lady Rowena?'

'The boy might have been killed to prevent him making a match with Lady Rowena.'

Sir Armand spluttered. 'My liege, you can't believe a word of it. Sir Eric is lying. He's an arrant knave—a cheat and a liar who has hoodwinked the Count and Countess of Sainte-Colombe into believing him to be a man of honour. Sire, Eric de Monfort is nobody. He is nothing.' Sir Armand clenched his fists. The look he sent Rowena was charged with such loathing she didn't doubt that if she wasn't in the presence of Eric and the king she would have been pummelled half to death. 'Tell us, my lady.' Sir

Armand gave a sickly smile. 'What does your so-called witness claim to have seen?'

Rowena found Eric's hand. 'The witness saw you, sir.'

Sir Armand's face went purple. 'How dare you? Your witness is a blasted liar.'

'No, Cousin, she is not. You were in Provins the night Mathieu de Lyon was killed. You were seen in the alley outside The Sun. You didn't wield the knife yourself, but she heard you giving orders to the man who did. Our witness states clearly that you were seen to point at a boy with curly brown hair, namely Mathieu de Lyon. You named him, sir. You ordered his death.'

A couple of strides brought Sir Armand within touching distance of Rowena. Eric stepped between them. 'That's close enough, de Velay.'

'Name your witness,' Sir Armand demanded. 'Who is she, a slut from The Sun?'

Eric's jaw tightened. 'Watch your mouth, de Velay.'

'Who is she?'

Rowena's head came up. 'I will not say, sir.'

'You will not because you cannot.' Sir Armand bunched his fists and swung to face the king. 'Your Grace, this tale of a witness is, like Sir Eric's tale of murder in Provins, a web of lies. Lady Rowena can't name a witness who doesn't exist.'

The king stroked his chin and caught the eye of a knight by the wall. In an instant, all the knights stepped in front of the door, making a wall of their bodies.

'I am not so sure,' the king said, sighing. 'I had hoped to resolve this matter today, clearly further enquiries are needed. Sir Eric, you will give me your word that you will remain in Paris until we have consulted with this witness.'

Eric bowed his head. 'You have my word.'

'Sir Eric, given what I have heard, I am afraid I have no choice but to set a guard over you. You and Lady Rowena will be given an apartment in the palace.'

'Thank you, Your Grace.'

'And you, sir.' The king looked at Sir Armand. 'You also must stay in Paris.'

'And I too must be under guard?'

'Naturally. I will take no risk with my god-daughter's life.'

Sir Armand brought his brows together. 'I take it I may use my own house?'

'If that is your wish. Do I have your word you will stay in the city?'

Sir Armand bowed. 'Of course.'

Rowena found herself holding her breath as a terrible truth dawned. The king was on the verge of asking to see Cécile and Cécile didn't have the strength for an audience with the king. The mere thought of meeting with him would likely overwhelm her. This could be disastrous. As if from a distance, she watched the king beckon her father forward.

'Lord Faramus, I am charging you with ensuring that the Lady Rowena's witness is brought from Provins. Bring her to the palace with all speed and be so good as to inform me when she has arrived.'

Rowena closed her eyes. Cécile couldn't come to the palace! She would be completely overawed and the king would be hard pressed to get a word out of her. He would learn nothing and this nightmare would never end.

When she opened her eyes again, Eric was taking his leave of the king. Dazed with worry and fatigue, she felt him tuck her hand into the crook of his elbow. 'Come, my lady, you have ridden many miles today. You need to rest.'

They left the chamber with four knights at their heels and walked through a frost-filled dusk to the walls of the Ecclesiastical City. As they passed through the gate to the merchants' quarter, the knights rearmed themselves and they marched through the failing light towards the Palais de la Cité and the apartment the king had promised them.

'Cécile,' Rowena muttered. 'Heaven help us.'

Chapter Fourteen

Eric let out an appreciative whistle as they were shown into their apartment in the Palais de la Cité. A small antechamber led directly to a luxurious bedchamber. Great logs flamed in the fireplace. A group of three lancets let in a shaft of evening light, which fell across a roomy-looking bed. The windows were glazed and framed by thick tapestry curtains to keep out the winter chill. More tapestries brightened the walls. And if that were not enough, a mountain of blankets and furs was piled on a coffer at the foot of the bed.

'Saints, what a place. We won't be cold.' Eric tossed his cloak on to the bed and sat on the mattress to test it. It had to be stuffed with feathers, he could sink into it quite merrily with Rowena in his arms. Now there was a thought. He smiled up at her, noticed that she was looking somewhat preoccupied and dismissed the idea.

Was she as worried as he that their marriage might not be allowed to stand? Well, since there didn't seem to be much they could do about it tonight, he would do his best to distract her. They hadn't been separated and they might have been.

He held out his hand. 'Being given these chambers takes the sting out of being put under guard. I would have objected if Sir Armand hadn't been accorded the same treatment. Did you bring Berthe?'

Shaking her head, Rowena walked over, the hem of the blue samite dragging on the matting. 'We left in some haste. Mother and I came alone, apart from our escort.'

'Very well, that does make it easier.' Eric set his hands on her hips, manoeuvring her until she was standing between his legs. 'Alard can sleep in the antechamber with the king's guard. We'll be safe in here.' Catching the sides of her veil, he tugged, forcing her to bend her head towards his. His eyes settled on her mouth. 'I know I told you to stay in Jutigny, but since you are here you could give me a kiss. You need to apologise for your disobedience.'

A plucked eyebrow arched. 'My disobedience?' Small hands closed on his shoulders. 'Sir, I am becoming wise to you. You are not the tyrant you pretend to be.'

Closing the distance between them, Rowena

gave him as pretty a kiss as he could wish. Murmuring his pleasure, wondering why one touch from this slight slip of a girl inflamed his every sense, Eric leaned back, hoping she would tumble with him on to the bed. Rowena resisted. He tugged a little more on the veil and gave her a suggestive smile. 'Come on, my love, I missed you.'

Her silver circlet glinted as she broke free with a laugh. 'Really, Eric, we've not been parted above a day. And Sergeant Yder will shortly be arriving with my things.'

'He can leave them in the antechamber.' Watching her retrace her steps to the fire, Eric laid a hand on his heart. 'A day without you seems like an eternity.'

'Eric, you really don't have to pretend. You don't have to woo me, we are already married.'

He was on his feet and sliding his arms about her waist before he had thought. 'Rowena, I'm not pretending, a day without you is a day lost.' He leaned his forehead against hers, slightly disoriented to discover that he meant what he said. 'It's true, my love. I am very fond of you. Inordinately fond.'

'Inordinately fond?' Her blue eyes were watchful. Wary. 'Did you mean what you said to the king?'

'Mean what? What did I say?'

'You don't remember.' Her voice was flat. 'You told him that you loved me.'

'*Mon Dieu*, Rowena, I don't know. I'd say anything to keep you.' She looked uncertainly at him and something inside him twisted. He tightened his grip. 'Rowena, I don't want to lose you, I can't lose you. You are mine.'

She continued looking at him and she didn't move, none the less he sensed her withdrawal. 'Possession isn't everything, Eric.'

The fire crackled and she gazed into the flames. 'I think you told the king the truth. You do love me. I will hold on to that and pray that you come to accept it.' She made an impatient gesture. 'However, this must wait, I really need to tell you about the witness.'

'Come to bed, my love, we can talk in bed.'

She made a clucking sound with her tongue. 'It's far too early to retire. In any case, this is important. Eric, our witness cannot testify. She isn't up to it. We will have to stop Father going back to fetch her.'

'Our witness isn't up to it?' Eric's stomach tightened. 'Hang it, Rowena, your father has to fetch her. We need her to make our case against Sir Armand.'

She looked up at him through her eyelashes. 'To save our marriage.'

He gripped her arms, realised he was gripping too hard, and relaxed his hold. 'To keep you safe.' Turning away, he shoved his hand through his hair. 'I will not spend the rest of my life haunted by the fear that each day may be your last because that man is trying to kill you. I won't have our lives ruined. Rowena, unless we can prove he was involved in Mathieu's death we will not be free of him.'

'Eric, please listen. Cécile—that's the name of the witness—cannot testify.'

'Why ever not?'

'If you'd met her you would understand why it would be impossible. I doubt that she could stand up to interrogation. Her testimony would be questioned and I'm pretty sure she would crumple. It's likely you may know her, she works at The Sun.'

Eric rubbed his forehead. 'Cécile, you say?'

'Aye.'

'The name doesn't ring any bells.'

'She has a round face and thick wavy hair. I think she's simple. Her mother's name is Marguerite.'

Eric felt his brow clear as he placed the girl. He remembered seeing Marguerite talking to a girl who answered to that description. He'd never actually spoken to her. He grimaced. 'I have her now, and I see what you mean. I've seen her in the kitchen and stable, she never comes into the body of the inn.'

'She's shy as a mouse.'

'Aye. Heaven help us, we need a credible witness. Cécile would do more harm than good.' He scrubbed his face. 'It's a pity you mentioned her. The king will be expecting sound testimony, he won't like it when he sees her. Lord, Rowena, what were you thinking?'

Rowena stiffened. 'You're implying I misled the king?'

'Didn't you?'

Blue eyes glittered, hard as sapphires. 'What choice did I have? I don't want her summoned to Paris any more than you do. If you recall, I did ask to speak to you on your own. I wanted you to understand about Cécile *before* mentioning her to the king.'

Eric touched her hand. 'Rowena, I'm sorry, I know it wasn't your fault. It is just that—hell burn it—we need someone reliable who will help us reveal your cousin's true colours.'

Rowena nodded. 'What do you suppose Cécile will do when faced with my father?'

He gave her a wry smile. 'Run?'

'It's not funny.' Rowena gripped his sleeve. 'We have to stop Father leaving for Provins. Where's Alard?'

He jerked his head in the direction of the door. 'In the antechamber with the king's guard.'

'We must send him after Father. Cécile cannot come to court.'

With a curt nod and a heavy heart, for he was desperate to remove Sir Armand from play, Eric went to speak to his squire. Alard would have to chase after Lord Faramus and tell him that it was pointless bringing Cécile to Paris. Much as he regretted it, he agreed with Rowena, Cécile was no fit witness.

The king would be apoplectic when he found out. Lord help them, with no witness, how on earth were they to prove Sir Armand was a murderous, manipulative swine?

Later that night Eric lay in bed with Rowena fast in his arms, idly watching the glow the dying fire painted on the tapestries and bed-hangings.

Rowena's hair gleamed like gold. Idly picking up a tress, Eric sifted it through his fingers—it was as smooth as silk. She stirred against him, pressing a warm kiss to his shoulder. Her breasts rested softly against his chest and a slender leg was hooked round his. A growing heaviness in Eric's groin made him realise he wouldn't mind another bout of lovemaking, but he made no move to press his attentions on her. Rowena was so delicate, she surely wouldn't be able to manage it again. Besides, he didn't want her to think him a rutting beast.

He couldn't understand it. They had had their joy of each other—twice—since coming to bed and his desire was far from slaked.

Would it never leave him? When he had entered this marriage he had promised fidelity and he had intended to honour that promise even though he had expected it wouldn't be easy. Yet easy it was. Since marrying Rowena, the thought of taking another woman to his bed was simply impossible. Wrong. Out of the question.

The fire flared as a log moved, its reflected glow turned her skin to gold.

'I love you, Eric,' she murmured, so softly that he barely heard her.

His heart clenched and for one cowardly moment he thought he might pretend he hadn't heard her. He wasn't ready for this and he doubted he ever would be. However, he didn't want her hurt. Carefully, he cupped her cheek with his palm and put lightness in his voice. 'Rowena, you know I adore you. Particularly when you are so disordered.'

Her head shifted. 'You adore me?' She gave a most indelicate sniff and lifted her head to stare into his eyes. She didn't look happy. 'You love me, Eric, as you told the king. It is just that you refuse to accept it.'

'Love? I can't afford love, my sweet.' He touched his forefinger to her mouth, tracing its shape.

Her brow wrinkled. She shifted her head and his finger fell from her lips. 'Why ever not?'

'Love leads to pain. Hurt. It's inevitable. I prefer adoration.' Bringing her close, he lowered his head and kissed her. She caught hold of his shoulder, gave a breathy, irresistible moan and opened her mouth in a response so passionate he was pushing her back against the pillows before he recalled his resolve to give her time to recover before he approached her again. Pulling back, he cleared his throat. 'We shall rely on this warmth between us, that is enough. We don't need love.'

The wrinkle in her brow reappeared, deeper than ever. Her gaze was serious, almost stern. 'You are thinking of your mother. Eric, I know she loved you.'

He forced a laugh. 'She said that she did. It was a lie. She left me. Abandoned me.'

'Eric, life for her was surely hard after your father's death.'

'Aye.'

'Perhaps your mother had no choice.'

Eric rolled away and lay on his back, staring at the ceiling. 'I was cold and hungry and she left me. Her own child.'

'Was there food in your house?'

'Very little.'

'Eric, I would be honoured to hear about how you arrived at Jutigny. Share it with me. What happened?'

Eric fell silent for a space. Shadows shifted, the fire popped. If he could tell anyone, he could surely tell Rowena. He swallowed. 'After my father died, my mother tried to carry on working.'

'You lived in Provins?'

'Aye, the house is in the Lower Town. As far as I know, it's still there.'

Rowena tucked herself against him and bumped her head against his arm. 'That must be strange. Do you go and see it?'

'I went back a couple of times when I became a squire. I haven't been there in years.'

'Go on. Were your parents merchants?'

'No.' Eric hesitated. He thought he could tell Rowena about his mother, but he had never told anyone how his parents had made their living. As a boy he had soon learned that most knights looked down on the people who worked their estates. They even looked down on merchants, some of whom had treasuries almost as large as the king's. In short, noblemen looked down on anyone who did not own land.

Eric's father hadn't owned as much as a yard of land, he'd been a baker. Bracing himself for her reaction, telling himself that since he didn't love her, her reaction was irrelevant, he took a steadying breath and watched her face as he said, 'My father was a baker.'

'A baker?' Her eyebrows lifted in surprise.

As far as he could tell, her expression held only that—surprise. He could see no shock and, thank the Lord, no revulsion. No mockery. He forced himself on, eyes focused on her face. He didn't want to miss the slightest change of expression. 'I remember the scorch of the oven, I soon learned to steer well clear. I remember the bright burn of the coals. Every morning the smell of baking bread reminds me of him.'

'I am sure. Do you recall what he looked like?'

He felt himself smile, how like Rowena to ask that. 'A blurred image only. After Father died there was little money. Mother struggled to carry on the business without him. It never seemed to work, she was no business woman.' Turning to face her, he took her head in both hands and gave her a kiss. 'Thank you.'

Her eyes were puzzled. 'For what? I've done nothing.' She leaned up on her elbow and drew a circle on his chest. 'Do you have any idea what happened to your mother?'

'I know exactly what happened to her.' Eric enfolded her hand with his, picked it up and studied it. Smooth and white, it was a lady's hand.

There was a small callous from riding; a few pinpricks from the making of his cloak and that was it. No ingrained dirt, no broken nails.

Eric had run the gauntlet of his questionable background all his life. He could still hear the taunts of that Jutigny head groom. *Gutter rat.* He'd endured prejudice and sneers like the ones cast at him earlier by Sir Armand when he'd stood before the king. *Arrant knave. Liar. Nobody.* Doubtless it would happen again. But not once had he suffered at the hands of Rowena or her family.

Oh, there'd been the odd cuff round the ear from Lord Faramus when he'd fumbled in the practice yard. More than one curse had been slung his way. However, the people who had come to mean more to him than any others had never abused him for his unknown parentage.

'One day a landless knight chanced by the bakery. In an effort to earn extra money, Mother had been spinning yarn for a friend. She was so engrossed in the spinning that she forgot the time and burned a batch of bread. The knight alerted her to the smoke pouring from the oven and that was that. Love. Did I mention that Mother was exceptionally pretty?'

'No, but I can imagine,' Rowena said softly. He looked enquiringly at her and she added, 'You are her son.'

Eric managed a faint smile and pressed on. Might as well get it over with now he had started. 'Three weeks later the knight asked Mother to go away with him. He wouldn't take me.'

She drew in a breath. 'That was harsh.'

Eric's throat closed and for a ghastly moment he could not speak. Tearing his gaze from Rowena, he stared up at the ceiling and cleared his throat. 'So I thought. Oddly, of late I've come to understand the man's objection. You know how it is for a landless knight. No security. Nothing save the hope of another commission and the chance of finding a fair man to call your master. There was no room in his life for another man's child. He wasn't rich enough to support me as well as Mother.' He shrugged. 'Mother made her choice. She told me she loved me and persuaded the knight to take us to Jutigny. The rest you know.'

Rowena buried her face in his chest and hugged him. 'Well, finally I understand why land is so important to you.' Her voice sounded muffled. 'God willing, you will one day hold more land than the King of France.'

Frowning, he tipped up her chin. 'Rowena? You must know that you are more important to me than the property.'

'God help me, I hope so,' she muttered. Easing away, she pushed back the bedcovers and reached for her shift. 'Excuse me a moment, I need to find the privy.'

The privy was out in the corridor, to get there Rowena would have to go through the chamber where Alard and their guards were sleeping. Eric watched her wind her cloak about her shoulders. 'I had better accompany you.'

She gave a shaky laugh. 'No need. Sir Armand is in his house with his own guard, and I trust the king's men.' The latch clicked and she slipped into the next room.

The corridor was lit by a row of candles in wall sconces. It was cold after the warmth of the apartment and goosebumps shivered along Rowena's arms. She hugged her cloak tightly to her and followed the fitful line of light.

A tear tracked down her cheek. With a grimace, she rubbed it away. She had told Eric she loved him and he hadn't responded in kind. Telling him how she felt about him had been a definite leap in the dark. She had realised she loved him some time ago and she'd been reluctant to tell him for fear that he'd find a declaration of love a burden.

This evening she'd changed her mind, thinking that a declaration of love might be exactly what Eric needed. His reaction—a retreat into his usual flirtatious self—had been disappointing. However, she wasn't surprised. Eric was living in the shadow of his mother's desertion. He'd had little love in his life and he questioned the love that he had had. Rowena had to make him leave his past behind; she had to make him see that whilst he'd been lost on that long-ago Christmas Eve, he had also been found.

Eric needed unconditional love. He needed someone to stand at his side through thick and thin. He needed to know she wouldn't let him down and that her love wasn't going to go away. She would simply keep telling him until he believed her. And she would pray that one day he would be able to reciprocate.

Eric's every action demonstrated that he held her in affection. And if affection was all that he could give? Then so be it. She would accept whatever he could offer. He was a good husband, he treated her as though what she wanted was important, as though she mattered. Her mouth twisted. It was more than she had expected from so strong a man.

Her father had never been perfect in that regard. His insistence on a betrothal to Lord Gawain when she hadn't been ready had driven her to the abbey, and when she'd been a child he had tried to put an end to her blossoming friendship with Eric. Her father could be a tyrant.

Not so Eric. He was strong. He wasn't a tyrant.

Coming to Paris had been worth it. Rowena had learned how much Eric wanted her to be his wife. She had learned that he valued her over her lands. He must do, for he had told the king—and everyone else in the conference chamber—that he loved her. This, from the man who professed not to believe in love. This, from the man who said he would give her adoration, but never love. His declaration before the council had been more than mere strategy, he had been telling the truth. It was up to her to make him see it. Eric loved her, he just didn't know it quite yet.

She wiped away another tear, she was determined not to let him know she'd been upset. She was making progress. He hadn't rejected her confession of love outright, weeks ago he would have done. She would keep faith and she would win.

As Rowena made her way back down the corridor, a small shadow leapt out of a darkened doorway. Her breath caught, but it was only a cat, shooting off in the direction of the stairwell. As she passed the doorway, she glanced sideways and almost stumbled.

A man was standing in the gloom, standing so still that if she hadn't glanced that way likely she would have missed him.

The man moved and a shock ran through her. It was Sir Breon.

White teeth flashed in a grim smile, a blade flickered silver. 'Good evening, my lady.'

Rowena flung her cloak at Sir Breon and ran.

Eric heard a heavy thud and lifted his head from the pillow. There it was again, a heavy thud, immediately followed by a muffled cry. It sounded like a woman.

Ice gripped his heart. Snatching up his sword, Eric dashed for the door to the antechamber. The other door, the one leading out in to the corridor was open. The guards were crowded round someone standing on the threshold.

'Eric!'

Dimly, Eric registered that he was stark naked. Not important. He pushed through the guards and gathered her in his arms. 'Rowena, Rowena,' he heard himself mutter as he kissed her hair. She was trembling head to toe and had lost her cloak.

'Sir Breon,' she said, her voice as shaky as her body. She pointed into the corridor. 'Out there.'

'What happened?' Eric's mind raced. Not safe. Rowena had been in the king's palace and she'd not been safe. He'd let her down, he should have accompanied her.

'He had a knife, I thought he was going to kill me. I threw my cloak over him and ran.'

'My brave girl.' Eric gripped her fiercely and held her eyes. 'We'll find him. Guard?'

'Sir?'

'I take it the palace gates are closed for the night?'

'Aye, sir.'

'Good, he won't get far. Just to be sure, alert the men at the gate, will you?'

'Aye, sir.'

Eric looked at his squire. 'Alard, take my lady back into our bedchamber. Stay with her. Bolt the door. Lady Rowena is not to leave that bedchamber until I return. Understood?'

'Yes, sir.'

He gave a wry smile. 'Before you lock the door, you'd better toss me some clothes.'

Alard grinned. 'Right away, sir.'

Eric peeled his arms from Rowena with some difficulty and gave her a gentle nudge towards the bedchamber.

She hung back, face strained and drawn. 'Eric, be careful, won't you?'

'Of course. You mustn't worry, there will be guards in this antechamber at all times. Sir Breon won't reach you.'

Her hand touched his. She leaned towards him and whispered, 'It's you I worry about, you dolt.'

Rowena's cloak lay on the corridor floor. Eric and the king's guard quartered the other apartments as quietly as they could. None the less, irritable lords and ladies had to be roused from their beds. It was to no avail, no one had seen Sir Breon. They quartered a great hall where great swags of holly and ivy acted as a backdrop for the colours of the king's knights. They roused servants and men-at-arms. No one in the hall had seen Sir Breon either, though he must have passed through it to get out.

Rowena worries about me.

They snatched up some torches and went outside in silence. The yard glittered with frost and starlight and compacted snow. Tracks criss-crossed the ground, they were so scuffed and mangled, Eric could read nothing from them. They scoured the stables, where Eric enlisted a groom with a pair of wolfhounds to help them in their hunt. They searched the cookhouse, a barn and a chapel. Nothing. Eric went to the gatehouse.

Rowena worries about me in the same way that I worry about her. Lord, the way his heart had sunk when he'd heard her scream!

He caught a guard's eye. 'Seen anything?'

'No, sir, not a thing.'

'Where in hell is he?'

Eric ran his gaze round the perimeter walls. They were the height of at least three men and visible as a heavy dark line against the starry sky. Here and there a torch blazed through the night. Sentries tramped the length of the walkway, their bodies and spears silhouetted against the stars, their helmets gleaming softly in the torchlight.

A wolfhound whined and strained at its leash. It was looking up at the walkway. One of the sentries had no helmet. No spear.

'There.' Eric pointed. 'Post a man at the bottom of each ladder.'

'Aye, sir.'

Eric sprinted for the ladder. 'It shouldn't take long.'

Eric fixed his sights on Sir Breon, the only man on the walkway without a helmet, and moved slowly towards him. He drew his sword and held his peace until he was on a section of planking that blocked Sir Breon's retreat to the nearest ladder. 'Guard!' Eric bawled. 'Over here!'

The sentries moved like lightning. Sir Breon looked wildly to his left and his right, and for a moment Eric thought he was about to hurl himself over the palace wall.

'It's too high for that,' Eric said, closing the distance between them.

Boots clattered along the walkway. Steel flashed and Sir Breon was surrounded. He threw his dagger aside and a guard bent to retrieve it. It was almost too easy, but it wasn't over yet.

'Where's your squire and your sword, de Provins?' Eric demanded, frowning as he studied Sir Breon's clothes, he was dressed as a merchant.

Eric's heart banged against his ribs, he was struggling with the most unchivalrous urge. By tossing down his dagger, Sir Breon had effectively surrendered and all Eric could think was that he wanted to run him through. This man had wanted Rowena dead. His sword quivered.

Sir Breon's face twisted. 'In lodgings. Didn't think they'd admit the wine merchant if he came with a squire and was armed to the teeth.'

Eric gripped his sword to prevent himself from doing Sir Breon serious injury. It flashed in on him that Sir Breon was the man who had wielded the knife against de Lyon. According to Rowena, Cécile hadn't named him as such, though that didn't rule him out since the girl never put her nose in the inn proper. She wouldn't necessarily know his name.

Step by step, Eric told himself. Rowena's safety was his prime consideration. He needed proof Sir Breon had been in the employ of Sir Armand. He needed Sir Breon's confession to that and he needed it before witnesses. *Reliable* witnesses. Somehow Eric had to trap Sir Breon into admitting his guilt over de Lyon's death.

'You will have to be questioned.' He glanced across the dark, glittering courtyard towards the palace tower. 'We'll do it in the guardhouse.'

Chapter Fifteen

Sir Breon stood, feet planted slightly apart, next to a table cluttered with wine cups and scattered breadcrumbs. Hands bound behind his back, he glowered at Eric. 'You can't hold me, you filthy peasant, I didn't touch her,' he said. 'She's lying if she says otherwise.'

Determined to ignore all insults, Eric flexed his fingers. *I will not hit him.*

Fortune was with him, two knights had been in the guardhouse when Eric had brought Sir Breon in—Sir Kay de Tirel and Sir Guivret Fitz Alan had been playing dice. Glancing at Sir Kay and Sir Guivret, Eric was pleased to find no mockery in either man's eyes, just a sharp attentiveness. Eric hadn't met either knight before. Fortunately they knew of him and his summons to court. They understood what was at stake here and, thank the Lord, they were reputed to be honourable men. They would know the truth when they heard it. They'd make ideal witnesses.

Eric was certain that Sir Breon was Mathieu de Lyon's murderer and he was determined to trap him into a confession. He would inform Sir Breon they had a witness to the boy's death and take it from there. Sir Breon didn't have to know their witness wasn't reliable. In any case, if he squeezed a confession out of him, their witness wouldn't have to be called.

'Lady Rowena hasn't said you tried to kill her,' Eric said, mildly. 'Merely that you were loitering in the palace corridor—uninvited, I might add. What were you doing?'

Sir Breon stared sullenly at a rack of shields. 'Satisfying my curiosity. I'd never been inside the palace.'

Sir Kay shifted, scooping the dice from the table. He tossed them idly from hand to hand. 'It's unwise to arrive without an invitation, sir. The king will have to be told.'

Sir Breon shrugged. 'It's scarcely a treasonable offence, surely? I did nothing.'

'That remains to be seen,' Eric said, softly. 'After you've told the king why you were hanging about near his goddaughter's apartment disguised as a merchant, you may find he has other questions for you.'

'Other questions?'

Eric crossed his arms. 'Aye. Such as how much you were paid by Sir Armand to murder de Lyon.'

Sir Breon's eyes flickered over the faces of the knights watching him and slowly shook his head. 'De Monfort, you're insane. An insane peasant whose promotion to the knightly estate is an insult to the rest of us.'

Eric made a swift negative gesture. 'It's not I who insult the knightly estate, de Provins, but you. A man who takes coin to kill an innocent squire—you're a disgrace.'

Sir Breon's lip curled. 'Your marriage to Count Faramus's whelp has turned your head. You can prove nothing.'

Eric braced himself to stretch the truth. He wasn't sure Cécile would be able to identify Sir Breon as the killer, certainly she couldn't name him. It was possible that she might recognise him though. He kept his gaze steady. 'Before you dig yourself deeper into the muck, there's something you need to bear in mind. We have a witness. You were seen outside The Sun the night de Lyons died.'

Sir Breon let out a bark of laughter and looked to Sir Kay. 'God's teeth, can't you see the man's lying? There is no witness.' He wrenched at his bonds. 'Set me free, de Tirel, for pity's sake. Surely we can discuss this in a civilised manner?'

'Our witness is prepared to testify that she saw you that night.' Eric pressed on. 'She also saw de Velay. Further, she heard de Velay order you to kill that squire. She is quite clear on all points. She saw you kill that boy.'

'She? Who is this she? A tavern wench? You would take the word of a tavern wench over that of a knight?'

Eric lifted an eyebrow and the bluff began. 'She's very convincing. Sir, the time for evasion is over, you know she is speaking the truth. Both you and Sir Armand were seen outside The Sun and Sir Armand was heard ordering you to dispatch that boy. For pity's sake, de Provins, you were *seen*.' He paused. 'Face it, you are our prisoner and you will be taken before the king. It will go better for you if you made a clean breast of things. Think about it. And ask yourself this question—are you prepared for the consequences of lying to the king?'

Sir Breon's skin paled. His jaw worked. The only sound was the clack of dice as Sir Kay rolled them in his palm.

Eric kept his face impassive, though he could scarcely breathe. He was sure Sir Breon was on the point of surrender.

Sir Breon sniffed. 'He'd be more lenient?'

Eric let the silence draw out. Eventually, he spoke. 'It's possible. He'd certainly be mightily relieved.' Eric wasn't going to add that a confession of this sort would mean that at the least Sir Breon would be stripped of his knighthood. 'The king wants this resolved quickly and a full confession from you would speed things along. Admit that Sir Armand gave you your orders to kill de Lyon. As I said, the king will be glad to see the back of this business.'

Sir Breon stared at the toe of his boot and, following his gaze, Eric found himself looking at some tell marks on the leather. Marks which betrayed the position where the straps for Sir Breon's spurs usually sat. There were no spurs tonight—clearly Sir Breon had thought to remove them before breaking into the palace. After this, he'd be unlikely to wear them again.

Sir Breon lifted his gaze, his shoulders sagged. 'De Monfort, it would seem the game is yours. Since there's a witness, I see the sense in your suggestion.'

Eric drew in a slow breath. 'You confess that Sir Armand ordered the boy's death?'

'Aye, damn you.'

'And that he charged you with carrying it out?'

'Aye to it all. Sir Armand paid well.' Face twisting, Sir Breon spat on the floor by Eric's feet. 'You should understand, you were a landless knight yourself not so long ago.'

Eric turned to Sir Kay and Sir Guivret. 'You heard his confession, sirs?'

'Aye,' Sir Guivret said. 'We'll speak up for you before the king.'

'Thank you.' Eric strode to the door. 'Sergeant!'

'Sir?'

'Sir Breon needs putting under lock and key well away from the king until such time as the king is ready to see him.' He thought quickly. 'I am not familiar with Paris and the name escapes me, but I seem to recall there's a stronghold just across the *grand pont*.'

'That would be the Grand Châtelet, sir.'

'That's the one, take him there.'

The sergeant saluted. 'Very good, sir.'

'Oh, and, Sergeant?'

'Sir?'

'When you've done that, I believe everyone in the palace will sleep more soundly if you rouse Sir Armand and install him in the Grand Châtelet too. Securely, mind.'

'Understood, sir.'

In the guest apartment, Rowena and Eric sat on the edge of their bed, facing the fire, a goblet of warm spiced wine in hand.

Rowena felt her mouth gape. 'He confessed? You got Sir Breon to confess?'

'Aye.'

'And he's locked up in the Grand Châtelet along with Sir Armand? How on earth did you do it?'

Eric grimaced into his goblet. 'Bluffed him. Told him about out witness and led him to believe her testimony was unassailable and that she had named him. Then I suggested that he considered how His Grace would react when he heard what she had to say.'

'You pointed out the disadvantages of being caught out in a lie to the king?'

'Exactly.' Eric took a small sip of the wine and his brows lifted. 'This isn't bad.'

She smiled. 'Thank you, I mulled it myself. Sent Alard down to the kitchen for spices.'

His eyebrows snapped together. 'You did what?'

'I mulled the wine.'

'*Bon sang*, Rowena, Alard was meant to be guarding you, not scouring the kitchen for spices.'

A small hand came to rest on his thigh. 'Eric, half the king's guard were in the antechamber, I was quite safe. Besides, I needed something to occupy my mind whilst you were gone. You didn't imagine I would be sleeping?'

'You disobeyed me again, *ma dame*.'

She made a small humming noise in the back

of her throat and sent him a sidelong glance under her eyelashes. 'I did, didn't I? Eric, I have to warn you, if King Louis ratifies our marriage, I won't obey your every word.'

'*If* the king ratifies our marriage? Rowena, with Breon's confession, there is no doubt.'

Rowena laid her head against his arm. 'Thank goodness. Eric, losing you would tear me apart. I love you so much.'

Green eyes watched her. Her declaration hadn't irritated him, on the contrary there was a hunger in them that she recognised. Eric wanted to believe her. He did love her, she was sure of it.

Carefully, he set his goblet on the coffer and nuzzled her hair. 'There are no lingering regrets for de Lyon?'

'I am sorry that he was killed certainly.' Sliding her arm about his waist, she gave him a hug. 'Eric, Mathieu was just a boy. I loved him with a young girl's love, and am very thankful you have got justice for him. But you are my husband. The love I feel for you is stronger than what I felt for Mathieu. I love you as my childhood playmate. You are my dearest friend. My heart. You are a man, not a boy, and I admit that gave me pause at the beginning.' Her lips curved. 'Mathieu was far more biddable than you will ever be.'

His eyes danced. 'Easier to control, eh?'

'So I thought. I was still smarting because Father had driven me into the convent and I had no wish to bind myself to another tyrant who would ignore my wishes.'

'Your father knew you weren't born to be a nun, he was right about that.'

'Sometimes Papa is far too impatient. If he'd given me time, I don't think I would have taken refuge in a nunnery in the first place.'

Eric ran his fingertip down her nose. 'For my part, I am glad you did. Otherwise, Lord Faramus would never have called on me to get you out.'

'Thank God that you did. Imagine, if you hadn't come to my rescue, I might be married to the man who had murdered Mathieu.'

Eric gripped her chin. 'Rowena, Sir Breon might have killed you.'

'I doubt that, I imagine the lure of the family acres would more than compensate for any bribe Sir Armand might have offered him.'

'Either way, it doesn't bear thinking about.'

'I hope the king hurries to judgement.'

His arm wound about her waist. 'So do I.'

Absently, Rowena ran the sole of her foot up Eric's calf. 'Getting Sir Breon to confess before those knights was a masterstroke. Add that to the gossip Alard winkled out of the king's guard—'

'What gossip?'

'Alard has learned that the king was petitioned

by Sir Armand's tenants months ago. They accuse him of bleeding his estates dry for the benefit of the Church. The governance of his lands has been called into question.'

Eric's eyes widened. 'It's that bad?'

'Apparently it's appalling. Sir Armand didn't stop at the usual tithes, he's stripped his land bare. His barns are empty. His peasants starving. His holding has become a wasteland and that is of no use to anyone. As you know, the king is a religious man and for a time the offerings Sir Armand gave to the Church must have blinded him to his true nature. However, no king wants to see peasants starving. No king likes to see workable land abandoned. Even if Sir Armand had nothing to do with Mathieu's death, he has ignored his responsibilities as a landlord. The king won't stand for that. My godfather needs to have confidence in the men who hold his lands. He has none in Sir Armand.'

'He has confidence in Lord Faramus.'

Rowena swirled the wine in her goblet and gave him a searching glance. 'So he does, they've always had a rapport. And since the king trusts Papa's judgement, that, too, will weigh in our favour. He will have no doubt that he may place his confidence in you, and that you will one day be a worthy steward for our French lands.'

'Yesterday at Notre-Dame, your father spoke most eloquently on my behalf.'

'I am sure that he did. He trained you, after all.' Rubbing her cheek against him, Rowena glanced up. Green eyes were watching her. The hunger in them was undiminished and she could see those gold flecks, but a shadow lingered. 'Eric, what is it?'

He shoved his hand through his hair. 'I can't forget that you were rushed into marrying me.'

Leaning past him, Rowena set her goblet on the coffer next to his and took his hand. Their fingers curled together and she felt a sweet ache in her belly. 'You're not still dwelling on that, surely?'

'It was not honourable to snatch you from the convent.'

'Yes, it was! Eric, whichever way you look at it you saved me from misery. I would have been miserable in the convent. I would have been miserable with Sir Breon.'

Putting a finger on her mouth, he shook his head. 'It was wrong to abduct you.'

She kissed his finger and watched his eyes darken. 'I loved it.'

A reminiscent smile flickered at the edges of his mouth. 'You struggled a bit at first.'

'Before I recognised you. Eric, I was dying in that convent. You were just what I needed. You are, and always have been, the most honourable man I know. Every day since our marriage I have become more and more grateful that you agreed to share my life. I'm glad you abducted me.'

He blinked and his gaze fell to her mouth. He looked at it with an intensity that told her he was about to kiss her. Rowena wanted that kiss. In a moment. They had something else to settle first and she knew this was the time. This talk of people doing questionable things with the best of motives was just the opening she'd prayed for.

Eric had no faith in love, he thought it always brought pain. She had to make him understand that his mother had loved him. And then would come her biggest challenge—she had to help him see that pain did not necessarily walk hand in hand with love. If Eric had grown up in a family, he would know these things. He'd been denied the rough and tumble of family life. He'd not had to learn to live with a tyrannical father whom you couldn't help but love, even when that father had driven you to hide in a convent where you would never feel at home.

Eric had relied on his charm to get by. Charm was also his shield, he used it to keep the world at arm's length. She was about to disarm him. She hoped. She wanted him to know that he didn't need charm where she was concerned. She wanted him to trust in her love.

She shifted closer and he cupped her head with his palm. Somewhere in the palace a door slammed. 'Eric, don't be so hard on yourself. You took me out of the convent with the best of intentions. People do bad things with good intentions every day. In a small way, you did it when you misled Sir Breon into thinking our witness was reliable in order to get a confession out of him. I've done it—'

'You?'

'I told the king I wanted to become a nun, when in truth I was deluding myself.'

His lips quirked into a wicked grin and he reached out to ruffle her hair. 'You like being disordered far too much.'

'With you I do.'

Twisting a strand of her hair between his finger and thumb, Eric leaned towards her. Pressing her hand to his chest, she ignored the purposeful light in his eyes and held him off. 'Eric, you need to think about this, it's important.'

'What? What must I think about?'

'People being forced to do horrible things with the best of intentions.' She took in a deep breath. 'People like your mother.'

His expression clouded. 'My mother?'

'Aye, Eric, your mother. Before she brought you to Jutigny your family lived in Provins, did they not?'

'You know they did.'

'Since you were so small when your mother left, it is unlikely you were then aware of my mother's reputation in the town.'

His brow furrowed as he stared past her into the fire. 'You're referring to Lady Barbara's passion for charitable works.'

Rowena nodded. 'Ever since my parents married, Mama has tried to help people. She ensures that food is given to the Provins Hospitallers for whoever might need it. She visits the sick.'

'Lady Barbara has a heart of gold,' he murmured.

'Don't imagine that you are the only child she took into her care. Why, two of the Sainte-Colombe cooks were rescued from a life on the streets. You, however, are the only boy who became a knight. I'm trying to show you that when your mother left you by the gate, she wasn't simply abandoning you. Eric, she left you in the very place where she knew you'd be safe. I'm sure she thought she was doing her best for you. I'm sure she loved you.'

Stiff-backed, Eric stared into the fire. His face was bleak. 'She was doing her best.' He scrubbed his face with his hands. 'Lord, Rowena, I was six. It was midwinter. I was cold and hungry.'

Rowena wanted to hug him and never let go. She wanted to tell him that she loved him with all her heart, but she knew that would not work. Not quite yet. She contented herself with leaning lightly against him and watching the flames alongside him.

'Your mother loved you.' Surreptitiously, Rowena glanced his way. He looked so serious, so unlike the carefree, flirtatious man she had married that she scarcely recognised him. Had she had gone too far?

He ran a hand round the back of his neck, and sighed. 'Perhaps she did.'

'Eric, your mother didn't simply abandon you. She took you to the one place in Provins where she knew you'd be safe. She'd worked out what your life would be like trailing after an itinerant knight who didn't want you and couldn't afford to keep you. She wanted more for you than that. I am sure she still loves you.'

'Wherever she is. She might even be dead by now.'

'Do you know her knight's name? Perhaps we might find her.'

He lifted his head and looked at her, eyes bleak. 'It's no use, Rowena, I thought of that when I won Monfort. Thought that if Mother and her knight were in difficulties they might make a home with me there.' He grimaced. 'I can't remember his name. I dare say I shall never know what happened to them.'

'I am sorry.'

The glow of the fire was fading, Rowena rose to add another log to the coals and came back to stand before him.

He took her by the hips and pulled her close. 'Thank you, my love.'

'For what?' She set her hands on his shoulders.

'For helping me see what my mother did in another light. Shameful though it might be, I'd never thought of it from her point of view.'

She pressed a kiss to his forehead. 'That's hardly surprising, what she did cut deep and you were little more than a baby. Think of it this way, you might have been lost that night, but your mother left you where she knew you would be found.'

'True.' Rising, he stretched and yawned. 'Rowena, my love, the night is half gone and it's been a long day. It is surely time for bed.'

He shrugged off his clothes, tossed them on to a coffer and shivered. 'Holy Virgin, it's cold.' He flung back the bedcovers. 'Hurry up, Rowena, we'll be warmer together.'

She smiled. 'So we will.' Peeling off her shift, she joined him in bed and settled against him. The bed ropes creaked as he reached to pinch out the candle and Eric's chest rose on another yawn. He really was tired. She kissed his chest. 'Eric, I love you.'

'And I you,' he said softly.

Rowena's heart missed a beat. Somehow she managed to keep very still. She even pretended to yawn. 'Hmm?'

A large hand ruffled her hair. 'You heard, witch.' His voice held a smile. 'I love you. I love you and I always will.'

Pulse jumping, for she hadn't expected a declaration until he'd digested their conversation, she lifted her head. Dimly, she made out his features in the firelight—his dark hair, that strong jaw, those high cheekbones. He was smiling and best of all his beautiful green eyes were looking at her with such softness—such *warmth*—that she felt the sting of tears.

A large hand slid from her waist, moving with slow, sensual intent over her buttock. He pulled her more tightly against him. 'Perhaps, before we sleep, we could try a little more disordering?'

* * * * *

MILLS & BOON®

HISTORICAL

AWAKEN THE ROMANCE OF THE PAST

A sneak peek at next month's titles...

In stores from 1st January 2016:

Available at WHSmith, Tesco, Asda, Eason, Amazon and Apple

Just can't wait?
Buy our books online a month before they hit the shops!
visit www.millsandboon.co.uk

These books are also available in eBook format!

'The perfect Christmas read!' - *Julia Williams*

Jewellery designer Skylar loves living London, but when a surprise proposal goes wrong, she finds herself fleeing home to remote Puffin Island.

Burned by a terrible divorce, TV historian Alec is dazzled by Sky's beauty and so cynical that he assumes that's a bad thing! Luckily she's on the verge of getting engaged to someone else, so she won't be a constant source of temptation... but this Christmas, can Alec and Sky realise that they are what each other was looking for all along?

Order yours today at
www.millsandboon.co.uk

1015_MB514

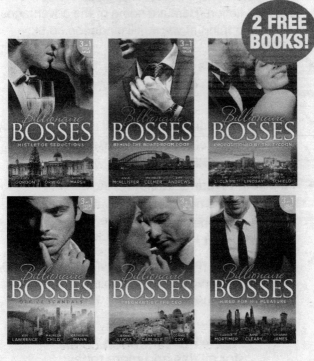

MILLS & BOON®

Why shop at millsandboon.co.uk?

Each year, thousands of romance readers find their perfect read at millsandboon.co.uk. That's because we're passionate about bringing you the very best romantic fiction. Here are some of the advantages of shopping at www.millsandboon.co.uk:

* **Get new books first**—you'll be able to buy your favourite books one month before they hit the shops

* **Get exclusive discounts**—you'll also be able to buy our specially created monthly collections, with up to 50% off the RRP

* **Find your favourite authors**—latest news, interviews and new releases for all your favourite authors and series on our website, plus ideas for what to try next

* **Join in**—once you've bought your favourite books, don't forget to register with us to rate, review and join in the discussions

Visit **www.millsandboon.co.uk**
for all this and more today!

MILLS_WEB